THE PRINCE REGENT'S SILVER BELL

Gladys McGorian

Walker and Company
New York

All the characters and events portrayed in this story
are fictitious.

First published in the United States of America
in 1987 by the Walker Publishing Company, Inc.

Published simultaneously in Canada by John Wiley & Sons
Canada, Limited, Rexdale, Ontario.

Library of Congress Cataloging-in-Publication Data

McGorian, Gladys, 1919–
The prince regent's silver bell.

I. Title.
PS3563.C3646P7 1987 813'.54 87-2006
ISBN 0-8027-0954-0

Printed in the United States of America

10 9 8 7 6 5 4 3 2 1

— 1 —

THE COUNTESS WAS sitting in the morning room, worrying. Embroidery lay in her lap. Pink thread fell from the needle in her hand, but not a stitch had she taken for above an hour. Beside her on the straight-backed sofa a fat white poodle was curled up, snorting in his post-breakfast nap.

She was not worrying about Continental affairs. After all, in that spring of 1814 that Dreadful Man had abdicated and had been banished to some island—Elba, was it? Surely, surely, that was the last they would hear of him. No, she was not worrying about Napoleon.

"Marriage," she said aloud, disturbing the poodle, who sat up and looked around. "It all has to do with marriage." The poodle yawned, revealing a pink tongue and a breath rank from eating mutton liver fed to her lovingly piece by piece by her mistress.

What concerned the countess was the welfare of three persons dear to her. Her orderly mind, with its Tory cast, put them in the order of political importance. First, the Prince Regent, who was treating his Princess so badly that the populace threw rotten vegetables at his barouche as he drove through London. Next, her elder son, Edward, already the fifth earl of Radburn, thirty years old, who ought to be getting married, but, please God, not to any of the prospects he had brought to meet her. And last, but equal to the others in her heart, Lionel, her earnest younger son, who had taken holy orders and really needed a wife to help him with his "living" over at Tweedstun on the edge of the Park.

Pauline, the countess of Radburn, was still lovely. Her broad, gently convex forehead now had a few horizontal lines, but they only accented its beautiful curve. Her cheeks were pink from living in the country, her waist perhaps a trifle thickened from bearing her two boys and doing adequate justice to the table for which Radburn Park was famous. But her carriage was still erect, her movements slow and graceful. She was known in the county simply as the countess, in deference to her regal bearing, her kindness, her unsullied reputation.

"Prinny's at fault. He doesn't set a serious example for the state of matrimony. Yes, Frou-Frou, you can put the blame on the Prince Regent himself." At this pronouncement, the countess rose, as though she had come into her monarch's presence, and the embroidery and needle dropped to the floor unheeded.

"He's extravagant and willful. Just think of that pavilion he built for Mrs. Fitzherbert at Brighton. As if that was not bad enough, I hear he is about to hire the architect, John Nash, to remodel it. He knows that these expenditures make his poor sick father sicker. The pavilion is just as fantastic as his mock-marriage to the lady for whom he maintains it. Yet I do like Mrs. Fitzherbert very much. So much more than—no, no, I must not get into *his* way of thinking. He should be setting an example of correct behaviour, no matter what. He is such a dear person. I wish, how I wish, he could be happy."

With Frou-Frou trotting at her heels, the countess restlessly went to the window, a floor-to-ceiling door of glass, which, like the frame of a painting, set off the smooth green lawn with a giant oak in the middle. However, she was not studying the expertise of Capability Brown, who had planned and executed this perfect landscaping. She was hoping that Prinny could become like that staunch oak, strong, enduring, protective, always there.

"And Edward."

Frou-Frou sat down, her shoe-button eyes alert under a pink satin bow, to hear what was coming, desirous that it had something to do with going outdoors.

"The title and estate have been his for some ten years now. It is time for him to marry and produce an heir. I long for a grandchild to fuss over and spoil a little."

She looked at the gold thimble on her middle finger, and a frown marred the perfection of her forehead. In preparation for the event of becoming the dowager countess, she had already repaired and decorated the Manor House, located midway between the Hall and Lionel's vicarage at Tweedstun. How many more embroideries could the Manor hold? Impatiently, she removed the gold thimble.

She would speak to Edward again. Her frown smoothed out and she smiled. It was imperative to be careful, for he liked to oblige her, and this past winter when she feared she might get the giddy duchess of Conroyallan as a daughter-in-law, she was sorry that she had brought up the matter of marriage at all.

You never knew with Edward; she had made mistakes with him before. He was volatile in a good-natured way, with wild enthusiasms. Just like Prinny, she thought, feeling a little proud. When Edward had come down from Oxford, where he had done excellently in the subjects that interested him and barely passed those that didn't, he had discarded books and taken to the outdoors, hunting every day that weather permitted and building a stable of thoroughbred horses.

Feeling that he had become too "county" and needed the polish of polite Society, she had opened her London house for him, and arranged that at the same time Lionel should take orders with the bishop of London, hoping that Lionel's presence would provide some kind of ballast for Edward. It didn't work out that way. Lionel studied from morn to night and visited not at all, rarely in fact seeing his brother. Edward plunged with glee into the London season and became the darling of hostesses. Pursuing young women with the gusto he used to expend on chasing fox and deer, he aroused alarm in the countess that he would become the rake his paternal grandfather had been.

The countess had then erred again.

The very minute that Lionel completed his studies with the bishop, she packed both her sons off to the Continent. The Grand Tour took them everywhere, everywhere, that is, except France, with whom their country was from time to time at war. The young men sipped at every other fount of culture on the Continent, spending months in Germany and Italy, but because it was forbidden to him, Edward wanted to see Paris. Somehow he persuaded Lionel to chance it with him. They had experienced no difficulty in entering France, due to an illiterate border guard who mistook them for Slavs because of their strange language, but it had required the intervention of a prominent Tory and a large sum of money to get them out again. Chastened, they returned home, Edward settling in at Radburn Park, while Lionel moved into the vicarage.

Edward's natural ebullience asserted itself, and he set out to build a racecourse a mile and a half long, with an opulent viewing stand, based on a design he had sketched while in Italy. This showplace attracted Prinny and the royal circle; at the race meeting held a few weeks before, the pick of London Society had descended on Radburn Park, and the little town of Tweedstun was engulfed with fine carriages, their well-dressed occupants demanding accommodations, and good ones, too.

No, the countess could no longer complain that Edward did not meet the *bon ton*. He was handsome, rich, and amusing, had already come into the title and estate, and unmarried ladies all over the county, nay, all over England and a number of foreign parts besides, made his interests their interests, which were mainly equestrian. One ladies' outfitter in London had developed a thriving business in producing well-fitted jackets and voluminous skirts hitched to one side for would-be countesses to ride sidesaddle.

But—and the countess groaned at the thought—the women who attracted Edward were the prettiest and the silliest! Thank goodness he hadn't proposed to the painted and patched duchess of Conroyallan, their house guest for six months! It was a miracle that he had not got himself entangled before this. Women apparently were as ready to forgive him (not that he asked them to forgive, not seeing that there was cause) as to fall in love with him in the first place.

"Why can't he take an interest in politics, as his father wished?" the countess asked Frou-Frou, who cocked her head to one side questioningly.

And then there was Lionel.

"He is dear, kind, and proper," the Countess informed her fat little pet.

Absorbed in his ministry at Tweedstun, on the edge of the Park, Lionel wasn't making any moves toward matrimony, either. He was a model of a vicar, helping the poor, visiting the sick, reading heavy tomes in the evening, and giving rather too learned sermons on Sunday morning. Quite shy, he attended the balls given in the neighbourhood, because his mother insisted on it, standing up politely with each girl in turn so that no one should be neglected by him. If he noticed that a plain girl was being overlooked, or that a pretty one was showing anxiety because forgotten by his brother, he would make it a point to stand up with her again. But the girl, while grateful to avoid the humiliation of sitting along the wall, knew very well that his intentions were simple charity and that nothing further would come of it.

"He is a good boy, none better," sighed the countess. Sincere in his religion, diligent in carrying out its precepts, with an understanding and sympathy of the human heart that she wished Edward could possess a portion of, he was too serious and often wooden.

"If the young women I observe are too frivolous for Edward, where on earth will I find one for Lionel?"

2

AT THIS MOMENT Edward, the handsome young fifth earl of Radburn, without a worry in the world, confidently raised his favorite rifle and adjusted it against his shoulder. The rifle was light, with a good balance, and he was well pleased with it. There was not the slightest doubt that he would bring down the snipe that Roscoe had disturbed from the marsh. Yet, at the precise height to fire, the muzzle wavered. The snipe, twisting in its flight and giving a sharp cry, escaped on the wind. Roscoe turned to his master questioningly. Following Lord Radburn's intense gaze, he made out in the purple distance across the downs a horse and rider moving at tremendous speed.

"Hand me my glass, quickly!"

Roscoe dove into the bag and found a folding telescope, one made by William Herschel. Swiftly, dexterously, Edward extended it and placed it to his right eye. The horse and rider disappeared behind a rise, and impatiently Edward awaited their reappearance.

It was the mount, not the rider, that had caught his eye. Only a fortnight ago, for the third year in a row, Edward's entry had lost the race for three-year-olds, and with it, the Prince Regent's Silver Bell. That meant he had never won on his own turf! Already he was planning next spring's events, and obtaining a really spectacular colt was a large element of that plan.

Just three years ago the Prince, having taken a fancy to the race meetings at Radburn Park, had had his own silversmith forge and engrave a silver bell, to be presented to the winner of the last race. That year, of course, it had seemed proper that he, Lord Radburn, should not win (after all, he was the host). The second year his entry had not been all that he had desired, and he was not surprised or disappointed when it came in fourth. But a fortnight ago! His colt, sired by the great Ormonde himself, had been easily edged out by Lord Easton's entry, a nondescript bay. It was inexplicable.

Across the downs, the horse and rider again came into view. "Magnificent!" was Edward's judgment. He handed the glass to Roscoe. "How old would you say?"

Roscoe squeezed his left eye, and the glass moved horizontally as he followed the horse. "Summat leggy. Could be two year, milord."

Excited, Edward took back the glass. The horse and rider seemed winged, alone in the universe, unreal in the haze of the distant downs. Not long ago in London, he had seen some sculptures brought back from the Parthenon in Athens by Lord Elgin. In those marble reliefs, horse and rider had been one entity, united in a spiritual whole that was uncanny and that had awed him with its beauty. This pair lithely crossing the downs had the same unearthly quality.

He focussed his glass on the rider. Something was odd. The saddle was forward on the animal's withers, and the rider, leaning over the neck, grasped the reins near the horse's mouth. This was the way Lord Easton's jockey had sat, and his lordship had explained that it was an American practice newly imported to England. Edward had scoffed, had thought it a rather ungainly position, but he had to face the fact that Lord Easton's entry had won the Silver Bell. He watched this horse and rider intently.

Skillfully easing speed, the rider brought the horse to a halt at the top of a knoll. Relaxing back in the saddle, he pushed back the soft tricorn from his forehead and surveyed the countryside. From one pocket he pulled out a knob of bread and broke off a piece with his teeth; from another he drew out a piece of paper that he examined whilst chewing hard. Swallowing, he looked up in the direction of Radburn Park. For a second, Edward thought the stranger was looking directly at him, then realised that the rider most likely was searching out the right-of-way. The animal stamped; the rider caressed his neck and spoke in his ear. Then he pulled down the tricorn decisively and turned the colt toward Radburn Park.

Edward conjectured that it was a horse from Tattersall's, being delivered by one of their specially trained jockeys. A gentleman would not ride that way, could not, if he were of any weight or size. Who could have purchased this animal? His closest neighbours were the Weywards of Coulder Hall, and the right-of-way led to their estate. Was Donald Weyward knowing enough to buy this exquisite creature? Or would he have money enough? Sir Donald had been getting into debt steadily for years and had lost heavily at the recent race meeting (as Edward had himself, but he could better afford it). No, the master of Coulder Hall would more likely be selling horses than buying them.

Edward simply had to get a closer look at the animal and find out whose it was. "Let's head them off!"

Picking up his rifle, he ran in the direction of the right-of-way. Roscoe followed more slowly with the bag, disappointed that the hunting was over. When Lord Radburn wanted something, all one could do was follow and watch him get it.

Horse and rider approached swiftly on the right-of-way. The animal's hoofs seemed not to be touching the ground.

Edward ran out on the right-of-way. "Halt!" he shouted.

Colt and rider veered to the right and kept going, as though a squirrel had been in their path.

Incensed, Edward raised his rifle and shot into the air. The horse shied, front legs pawing the air, the whites of his eyes showing in shock. The rider, nearly thrown off from his unusual position, clung with arms and knees to the terrorised animal.

"*Imbécile!*" he shouted, outraged. He leapt from the

horse, and with a look of disgust at Edward, turned his back on him and stroked the colt gently.

"*Chéri, calme-toi, calme-toi*. It's only a stupid man with a gun." The horse shuddered. "There, there, *mon bon* Fantastique. *Calme-toi, chéri*." He brushed aside the forelock tenderly and leaned his cheek against the colt's head. The horse steadied.

The fifth earl, infuriated at being spoken to like this, lifted the rifle again. But he was an honest fellow at heart and knew that he was acting irrationally. The courage of the lad to turn his back on a rifle! Edward lowered it with reluctant admiration. The boy's clothes were worn and dusty, the gloves threadbare, and the boots shabby, but he had a manner, and how he could manage a horse!

"Haven't you any sense?" The boy turned around accusingly, and Edward looked into stormy dark blue eyes. Freckles stood out angrily on an upturned nose.

Again Edward felt a stab of resentment, but controlled it. He had deserved that and was sheepish at having frightened such a fine animal. At close range the colt was a real beauty, dark brown, not black as he had first thought, but the mane and tail were full and black as only shiny black can be. The head was majestic.

"It's rather nervous," he said, wanting to find fault, not wanting to apologise.

"Nervous, *non*. Sensitive, *oui*. Don't you know anything about horses?"

It was a rhetorical question, spat out, and it hurt. The boy turned again to the horse, who had begun to move about restlessly. "*Chéri, mon beau cheval, calme-toi*," he crooned.

Roscoe, hidden by bushes, sized up the situation for himself. He knew that lingo when he heard it, he did! The boy was a Frog, the Enemy, probably had stolen that thoroughbred, and was up to no good. The way he spoke to Lord Radburn! Roscoe crept through the foliage until he was just back of the fellow.

Edward spoke sharply, "You might at least be civil. This just so happens to be my property."

"And I am on the right-of-way! This *your* land! Do you always act the highwayman?"

Roscoe had had enough of lèse majesté from this foreign ragamuffin! He came up from behind the boy, seized his arms, and pulled them together behind the lad's back.

"Here he is, milord!" he shouted, gloating. "What shall I do with the varmint? A Frenchie, by the speech of 'im."

The boy twisted and turned his grasp. Roscoe showed his teeth, holding him with only part of his strength. But his prisoner bent over and stomped backward with all the power he could put behind a wooden heel and sharp spur. With a yelp, Roscoe let the boy go. In the turmoil the tricorn fell off and auburn curls cascaded over the boy's shoulders as far as his waist.

Edward recovered from surprise quickly and his dark eyes sparkled. "Well, well, what have we here? Let him—her alone, Roscoe."

Roscoe didn't need to be told. He retreated, hopping on one foot as though the red curls were fire itself.

Edward laughed an easy laugh, then assumed a bland expression as he saw the fury on the flushed face.

"Tell me, *gentle* lady," he said, "where are you delivering that horse?"

"Delivering the *horse?*" the girl said. "I'm delivering *myself!*"

Edward could not control his laughter. He leaned back and roared. "It's too much!" he gasped.

The girl glared, then her lips too began to twitch although she remained wary.

"Perhaps I can direct you," choked Edward, "if you tell me who you are and where you are going."

"My name is Katherine Martin"—she gave the name the French pronunciation—"and I need no direction. I am on my way to Coulder Hall at the top of the road. Lady

Harriet Weyward is my aunt, and I am to live with her for exactly one year."

"So you are the Katherine Martin I've been hearing about!" He gave the name the English pronunciation. "What was it that Lady Weyward was telling my mother the other day? Something about a will." He frowned, trying to remember.

"Yes. My uncle's. He died recently in the West Indies and left me his fortune if—if I can prove that I can conduct myself like a lady."

Their eyes met irresistibly, and merriment broke out on both sides.

"My poor girl!" he said, trying to speak while laughing. "And is your Aunt Harriet to decide this?"

"No, a committee of three solicitors will make the decision. They will visit Coulder Hall twice and—examine me. I imagine that the opinion of Lady Weyward and my cousins will be taken into consideration."

"May I ask—excuse me, Miss Martin, for the impertinence—" he said, broadly smiling, "what gave your uncle the idea that your manners might need . . . mending?"

"I don't know," said the girl. "I was only nine years old at the time of Uncle's visit. He and I became great friends. I don't remember that he was at all critical. But at Newmarket we live humbly, in a cottage, not at all on the scale that life must be led at Coulder Hall. I suppose he thought that I'd need polishing."

His grin annoyed her. "Don't laugh. I feel very bad about it. I assure you that I don't ordinarily stomp on people's feet, but I did have provocation."

Roscoe had recovered and was looking ashamed. "I be sorry I mistook you, Miss Martin."

"Your uncle has sent you to the right place. Lady Weyward is a stickler for every little nicety known to polite Society. Not one lapse escapes her critical eye. She will, no doubt, be an absolute martinet."

"You don't intimidate me," said the girl proudly. "I'll get by. Fantastique and I will manage." She fingered her hair for loose pins and piled it up again on top of her head.

"Fantastique," murmured Edward. "Very well named, indeed. To whom does he belong?"

"To me, of course."

"To you! Girls don't own thoroughbreds."

"This girl does. My father gave it to me as I was leaving. He was the finest two-year-old in the Newmarket stables, and the last one belonging to my father. It was a tremendous gift."

"Indeed a tremendous gift. I agree! Would you consider selling him?"

"Certainly not," said the girl, jamming the tricorn over her curls and down on her forehead.

Sudden light came to Edward. "Is your father Guy Martin, the trainer at Newmarket?"

"Yes, you have heard of him?"

"I should say!"

The girl looked appeased, even pleased. She allowed Edward to help her up onto the saddle. "Thank you, Lord—"

"Lord Radburn, at your service, ma'am." He bowed a little too obsequiously.

She pulled on the ragged gloves. "I bid you farewell, Lord Radburn."

Edward cleared his throat. "Excuse me, Miss Martin, may I offer a suggestion with regard to your—endeavour this year. I must tell you that I am certain that Lady Weyward would not take kindly to your masquerading as a boy."

"Masquerading as a boy! Who is masquerading as a boy? I always ride in these clothes!"

"I assure you that it is not done in this county. Young women—ladies—rarely ride at all, and if they do, say, for the benefit of the exercise, it is sidesaddle, and with a chaperon."

"Sidesaddle! Monstrous! Not ride at all! Well, I shall have to change a thing or two in this benighted county."

"What if you don't change the mind of Lady Weyward? How about your inheritance, Miss Martin?"

She couldn't abide his smile. "I'm not inclined to believe what you say."

Edward opened wide his arms in helplessness. "As you wish. But I swear to you it is true, however foolish. Is it not so, Roscoe?"

"I be in this county fifty years, man and boy, and I never did see a lady go riding astride. Nor alone. Afore today."

She could see that Roscoe meant what he said. *He* wasn't laughing at her.

Edward saw her hesitancy. "Would you trust my mother's opinion? She is a wise and kindly person. Although not stuffy nor overcorrect, she is indeed a lady in every sense of the word." There was no immediate rejection of his idea, and he furthered his advantage by saying, "Besides, I for one am hungry. Aren't you? Come and have elevenses with us and we'll talk it over. Or are you awaited at Coulder Hall?"

"Not until late afternoon. Fantastique made excellent time."

"I am sure of that! He's a magnificent beast." He took the reins out of her hands. "Come meet the countess," he said authoritatively. "We shall be your nearest neighbours for a whole year, and you'll have to get acquainted with us sooner or later."

The horse turned his head around to her questioningly, but she gave no response. Doubt was sapping her reserve of confidence. Were they right about her appearance? Would she make an unfortunate impression on Lady Weyward? This fine Lord Radburn with his maddening good humour might be making a fool of her. But then Roscoe—his lined, honest face had no trace of amusement in it.

She made a decision. "*Oui*, Fantastique, *suis*. Follow him, love. We'll have to see if they are telling the truth."

—3—

THROUGH A COPSE of trees, seemingly natural but actually carefully arranged by the talent of Capability Brown, Edward led the way to the Hall, an anticipatory smile hovering about his long, undulating mouth, his dark eyes alight with the prospect of fun ahead.

Radburn Hall that morning seemed rather like a maturing matron, at ease and comfortable, with serene memories of her marriage and with her charming offspring showing off to advantage about her.

The Hall lay on level ground, self-contained, perhaps a little severe, mild sunlight picking out the yellow fungus on the cold grey stone. The square central part was the oldest, built by the first earl, a soldier, whose intention was to have his house look solid and impregnable. From the great stone gate, worthy of a Caesar, stretched a road for a quarter of a mile straight to the steps of the Hall.

The second earl, burdened by a large family and regal entertaining, added two side wings, which softened and improved the outline of the house. Depleted funds prevented his making any further changes. The third earl was never there. London was his habitat, for he was a notorious rake. Poor relatives were permitted to live in the Hall, but the Park became a wilderness of neglect.

His son, the fourth earl, was a throwback to the first. Army life and shrewd investments enabled him to pay his father's debts and to build a fair fortune of his own. Marrying the beautiful and affluent Pauline Forestier gave him the incentive and finances to renew and embellish the Hall. His wife loved the countryside, and it was at her instigation that he called in Capability Brown, who remade the gardens and park, added a lake and boathouse, an orangery and pinery, and extensive stables.

To these embellishments, the fifth earl, our Edward, had added the racecourse with a viewing stand, which was honoured with the attention and attendance of His Royal Highness, the Prince Regent. Radburn Hall and its Park had reached a summit of perfection.

Edward turned to look at his captive. He thought that he had subdued her; actually she was plotting rebellion. She was asking herself whether it was really necessary to confer with Lord Radburn's mother before presenting herself to Aunt Harriet at Coulder Hall. What was the difference between the ladies? What was so shocking about wearing pants and boots and riding astride Fantastique? Surely it was only intelligent, especially for a fairly long journey with practically no money. Her aunt would certainly understand that to obey fashion in such a case would be folly.

All that was necessary was to give Fantastique a nudge with a spur, and they could bolt away from the opinionated Lord Radburn, pulling the reins out of his hands. Better than slavishly following where he led.

She almost did it.

But that prickle of doubt came back to nag her. What if what he said was true, that her Aunt Harriet observed the proprieties to the letter? If she made a bad impression at the outset, it might be irrevocable. Her aunt might say that she was an impossible charge and send her away! Reason triumphed over rebellion. After all, she wasn't a prisoner; she would only have to stay long enough to meet the countess and gain her impression.

They were now out of the copse, with a view of the Hall. The countess, absently gazing out of the window, saw the procession approaching. Edward has bought another colt, she thought, and it looks like a beauty. If only his judgement of people was as good as his judgement of horseflesh!

Edward stopped before the main steps, and the rider, refusing his help, slid easily down from the horse. Roscoe took the reins and started to lead it away.

"Let him be!" said Kate, feeling that she was being deprived of her last friend.

"Pray be not alarmed," said Edward smoothly. "We have the most modern stables in the county, even better than the Prince Regent's, to my mind. Fantastique will be well taken care of. Roscoe is a groom of long experience."

"I shall be here only for a few minutes."

"Possibly; possibly not. It depends on my mother, I should say."

She glared at him, furious at his arrogance.

Roscoe took off his cap. "Excuse me, miss, but this here colt needs rubbing down. He's wet with sweat, he is. I'll wager he be hungry and thirsty, too."

This homely advice appealed to Kate. She examined Fantastique, who had indeed been ridden quite hard.

Roscoe twisted his cap. "I knew your father, miss, when he was trainer in the stables at Coulder Hall. Nobody was ever better with horses than Guy Martin. He had a kind of gift you might say, miss."

This praise of her father completed her capitulation. She nodded assent. Patting Fantastique, she whispered, "*À bientôt, chéri. Sois sage.*"

Two footmen in livery stood at the door. "Where is the countess?" Edward asked the man who opened it for them. He gestured to Kate to precede him.

"In the morning room, milord."

"Pray wait here, Miss Martin. I'd like to speak to her first."

Edward strode through the great hall, his heels resounding on the wooden floor. The planks were marred from the heavy heels of boots and the sharp claws of countless dogs. Several hounds asleep near the fireplace stirred awake and followed him.

At the end of the hall he tapped on a door and opened it without waiting for a reply. Kate heard a woman's voice saying, "Edward dear, keep those big dogs out of here. They frighten Frou-Frou."

He obliged, and at his command the dogs retired to the fireplace, circled round, and made themselves comfortable again.

Kate looked about her, feeling small in this immensity. The hall was two storeys high, the lower half panelled in dark wood and decorated with armorial bearings and deer antlers. The upper half was covered with enormous paintings depicting hunting scenes. One would be able to see them better, Kate thought, from the minstrel's gallery at the end; I should like to examine them one day. Hearing Edward's laughter behind the closed door, she flushed and glanced at the footmen, but their faces were passive.

Edward came out smiling. "Come, my mother is anxious to meet you." He glanced at her battered tricorn with mock puzzlement. "Now, what to do! On the one hand, as a *lady* you may keep your hat on. But as a *boy*, on the other, you should take it off. Quite perplexing!"

Unceremoniously, he solved the problem by pulling the hat off and thrusting it into her hands. As before, the hair came tumbling down. She gave him a look, thunder on her brow, lightning in her eyes, as Edward opened the door and permitted her to precede him into the room. Her glance at Edward was not lost on the countess of Radburn.

"Mama, this is Miss Katherine Martin, who is to be our neighbour at Coulder Hall."

"Miss Martin, I am delighted to meet you! At last. I knew your parents, you know. Do come over and sit by me. Frou-Frou, you must get down."

Kate curtsied as well as she could in pants and boots and obeyed her hostess. From the countess's manner, no one would think that the girl presented to her had been riding for days, was dressed in pants, had unkempt hair and none too clean a visage.

"Tell me about your dear parents. I have had no news for years. Do they still live in Newmarket? Are they well?"

"No, ma'am, I'm afraid not. Mama passed away while Papa was in France. She thought they had killed him, you see, and gave up wanting to live. Actually, he had been shut up in the Luxembourg Palace without the privilege of writing—without *any* privileges. He was barely kept alive, and it was cold. Every morning he waited for the sound of the tumbrel's wheels, but it never came. Then one day, without explanation, they released him. He came directly home, but by then it was too late. Mama was gone."

"Dear Meg gone! How sad! So Guy returned to France! During one of the so-called periods of peace, no doubt. Did he think to reclaim his title and estate?"

"Oh, no, nothing like that! Papa considers himself English now. But he and Mr. Tattersall—do you know Mr. Tattersall, of Hyde Park Corner?"

"Indeed, Edward speaks of him constantly."

"Well, because of the peace, they decided that Papa should go to France, taking six English thoroughbreds, with the idea of improving the stock with French thoroughbreds. And he was to bring back a half-dozen of the best French studs."

"What a capital idea!" exclaimed Edward.

"Also, he was to look into the feasibility of establishing a racecourse or perhaps a steeplechase over there, perhaps at Chantilly or the Champs des Mars."

"First-rate!" approved Edward.

"The horses travelled beautifully, but when the party reached the gates of Paris, the horses were seized by the authorities and Papa taken to prison."

"They discovered he was the Vicomte de St. Martin," hazarded the countess, "and were taking no chances."

"Perhaps you are right. Papa is not sure himself. Certainly they found that out later. But it's possible that some official in the government had cast covetous eyes on that string of thoroughbreds. They were outstanding, you see.

English horses are much larger than French ones, and they attracted a lot of attention on the journey. Papa thinks that someone was ready to accuse him of just about anything to get possession of them."

"Very likely!" interposed Edward. "What was the charge?"

"No charge. No accusation. No trial. He was locked up and forgotten for two years. There was little food and no fires in the winter. He became very ill. Then one day they just let him go with the proviso that he return to England at once. He was happy to comply."

"Poor Guy! To go through that experience and then to return home sick and find that his wife had passed away!" said the countess sympathetically. "Is he better now?"

"No, ma'am. He is very thin and bent, with a bad cough. He runs fevers, every night."

"Ah, consumption. Does he take good care of himself?"

"Not very well. He insists on going to the stables every day, even in bad weather. That is why I must—when I learned of Uncle William's bequest, I thought I must *make* myself worthy."

"Just so," said the countess.

Silence fell.

"Do you like chocolate, Miss Martin, hot chocolate?" asked the countess. "I always have some at eleven."

Kate hadn't had chocolate since Uncle William had bought it for her when she was nine, but she remembered how delicious it was. Besides, she was so ravenous anything would have done, even the last hard piece of bread still in her pocket.

A tray was brought in and set on a table before the countess, with a steaming pot of chocolate, various little baked goods, light as air and kept warm in linen covers, and pots of butter, orange marmalade, and Devonshire cream. The countess poured the chocolate into large cups while Edward assumed charge of preparing heaped mounds of dripping deliciousness for Kate and himself, with more restrained ones for his mother, who gave them all to Frou-Frou anyway.

The feast over, the sated little dog yapped to go outside. The countess smiled indulgently. "Would you like to walk in the garden, Miss Martin? I am afraid to let Frou-Frou go out alone. She gets into all kinds of trouble."

Edward opened the tall doors for them, giving the animal a disgusted look as it waddled past him.

"Edward, go away," said his mother, wondering whether he or Frou-Frou was the most spoiled. "I want to talk to Miss Martin alone. Look out for your brother. I am expecting him for dinner."

The sun had warmed the flowers and greenery, and sweet odours wafted on the slight breeze. An unseen gardener was pruning the hedges, and the clip of his shears attracted Frou-Frou, who padded off to investigate, stopping on the way when some novel sight or sound or smell excited her senses.

"This, then, is your first visit to Coulder Hall, Miss Martin?"

"Yes, ma'am. Mama and Lady Weyward were never close. They did not visit."

The countess made no comment but asked, "Who looked after you when your dear mama passed away and your father was in—Paris?"

"The Tattersalls, ma'am. Mrs. Tattersall was most kind. She wrote to Lady Weyward as my nearest of kin in England, but Lady Weyward replied that it was not convenient for me to come."

"Ah!"

"Mrs. Tattersall was about to write to Uncle William in the West Indies, but just then Papa arrived home. It was like a miracle—I wasn't an orphan anymore! It is so good to have Papa again! We returned to the cottage in Newmarket. We manage."

"Of course. How old are you, my dear?"

"Seventeen, ma'am."

"And you have 'come out'?"

"Come out of where, ma'am?"

The countess laughed. "A fair question. It is the custom to have a ball in honour of a girl at just about your age. It means essentially that she is ready for marriage."

Kate was aghast. "Infamous!"

The countess nodded but was smiling. "Still, it is very enjoyable to have a ball in one's honour. And it serves a purpose."

Outraged, Kate said, "Mr. Tattersall sells his *mares* in a more civilised manner! Besides, I don't want to get married."

"What *do* you want, my dear?"

"I want Papa to get well. It was so awful when I thought I was all alone in the world. But now I have Papa back! He must rest, not go out in the rain and wind. I hear that there are fine doctors in London. Mr. Tattersall offered to send for one, but Papa would not hear of it because he is so indebted to Mr. Tattersall as it is, because of the horses stolen in France. That is why I *must* become eligible for my inheritance. Papa would not say no to *me*."

"Those are fine sentiments and I admire you for them. Yes, I would like to see you inherit, too."

They reached a shaded avenue which approached the Hall from the west. Trees on either side bent towards the road like courtiers, carefully cultivated that way by the fourth earl's landscape artist. The countess looked about for Frou-Frou, but she wasn't to be seen.

"Would you be willing to follow my advice?"

"Oh, yes, ma'am, if you would be so kind! This morning I realised—that is, Lord Radburn told me—that these clothes are not suitable, nor is riding astride, he said. Actually, Papa told me so, too. He wanted to sell Fantastique—Fantastique's a colt—and buy me clothes and pay for a coach and a companion. Sell Fantastique! I would not have it. I said I would ride Fantastique and beware of strangers and all. He said, 'That's my brave girl!' and that

Fantastique was mine—my very own!—that I deserved him. So off I went alone. At London, I spent the night with the Tattersalls. They seemed surprised but didn't stop me. Now what am I to do?"

For a moment the countess was distracted. "Where on earth can Frou-Frou have gone!" She looked along the bushes that ran the width of the Hall, but no little white dog was in sight. She returned to the more important problem of helping Kate.

"Let's see—first of all we'll save this day. We'll make up a story that Edward met you aboard the mail coach in which you were travelling with an elderly companion. He introduced himself and, when he discovered who you were, offered the use of his coach, which was waiting at Lewes with his mother aboard. The offer was graciously accepted, and the elderly lady, finding that she could get a return coach immediately, did so, feeling that she was leaving her charge in good hands. In this way, you went first to Radburn Hall, had dinner there, and then we brought you to Coulder Hall."

Dismayed, Kate gasped, "But will Lady Weyward believe such a story?"

"She will if I say so," said the countess serenely.

"But my clothes, how can we explain them?"

"We must find you a suitable frock. The housekeeper will help you. In the upstairs corridors are armoires filled with clothes of every sort, jettisoned or forgotten by former occupants. We recently had a duchess with us—she stayed six months, my dear—who, when she left, abandoned her entire wardrobe, claiming that after six months, it would no longer be fashionable in London."

"Good God! Could that be true?"

"I'm afraid the vanities of Society are endless, my dear."

A ferocious yapping drew their attention. A hare started up from under the hedges, followed by an enraged and excited Frou-Frou. The hare, going at not nearly his full speed, was soon far ahead of the overfed pet, his long hind legs coolly taking him out of reach. He had recognised this noisy nuisance from other occasions and knew that just a little effort would place him in safety from it. A convenient hole inside the copse would serve him well.

"Oh, Miss Martin, save Frou-Frou!" cried the countess. "If she goes too far, she'll get lost!"

Kate set off after the poodle, catching up to it just as it dived recklessly into the hole after the nonchalant hare. Alas, only the front half of Frou-Frou could fit, her overfull stomach jamming itself in the opening. Kate knelt and tried to pull the dog's hindquarters back, but as the animal was still straining forward, they were at cross purposes.

Kate sat back on her heels, knuckles on hips, surveying the problem. Frou-Frou's rear legs were moving back and forth, casting up earth at her rescuer, her middle only becoming more firmly entrenched.

The crackle of twigs breaking under horse's hoofs diverted Kate from her assignment. A man, all in grey on a grey mare, appeared through the trees. Seeing Kate on the ground before him, he pulled on his reins and doffed a high-crowned hat.

"Good morning, miss," he said pleasantly. Without the hat he seemed younger, not more than twenty-two or twenty-three, although steel-rimmed spectacles gave him a sober, academic expression. At the sight of half a dog in the earth, hind legs wiggling, the rider smiled.

"I see Mama's little monster is in trouble again." He swung a long leg over the mare and jumped down. "Perhaps I can help."

With his crop he poked the ground before the animal. "If you will hold her hind legs together, something like a chicken trussed for the oven, and keep her from falling in farther, I'll excavate with my crop."

Working together, they got the job done. Frou-Frou was extracted, blinking at the light and sneezing because of the earth in her nostrils. To avoid any further misadventures, Kate held on to her tightly, disregarding the dirt embedded in the curly coat.

They both stood up, the young man brushing earth and leaves from his clothes. He was tall and very thin. "Permit me to introduce myself," he said. "Lionel Vinnay, at your service. I am the vicar at Tweedstun."

Kate managed a curtsey, still clutching the dog. She flushed in embarrassment at the appearance she must be presenting, in clothes that, as she had been informed several times that day, were all wrong, not to say scandalous; her red hair in disarray about her shoulders; an overstuffed dirty dog in her arms. Lionel didn't seem to notice.

"My name is Katherine Martin. I am—visiting at Radburn Park—on my way to Coulder Hall where my aunt lives. Frou-Frou chased after a hare—I chased after Frou-Frou—" Kate found herself as out of breath as Frou-Frou, who was panting after her exertions.

"That little dog causes more disturbance in this county than Napoleon. I am happy to meet you, Miss Martin. Are you staying to dinner with my mother?"

Kate nodded.

"Fine, I shall see you soon again, then." He swung up into the saddle and turned the mare in the direction of the stables.

At the edge of the copse, he looked back. Finding her gazing after him, he lifted his hat to her and rode on.

Kate bit her lip. "I am doing everything wrong. A lady would not be found staring so."

She gave Frou-Frou a poke. "And you aren't helping any."

— 4 —

Mrs. Wilcox, the housekeeper, with keys clinking in the folds of her skirt, led Kate upstairs and into the central hall of the west wing. Most people found Mrs. Wilcox tight-lipped and formidable, but she set herself out to be friendly and helpful to Kate, the result of a conversation with her brother Roscoe, who had informed her that the girl was the foal of the esteemed Guy Martin. Kate could be as eccentric as she pleased, and it would be all right with Mrs. Wilcox.

The hall stretched the width of the house and was lighted by tall mullioned windows at either end. Bedrooms opened up on both sides, many bedrooms, built to house the second earl's large brood of children and constant visitors. Between the doors were armoires and cupboards, some of the cupboards reaching almost to the ceiling and requiring the use of a ladder to see what was in the top drawers.

Mrs. Wilcox stopped before an especially large armoire, efficiently produced the right key from the bunch, and swung open massive doors.

"These belonged to the duchess of Conroyallan, miss. Stopped here half a year, she did, fluttering her lashes at Master Edward and saying things to make him laugh. Monstrously giddy she was. Left in a huff the day after the race meeting." Mrs. Wilcox lowered her voice, although they were alone. "Some folks say as how *she* popped the question, and Master Edward just laughed hearty in the way he has, as though she had said something witty-like.

She left so suddenly she didn't even pack her trunks, saying she had been here so long that her clothes were out-of-date. Pretty they are, though. Look at this, miss."

She held up a fragile ballgown made of mull-mull, in shell pink, with satin roses around the hem to give it weight. Kate gasped in admiration of its gossamer beauty but, not being informed in these matters, could only suppose that it was hopelessly unfashionable.

"Indeed, it is lovely. However, my need is for a travelling dress and cloak."

Mrs. Wilcox, well trained enough to ask no questions nor exhibit any curiosity, brought out several more costumes, with materials so fine and transparent and with necklines so low that Kate blushed at the thought of wearing them. She kept shaking her head. From the depth of the armoire Mrs. Wilcox then produced a dress of a heavier fabric in deep blue. There was a cloak with a hood in dark blue that would go with it. It was the nearest thing to what Kate wanted.

"Do you suppose these could be removed?" she asked, indicating with dissatisfaction bands of ruffles that encircled the neck and bodice.

"I think so, miss. My daughter Lucy is handy with scissors and needles. She could do it nicely. But the dress will then be very plain, miss."

"That's exactly what I want," said Kate decisively.

"Very well, miss," acquiesced Mrs. Wilcox, folding the dress and cloak over her arm. "Come this way, and we'll tell Lucy and see if she needs to make any changes in the fit. She can do them while you have your bath."

She led the way through a pink and blue and gold gilt bedroom, and beyond to a boudoir that seemed to be all mirrors and bows. These were the duchess's rooms, I'll wager, thought Kate. In the middle reposed a curved metal bathtub. Mrs. Wilcox pulled a cord on the wall; not only did daughter Lucy arrive with a sewing basket, but she was followed by a parade of maids bearing pitchers and buckets of steaming water. While Lucy deftly inserted pins in the blue frock to fit a figure slenderer than the duchess's, the others filled basins in which to wash Kate's luxuriant hair and filled the metal tub into which they tossed bits of lavender.

Kate emerged from the ablutions feeling like a boiled lobster and nearly as lifeless. Mrs. Wilcox mopped her dry and helped her into delicate white linen undergarments with interlaced ribbons around bosom and waist that could be drawn to fit. White stockings with a clock design up the sides were found of the right size, and her feet were inserted into soft black heelless slippers. The blue dress, now bereft of its finery, was slipped over her head.

A maid with a brush in either hand vigorously brushed her hair dry, and still another appeared with pins and ribbons and began to dress it, piling some of it high with curls dangling at the side. "This is the way the duchess liked me to arrange her hair," said the maid, "although she needed to use rats."

"*Rats?*"

"Extra pieces of hair, miss. But you don't need none, not with all you have."

Kate surveyed herself in the oval mirror. "Oh, no," she said, seizing a brush for herself and smoothing the hair down, using a single blue ribbon to hold it back. "There, that's better."

"As you wish, miss," said the maid doubtfully.

At last she was ready, and Mrs. Wilcox preceded her handiwork downstairs to the small drawing room, where the countess and her sons were enjoying glasses of Madeira before dinner. Both men stood up as she entered and looked at her with interest. She knew that they had been discussing her.

"Yes," said Edward, "just about right."

Mrs. Wilcox withdrew, satisfied.

Edward continued his examination by walking around Kate. "Just *about* right," he said, an element of doubt entering his voice, as though she were a mare he was considering purchasing, but perhaps there was some hidden fault somewhere.

"Would you like to examine my teeth or inspect my shoeing?" asked Kate.

"Don't be impertinent, my girl. But a little severe, no?" he said, noticing the unadorned dress and simple hair arrangement.

"That's because I *am* severe," said Kate, giving him a fierce look.

"*Ed*ward," protested the countess, "fetch Miss Martin a glass of Madeira, and stop pacing." She turned to Kate. "Do sit down, my dear, and ignore him. The simplicity of dress and hair is absolutely correct for your age and for the purpose of travelling in a mail coach, which is what you are supposed to have done. Besides, it suits you entirely, and it wouldn't many women. You have an instinct for dressing well, the *je ne sais quoi* that the French always have."

"Thank you, ma'am." Kate was glad to sit down, for she was feeling weak from the scalding bath.

Lionel spoke up. "The colour of the dress brings out the blue of her eyes."

"How gallant, Lionel!" exclaimed the countess. It was not the most elaborate of compliments she had ever heard, but considering that it was Lionel who made it, she felt her younger son deserved praise.

He was encouraged to continue. "Her eyes are the colour of lapis lazuli."

"A lovely comparison," said the countess approvingly.

Edward held out a glass of wine to Kate, looking deeply into the lapis lazuli eyes, his own dark ones shiny with amusement. Kate lowered her lashes abruptly. The countess was pleased again. Her elder son had not made his usual snap conquest; clearly the girl was annoyed, and a rebuff would do him good.

Edward was not put off. "Remember that altar we saw in Rome, Lionel, made completely of lapis lazuli? San Giovanni, was it? Her eyes are very like."

"I don't enjoy being compared to an altar."

"It was Santa Maria Maggiore," corrected Lionel, "and it was very beautiful and impressive, Miss Martin."

"Thank you for speaking *to* me, Vicar, and not *about* me. I was beginning to feel like an object and not a person."

"I think you are very much of a person," replied Lionel. "Very real."

Kate managed a smile and sipped at the Madeira.

"Now," said Edward, with the air of taking charge, "I think we should get the story straight. I met Miss Martin on the mail coach to Lewes. There we transferred to our coach, in which my mother was waiting. The elderly companion returned home. Miss Martin stopped for dinner at Radburn Hall, then I drove her on to Coulder Hall."

"I intend to go with you," said the countess, "to lend my weight to the fiction."

"I, too, shall accompany you," put in Lionel.

"I want you to," approved the countess. "We'll wait upon Lady Weyward *en masse*."

"One more thing," said Edward. "What about luggage for Miss Martin?"

"I sent off a small trunk," said Kate, with dignity. "It should be there by now." She took another sip of the Madeira, feeling close to tears.

"If you have need of a more extended wardrobe, Miss Martin, I invite you to take further advantage of the armoires in the west wing . . . why, whatever is the matter, my dear?"

Tears were coursing down Kate's pale cheeks, and the eyes that so recently were compared to lapis lazuli were as awash with saltwater as the stone itself in the depths of the sea.

"I'm sorry," gulped Kate, trying to get hold of herself. "It's been an unusual day—the hot bath drained my strength—I'm not used to fortified wines. . . ."

Edward looked at her in amazement. "Good God," he said.

Lionel spoke gently. "There's more to it than that, isn't

there?" He removed a handkerchief from his cuff and handed it to her. "Why don't you tell us? We *are* your friends, you know. Perhaps we can help."

His sympathy loosened the tears in reserve, and she made good use of his handkerchief.

"My dear," said the countess, "pray tell us."

"It's just that"—she swallowed hard and crumpled Lionel's handkerchief into a wad—"I don't like being a lady!"

"Good God!" repeated Edward. "Is that all!"

"*All!*" she flared up at him. "*All!* It's monstrous, that's what it is. It's all lies and deceit, sham and hypocrisy, falsity and subterfuge. That's the lesson I have learned this day! Oh, I'm sorry, Countess. You have been very kind to me, and you must believe that I am very grateful to you for your efforts on my behalf. But I can't go on with it, it's all *wrong!* I want to go home!"

"Good God!" said Edward a third time. He turned to his mother for help. "Mama, tell her that she is mistaken."

The countess remained silent.

"Tell her that what she says is nonsense!" pleaded Edward.

"No," said the countess slowly, "it is not nonsense. I, too, have often thought those things that Miss Martin has so bravely put into words."

"Mama!"

"Edward, think of the ladies you know. Aren't you aware that their pink complexions are not always the endowment of nature, that the high-piled hair is not all their own, that mull-mull and silk and satin are more flattering to face and figure than linsey-woolsey? Don't you realise that high spirits are often false, that clever remarks, seemingly off-hand, are prepared well ahead of time? Have you never met ladies who claim friendship with prominent people that they have met just once, or not at all, and some who pretend to have more of a fortune than is actually the case?"

"I suppose that some ladies are like that."

"I, myself, have lied, was planning to do so this very afternoon, as you see. Often have I resorted to falsity and subterfuge."

"Mama!"

"It's true, Edward. And what Miss Martin says is well taken, at least in part. And that is the part we have so cruelly and crudely exhibited to her this day. Now we must somehow set it right, before she gives up on this whole charade and returns to Newmarket. And that would be a great loss to her, to her father, and to us who would enjoy her company. We must not allow it to happen."

"It would not be fair," put in Lionel.

"Miss Martin, as I understand it, your Uncle William has left a will that bequeaths to you his entire fortune—which I also understand is more than substantial—if you will live a year at Coulder Hall with your Aunt Harriet and if at the end of that time a committee of three solicitors finds that you are indeed a 'lady.' Otherwise, this fortune goes to his business partner in the Caribbean, who is equally as rich as William was and does not need it.

"Already a generous sum of money has passed to your aunt for your support for this year, but other than that the Weywards have not been included in the will. I think I can explain that. Harriet jilted William for his elder brother—so why should he leave her anything, or her children? When I came to Radburn Hall as a bride I met them all. William was no one's fool, believe me. Except in love. He was terribly cut up when Harriet married his brother Joseph. He left before the wedding, never did marry, and returned only once for a visit. Were you fond of your Uncle William, my dear?"

"Oh, very! He was so kind to us. I cried when he left. I loved him."

"And I believe that he loved you and wanted you to have his fortune. Yet he was shrewd, was your uncle, remember that, and he did make this stipulation about your being a 'lady.' "

"Yes," said Kate miserably.

"Being a 'lady' does entail wearing clothes that are generally considered at least suitable. In fact, being a 'lady of fashion' carries a weight that you wouldn't believe, that goes far beyond the matter of the clothes on one's back. A 'lady' influences others in all kinds of ways, for better or for worse. What starts out as a discussion of her clothes extends into a criticism of her manners and a dissection of her morals."

"Oh, dear," said Kate.

"You, within the year, at the age of only eighteen, could be an heiress of great wealth, and as such, a person of consequence. Everything about you would be noted, and not only noted but copied, *aped*, and this is a responsibility. You would be an influence, a power for good or evil. Therefore, you would have to take heed in everything, be prudent, always weigh an action in terms of its consequence."

"What about freedom?" Kate sounded as though she were strangling.

"Freedom of a kind. Think of people you would be free to help—your father for instance, are you not now thinking of him? You would have freedom to make decisions about an array of opportunities that now are not open to you. But of course they must be correct decisions, not carelessly thought out, not selfish."

"What about happiness?"

"Oh, well, happiness—" The countess seemed about to disregard happiness, until she looked into Kate's earnest face. "Perhaps if you are lucky—yes, why not? I was. And there would be satisfaction. Responsibility, well handled, brings satisfaction."

The countess's words left them all thoughtful.

Lionel was the first to break the silence. "Well, Miss Martin, are you still willing to go through this year of probation, beginning with this afternoon of playacting and deception, and ending possibly with a lifetime of self-imposed restrictions?"

"It would require courage," said Edward, with a rare show of understanding, "but the stakes are great."

"Your uncle wanted it," said the countess. "It was his dying wish."

"Well?" asked Lionel quietly.

Kate swallowed a sigh. "I'll try," she said meekly.

Cosgrove the butler opened the double doors. "Dinner is served, my lady."

Both men stood up and offered their arms to Kate. She looked from one to the other and chose Lionel. Edward, ruffled, assisted his mother.

The countess looked pleased.

— 5 —

FOUR WHITE HORSES, hitched to the countess's carriage, stomped their hoofs and switched thick untrimmed tails. The coach was a gift from Edward to replace the heavy and uncomfortable one built on cross beds. This new one was the latest thing, designed by Obadiah Elliott. It was light and hung upon elliptical springs, so that an occupant's upper and lower teeth did not crash together painfully, even when jolting about on rough roads. Not only that, the coach was beautiful to look at. Gilded angels decorated the four corners of the roof, and there were elaborate carvings about the panels of the doors. Forest scenes with nymphs had been painted on the panels by an Italian artist whom Edward had met on his Grand Tour. As outriders, Edward and Lionel were already mounted, one on either side. Not even a queen could arrive at Coulder Hall in a more elegant or ornate equipage than had been made available to Kate.

Dressed in calling clothes, the countess approached, as two footmen lowered the small steps and assisted her into the carriage.

A flurried Cosgrove ran down the front steps. "My lady," he said, "I can find Miss Martin nowhere on the main floor. I have been in every room."

"Nor anyplace upstairs neither, my lady," the housekeeper gasped behind him.

The countess called to her sons. "Edward! Lionel! Alas, I'm afraid our little bird has flown after all. Our servants say she is not in the house anywhere. Oh! I am so disappointed. I had formed an attachment to her."

Lionel drew up to the coach. "I cannot believe she would run away. She had a moment of weakness, reasonably so, but she gave her word to try."

Edward said confidently, "I'll wager I can find her for you."

He set off for the stables and found Kate at Fantastique's stall. Trusting the ministrations of no one but herself, she had come to see to the condition of the colt. She could not fault Roscoe. Fantastique was clean, dry, and smooth, and was sleepily blinking his eyes after his meal.

"*Sois patient, mon petit.* Just a little patience and we shall be together again."

At the approach of Edward, she stiffened.

He smiled. "Satisfied?"

"Yes," said Kate. "Roscoe does excellent work."

"I'll tell him your verdict. He will be pleased to hear your opinion."

Kate frowned, not certain whether he was mocking her or not, but thinking he most likely was. Outrageous man! She turned her back on him and stroked the colt. "*À bientôt, mon cher.* I'll come back for you as soon as I can."

"Wouldn't it be better for him to remain here—for the year? Lady Harriet might not care for the expense of having another horse to look after. And, as you say, Roscoe is a first-rate stableman."

"I will think about it."

"As you please, Miss Martin. But remember the colt. You will not find the same amenities at the stables of Coulder Hall, I assure you."

Kate did not deign to reply to this, feeling that she was as good a judge of these matters as the opinionated Lord Radburn, any day.

"Is it time to go?"

"Indeed, the countess is awaiting you in the coach. Everyone has been looking for you."

"How did you know I was here?"

"Like minds."

"I hope not, Lord Radburn!" Kate said fervently and walked quickly to the door. Edward only laughed.

Adelaide Weyward was the only member of the family at Coulder Hall awaiting Kate's arrival with pleasure. Every few minutes she ran from the schoolroom to the hall windows that overlooked the drive. Mrs. Mitchell, reading aloud from an easy history of the Tudors, was annoyed with her charge, as usual.

"Adelaide, come here this instant! If you do not settle down, I shall have to inform Lady Weyward, and you know what that will mean."

Adelaide knew all too well what that would mean. Meekly she returned to the schoolroom.

"May I keep the door open so that I can hear her carriage?"

"You may *not!* Shut that door, sit down, and stay *sat.*"

But the unmistakable noise of many horses' hoofs and carriage wheels setting up sparks on pebbles drew Adelaide recklessly back to the hall window, regardless of the consequences. The elaborate coach of the countess was drawing up to the steps, with Edward and Lionel as outriders. Adelaide was disappointed. Although she was always happy to see her neighbours, as they were kind to her, especially Lionel, this time she regretted that it was not her only cousin come to stay. She watched the footmen assist the countess down from the coach. Then, oh joy! a glorious surprise, a young lady dressed in a deep blue cloak with a hood barely covering bright red hair, just like hers!

"Mama! Donald! Lydia!" shouted Adelaide, tearing down the hall, evading the ample form of Mrs. Mitchell, who tried to block her. "Cousin Kate is here! She has arrived at last!"

Down the staircase she flew and burst into the drawing room, where the family was assembled. "She's here!"

"Adelaide! How dare you enter in such a manner? I won't have it!" The frown lines between Lady Weyward's eyebrows deepened as she regarded her youngest. "Why, oh why, have I been cursed with such a backward daughter? What am I to do with her?"

Lydia looked up irritably from the novel by Mrs. Radcliffe that she was reading. "Where is that Mitchell woman? Isn't she supposed to be guarding her?"

Donald, *Sir* Donald since the death of his father, regarded Adelaide with disdain. "She ought to be locked up. There are institutions for cases like hers. Why do you not put her away?"

Adelaide looked from one to another of her relatives, the colour and happiness draining from her face, fear in her eyes. Mrs. Mitchell entered, one hand dramatically over her heart to emphasise that hurrying was not good for her. She found her charge hangdog and pliable.

"No supper for her tonight," ordered Lady Weyward.

Mrs. Mitchell led Adelaide back up the stairs, complaining that the steps and Adelaide in particular would be the death of her. They had reached the top when the visiting party entered the hall. Kate, allowing the butler to remove her cloak, felt her glance drawn upward to a small face that, although framed by cheerful red hair, was as far from cheer as a young face could get. It was pale, and in the eyes was silent terror.

That child looks the way I feel, Kate thought and smiled ruefully up at her. After a second of surprise, the smile was returned with interest, a beautiful guileless smile. In an instant they were collaborators against an unjust and bewildering world. Kate raised her hand and wiggled her fingers in greeting, and the girl would have responded but was jerked out of sight by Mrs. Mitchell with a rough, "*Come on*, then."

"That's Adelaide, your youngest cousin," explained Edward, noticing the exchange. "She's a bit simple."

Kate wanted to ask him more, but the butler had opened

the double drawing room doors and was already announcing the countess.

Lady Weyward started up as the countess swept in. Without meaning to, without a word or a gesture, the countess always made her feel inferior. It was because the countess knew of her humble origins as the daughter of a tradesman, knew that she had married for a title and inheritance, callously jilting the man to whom she had promised herself. So Lady Weyward disliked the countess, that dislike carefully disguised because of the countess's powerful social position.

Lydia was fluttery, not at meeting her long-lost, newfound cousin, but because Lord Radburn had accompanied the countess. Her cap was set for him, had been since childhood, and although he was carelessly courteous, he never gave her any hope. Lydia arranged her face and posture becomingly.

With the gesture of a connoisseur, Donald lifted the single eyeglass that dangled from his neck on a ribbon and secured it in his right eye. He did not need the eyeglass to see better; it was worn because, although he had straight features, his eyes were set too close together and the monocle helped to disguise this defect. Besides, to raise it to his eye and peer at something from a height was a condescending gesture that he enjoyed assuming.

With a backward tilt to his head, he examined the flushed girl being presented to them as though he were sniffing her. It was not because he found her attractive that he was pleased with his cousin; it was because she reminded him of Adelaide. The resemblance caused him to think that Cousin Kate, too, might be mentally weak and easily manipulated by threats or by one of his smiles bestowed as a great reward. The going would be easier than his mother had thought.

Lady Weyward rang for tea. As they waited, Edward explained with amused relish how it came about that Kate had arrived at Radburn Hall first, while Kate herself sat silently in anguish.

Not one of the Weywards doubted the story.

"How convenient that was for our dear Kate!" said Lady Weyward with a smile, thinking how the family had been saved from paying for the coach from Lewes and from the expense of putting up the companion.

"How pleasant it was for us to have Miss Martin!" said the countess.

Lady Weyward studied the countess. Clearly the girl had won her approbation; if the countess found her likable, perhaps those solicitors might. She glanced at her son, who was looking remarkably self-satisfied. She did not feel as sanguine about the situation as Donald did, and the lines of dissatisfaction in her face deepened.

While the wrinkles of discontent had not yet marred her smooth visage, Lydia, a younger version of Lady Weyward, looked at Edward, who was looking at Kate, and discontent marred her heart. How often she had daydreamed about meeting Edward accidentally in the very way he was now happily describing, and in all these years it had never happened. Instead, it had to happen to this raw girl on her first day in the county, and Edward obviously had enthusiastically aided and befriended her. Maddening! And just now when the field was clear after the departure of the duchess of Conroyallan. This girl isn't even pretty, Lydia thought. I have never cared for red hair; thank heaven *I* did not inherit it. She has freckles and her gown is plain, obviously not from London. Yet there is something about her—what is it? Style? No, no. Couldn't be.

With narrowed lids she watched Edward turn to Kate as he embroidered his narrative. He stopped and smiled. The girl did not respond but remained motionless, her eyes on the floor, looking uncomfortable. No charm, thought Lydia, she hasn't an ounce of charm. Why, she hasn't said two whole sentences since she entered the room. With astonishment she saw Lionel reach out and squeeze one of Kate's clenched fists as though to comfort her, and Kate responded to him with a tremulous smile. Lionel! Is Lionel smitten? Well, she can have *him*, that stick! But she had better leave Edward alone.

Tea was served. To Kate's relief, the conversation turned to topics other than the fictitious account of her fortuitous arrival. Edward led the discussion of the recent race meeting at Radburn Park and the upsetting results of the last race.

"I was certain my entry would win," he said. "It seemed a sure thing."

"You made quite a few of us think so," said Donald bitterly, "and we lost our shirts."

"I *am* sorry," said Edward, not sounding very sorry. "At first it seemed unreasonable to me that Lord Easton's colt should get and keep the lead the way that he did. It was only a moderate horse, and mine had a stud fee of fifty guineas. I'm beginning to believe that it has to do with horsemanship as well as horses, a redistribution of the weight of the jockey."

"It's the new American method," said Kate. "Not long ago Papa brought over an American to teach his jockeys the Sloan method. It consists of throwing the weight of the body forward onto the withers. You must pull up the stirrup leathers. I will show you if you like—" She caught a gesture from the countess, a barely perceptible shake of the head.

"You will *show* him?" asked Lydia, picking up the slip. She pretended to be horrified, raising her eyebrows; actually she was annoyed that Kate continued to have Edward's undivided attention.

"I meant that I could instruct his jockey," revised Kate, sadly realising that now she could not show him, much as she would be glad to. "The horses like it better that way. Also, it permits them to race from the start, instead of conserving strength for the last lap."

"But doesn't this method take more out of a horse?" Edward asked.

"Of course. Bigger demands are made on it. One must look for endurance in a horse as well as speed; he must have a strong constitution and courage to keep going. The horse's temperament becomes a factor."

Donald's monocle popped out, revealing his eyes—not his best feature. Kate did not sound at all like Adelaide. She was direct, vigorous, emphatic, not the least sickly in mind. Lord Radburn was leaning forward with rapt attention while she informed him of a thing or two. About horses!

Now the three Weywards were alarmed.

"This is a delicious dish of tea," said the countess tactfully. "Do you mix it yourself?"

"We have it mixed specially in London," said Lady Weyward, pleased with a compliment from the countess, "and we are very particular in the brewing. Let me tell you."

The two older ladies discussed tea and its steeping. Alert to his mother's cue, Lionel turned to Lydia.

"Where is Adelaide today? Is she not well?"

"Well enough—in body," replied Lydia, still keeping her eyes on Edward, who persisted in discussing horses with Kate. "Otherwise very bad. She is disobedient, dresses carelessly, runs through the house screaming, and cannot learn. Mrs. Mitchell says it is impossible to teach her *anything*. She is an embarrassment to us all. Donald was saying only today that we shall be forced to have her sent away." Reluctantly she turned her gaze from Edward to Lionel. "As a vicar perhaps you have heard of some institution or other?"

"I have, certainly, all of them horrors. Surely Adelaide is not that bad. I know that she would be desperately unhappy if she were committed to any of them."

"Serve her right! Aren't *we* unhappy? She is a great burden to us. Why should we allow it?" Her voice rose stridently.

Lionel examined her through steel-rimmed spectacles. "I understand," he said.

"And you will help us find a place?"

"It isn't that simple. There is a question of certification."

"That's easy. Dr. Gilford will sign anything we say."

"Other physicians would have to be called in."

"Perhaps they could be brought to sign, with—encouragement." She looked at him slyly from the side of her eyes. "Say of a monetary kind?"

She was suddenly aware that everyone else had become silent at once, as happens with groups sometimes. They had all heard the last remark. Edward was staring at her. So was Kate.

Lydia laughed nervously. "It must be twenty of, or twenty past, the hour," she said, "if you are superstitious."

"Superstitious or not," said the countess, who had grown weary of the Weywards, "it is time for us to leave."

Lady Weyward jealously observed the cordiality of the countess's farewell to Kate. "Won't you come again for chocolate, say Thursday at eleven? I know how much you enjoy it. We must get better acquainted."

Donald, his eyepiece restored but not his self-confidence, saw Lionel take Kate's hand and heard the words, "I have something to ask you, Miss Martin. But not here and now. Later." Good Lord, thought Donald, does this chap think to propose? Lionel must be assuming she will inherit.

Lydia watched Edward bow to Kate and strained her ears to hear what they were saying.

"Your advice this morning was correct, Lord Radburn," Kate admitted. "I can see that."

"Please don't thank me."

"I didn't know that I was thanking you. I merely said that I see that you are correct."

Edward grinned. Does he never take his eyes from her? worried Lydia.

Mrs. Mitchell heard Adelaide's prayers in a bored way, then followed her mistress's precept of meanness by taking away Adelaide's candle. "You don't need no candle when you are in bed," she said crossly. She wasn't saving the candle for the sake of Lady Weyward's budget. It was a new candle, and she would stow it away with some others in a bottom drawer for her own use later on at home. *Candles don't come cheap*, she thought to herself, *and Lady Weyward don't pay me enough.*

Adelaide lay in bed trying not to notice how her stomach was rolling with hunger, her eyes squeezed tight so that she would not see shadows moving in the corners of the room. With Mrs. Mitchell gone, she threw caution aside along with her blanket, leapt out of bed, and went down on her knees to say an extra urgent prayer.

"Oh, God," she whispered, "don't let them send me to an institution!"

She returned to bed and was pulling the covers over her head when she thought of another petition. Resolutely not looking at the shadows, she again climbed out of bed and went down on her knees.

"Dear God," she prayed, "please make Cousin Kate like me even though I am very naughty."

Back in bed, another need relentlessly occurred to her, and once again she dared the threatening darkness to pray, "Dearest God, help me to forget how hungry I am!"

— 6 —

As WAS HER habit, Kate rose at dawn. In the chill room, she poured some cold water from a pitcher into a basin and washed very quickly. It was a small room, located opposite the schoolroom, which had been occupied by Lydia as a child. Kate's trunk had arrived, and she selected from it a dress she thought would be suitable for mornings at Coulder Hall. It was of white cotton with blue stripes, in an old-fashioned style with a full skirt, handed down to her from her mother. A sturdy pair of shoes and the duchess's cast-off cloak and she was ready to inspect the stables of Coulder Hall.

The house was still as Kate descended the staircase and crossed the hall.

"Miss Meg?" asked a cracked voice.

Startled, Kate paused and looked toward the door leading to the kitchens. A hunched shapeless figure of an old woman dressed in black, with a white starched cap that did not quite succeed in holding down the wispy white hair, was peering into the hall.

"Be ye Miss Meg?" asked the old voice.

Kate moved into a shaft of morning sunlight that shone through a window set high in the wall. Sunbeams lit up the red hair and the young eager face. The woman moved closer, trying to see with eyes whose brown irises were ringed with white.

"Ye be Miss Kate, newly come to visit! Forgive an old woman. Sometimes early in the morning, afore I've had me tay, it seems like I'm living twenty years back. When I seed you tripping down the steps just now for all the world like Miss Meg, it seemed like the old days when we was all happy and full of hope. Afore Lady Weyward come to be mistress here, that is. Shouldn't be saying that, but I'm old now and can say anything I like. She don't like it, but she don't say nothing, afeared of the other servants."

"Nurse Amelia? Is that you? You were Mama's nanny until her marriage?"

"That I be, miss, and that I was. Many's the time I be sorry that I didn't run off with them like they axed. But I was married meself, and Ben Hanscomb, him that was me husband, Lord rest his soul, he was too timid-like. He said Guy Martin, gentleman though he was in a funny foreign way, didn't have a bean nor was like to have. Excuse me, miss, for speaking so frank-like. It's me way."

"Not at all, Nanny. Your husband was correct. Papa never did succeed in rebuilding his fortune. But we have all been happy, anyway. We would have loved to have had you at Newmarket. Your husband might have found good work there. Newmarket is a busy, thriving place for those fond of horses."

"All might-have-beens, miss. Too late now. But here *you* be at last, and things is looking bright again."

"I must tell you that Mama—"

"Ain't with us no more. So I heard, miss, and sad I was at the news. The Lord taketh them that he loveth. The good die young. But here I am keeping her Miss Kate in the cold hall. I talk a lot, don't I? Can't help it. Would you like a nice hot cup of tay? Just set it on to steep and it oughter be good and black by now. If you don't mind coming into the kitchen. No one is about yet. I allus gets up early and sets the kettle on and has a peaceful cup of tay afore the rest gets moving."

Kate followed the old nurse into the cavernous kitchen and accepted gratefully the big steaming bowl set on the long scrubbed planks of the table.

"Nice and strong, ain't it, miss? I allus make a good black cup. Keeps me going, tay does."

They both drank appreciatively.

"Now, where be ye off to so early in the day? Don't tell me, you're off to the stables, like Miss Meg afore ye."

"You don't know how much it pleases me to be told I am like Mama. You couldn't pay me a nicer compliment."

"Ye be very like her, hair, figger, and disposition to boot. Off at dawn to see the horses! But ye won't find the stables like they was when your papa had charge. Master Donald, he don't really care about horses. Just to ride on to get someplace, and something to bet on at the race meetings. And he don't have no money no more to keep things up, what with his gambling and drinking and whoring. Excuse me, miss, using such a word in your presence."

"Donald! He looks so proper!"

"Oh, butter wouldn't melt in his mouth to look at him here at Coulder Hall. But in the coast towns it's another story, so I hear, miss."

"Well! That's something to know."

"Yes, miss, just as well you do know and keeps your distance. He ain't bad looking, is Master Donald, in a wishy-washy way. But I sees ye're anxious to be off. The quickest way to the stables is through here, miss."

She led the way through the pantry and a cold-storage room to a back door. "Breakfast is at nine in the breakfast room. Best be on time, miss. Her ladyship can be a stickler on little things. The big ones she don't see."

"Thanks, Nanny."

"Any time you wants something, I'm allus here, puttering near the fire to keep me old bones warm. Some'n else, miss. Just as well not to let Lady Weyward see you care much about horses, or care about anything. She can twist things something awful. Keep yourself to yourself, as they say."

Kate nodded and set off in the early morning mist toward

the stables. On an impulse she turned around and ran back to the squat figure, threw her arms around her, and kissed her.

"That's from Mama," Kate said and skipped off. She followed a path, nearly grown-over now, thinking of her mother taking the same way many years before.

The stables were large, but the wooden doors were weatherbeaten and decayed. Rusted iron clasps creaked as she pulled open one side. The foul odor of unclean, unventilated stables drove her back. Opening both doors as far as they would go and propping them with stones, she took a deep breath and braced herself to reenter. To think that her father had once been in charge of these fetid stables! He would have apoplexy if he could see and smell them now!

Only five stalls were in use. Four drooping chestnuts, obviously matched to draw Lady Weyward's coach, occupied adjoining stalls. On the other side of the stables, the fifth horse, a large powerful roan, was angrily twitching flies from its back. Donald's, thought Kate. The chestnuts drowsily let her open the upper parts of their hatch doors and began to stamp and neigh as the morning air revived them. As she released the catch on the roan's stall, he moved threateningly. "Like master, like horse," Kate muttered. The mean-tempered roan told her as much about Donald as Nurse Amelia had.

In the corner was a barrel of water, and she filled the troughs. Each animal drank thirstily and looked for more. Searching about for some hay or oats, she tripped over an object in the straw and nearly screamed when she saw that it was a man's arm. The arm, however, was attached to a body in stableman's clothes, and that body groaned and went on sleeping. The other arm cradled a jug, the cork gone, its contents obviously transferred into the inert form half covered with straw. Kate was tempted to kick him but instead muttered another proverb: "Let sleeping dogs lie."

Finding some hay, she filled each animal's pouch, warily

in the case of the roan. The groom will wonder who did all this, she thought, and giggled. Let him worry about pixies and hobgoblins whilst nursing his hangover!

Before she left, she glanced around the stable again. If only I could get this place back in shape again, she said to herself. But I am not in charge here, am I? If I could get my inheritance, that is, if I behave myself, I could suggest—I could make changes. A force for good, the countess had said; I might be a force for good, starting here, with my relatives' stable.

Back in her room, she hurriedly unlaced the heavy shoes, replacing them with the dainty flat ones formerly belonging to the duchess, and made herself clean and presentable. The clock on the mantel of the breakfast room was striking nine as she entered.

Her aunt and two cousins were already at the table. Donald and Lydia nodded to her coldly, and Donald retreated behind a newspaper. Lady Harriet said formally, "Good morning, Katherine. It might be just as well if you begin to observe our customs as soon as possible. You should arrive for breakfast *before* nine so that the servants can begin serving on the hour. They have other work to do, you know, and cannot wait about for layabeds. I am a firm believer in early rising."

"So am I, Aunt," said Kate. Lady Weyward gave her a sharp glance, but the girl's attention was on the boiled egg in front of her, of which she broke off the top dexterously.

"Will Cousin Adelaide be down for breakfast?" she asked, thinking of the sad-faced girl she had not yet met.

"Adelaide no longer takes meals with us. I must tell you, although you will no doubt find it out soon enough for yourself, that Adelaide is not normal."

"Not normal in what way?"

"She is noisy, disobedient, and cannot learn. Generally she is a pest around the house. Pray let us not discuss her. It is *too* distressing."

The rest of the meal passed in silence except for the clink

of silver against china and an occasional "Pass the salt, please." Several times Kate intercepted a look in her direction from Lydia. When she answered with a smile, the appraising eyes were lowered.

As they rose from the table, Lady Weyward said to Kate, "Can you find employment of your own this morning?"

"Yes, Aunt, I plan to write to Papa to tell him that I have arrived safely."

"Very good. You see, we are going to have a family conference and must not be disturbed under any circumstances."

"I shall not disturb you, Aunt."

She watched as Lady Weyward, followed by Lydia and Donald, entered the library. The door was firmly closed. So I am not "family," thought Kate. She went up the stairs to her room, relieved that she had the morning to herself.

In the library they gathered at the fire, Lady Weyward taking a comfortable chair while Lydia sat in the settle close to the fire. Donald paced restlessly back and forth. The library had a ravaged look, for the classics that once lined it had been sold. Nobody read them, Lady Weyward had reasoned, and they only gave the servants more to dust. She had got a good price for them, too.

"Whew!" said Lydia. "Did you see that frock? A full skirt and built-up neckline—ten years old at least!" She smoothed out the straight lines of her morning gown and pushed down the décolletage that kept riding up. It was a style made popular by Josephine of France but sewed badly by a local dressmaker.

"The Messrs. Pierce, Price, and Sharpe are not going to judge her on the fullness of her skirt!" said Donald irritably. "At least she looked decent and warm!" Like many libertines, he often adopted a righteous tone.

Lydia hissed like a cat but raised her scarf around her shoulders—the truth was, she felt chilly.

"Stop quarrelling!" interposed Lady Weyward. "It will

get us nowhere. Donald is right. We must try to judge her from the standpoint of the solicitors. From what we have seen of her so far, would you say that she appears a *lady?*"

"You'd have to," said Lydia reluctantly. "It's 'yes, Aunt' and 'no, Aunt' and 'just as you say, Aunt.' " She mimicked someone toadying.

"Unfortunately, she *doesn't* sound like that," said Donald. "She is perfectly civil."

"Why are you taking her side?" his sister demanded, flaring up. "What is this magic she has over men? Donald, Lionel, even Edward!" Her voice was shrill. "They have fallen like ninepins in a game of skittles."

"Perhaps it's because she has a pleasant disposition, not like some I know."

"Children! Stop it! Stop it this instant! You both agree, then, as matters now stand, that she is likely to inherit?"

They were both silent. Donald paused in his pacing. "I suppose so," he muttered unwillingly.

He resumed walking, saying sulkily, "We are as closely related to Uncle William as she is. And I am the oldest and a man."

"Huh!" said Lydia scornfully. "You fancy yourself the male heir. Perhaps Uncle William heard how fast you went through your father's inheritance. That would be enough to put him off! But I am her senior by two years. *I* should be the one to inherit!"

"But you weren't mentioned in the will at all, were you?" said Donald nastily. "Perhaps he heard about your haughtiness!"

This time Lady Weyward said nothing, allowing her children to bicker, knowing quite well why their Uncle William had not felt inclined to remember them in his will.

Lydia turned to her mother. "What did you mean by 'as matters now stand'?" Her tone exactly duplicated Lady Weyward's.

"We thought . . ." said Lady Weyward, lowering her voice. Since the books had been removed, the library had an unfortunate tendency to resound. "Donald and I, that is, thought we could—manipulate—the situation, you see."

"No, I don't see."

"Well, she will inherit if she can prove herself a lady. But suppose, although her manners were adequate, she appeared a little—" Lady Weyward made circular motions next to her temple.

"Like Adelaide?"

"Like Adelaide."

"But still, even if Kate doesn't inherit, then the fortune goes to Uncle's partner in the West Indies. What's the point?"

"You miss the point, as usual," said her brother, with a superior air. "What we can prove is a streak of madness in the family. Adelaide, Kate, Uncle William. I know a very clever solicitor"—Donald put a forefinger next to his nose to indicate cleverness—"who is prepared to overturn the will on the grounds that Uncle William was not in his right mind when he made it. It *is* a very strange document."

"You fool! You'll ruin my chances!" shouted Lydia, making the empty shelves reverberate. "I don't want madness proved in this family! I want to marry—and marry well!"

"Only yesterday you were inquiring of the vicar of ways to put Adelaide away. Why the change?"

"Having a backward sister is one thing, and if she could be put quietly out to pasture somewhere, good riddance to a bad embarrassment. But a *streak* of madness is something else. People will look for it in *us!*"

"I wouldn't worry about that," said Lady Weyward in a soothing voice. "After all, a streak of madness appears in the best of families. Look at the old king—they have to strap him down periodically. The same with some of his cousins in Germany."

"*We* are not the royal family!" said Lydia vehemently.

Lady Weyward felt insulted. She was tempted to say that Lydia's real father was nowhere near as highborn as the father she thought was hers, being a certain draper's assistant in Lewes—who happened to be Donald's father, too. The irony was that Adelaide, who was most certainly mad, was the only true child of Sir Joseph Weyward. Lady Weyward clenched her lips together in the effort to hold back this information.

"I won't have it!" stormed Lydia. "Think of something else!"

"It has its risks," said Lady Weyward, through tight lips, "and it would cost to pay the lawyers. Well, Donald?"

He stopped pacing and sighed heavily. "So be it," he said in a resigned voice. "I'll marry her."

Lydia gasped. "*You*—will marry her!" She began to laugh. "*You* will get her to marry you!"

"Donald has had many conquests," defended his mother.

"If he *pays* for them," said Lydia coarsely, "at Liz Hamilton's!" Her laughter had a hysterical ring.

"Lydia!" protested their mother.

"Better Kate marry me than Lord Radburn," said Donald ominously. Lydia's wild laughter ended in a croak.

"Touché," said Lady Weyward smugly, happy that her daughter had had a proper comedown. "Now, are we agreed that the easiest course is simply for Donald to marry Kate? The actual marriage should wait until after she gets the money, to make absolutely sure that she inherits. We wouldn't want a penniless bride on our hands."

"I am agreeable," said Lydia, "if he can do it."

"I am agreeable," said Donald, "although, of course, it will be a sacrifice on my part."

"Since you are both agreed, it is high time to set yourselves out to be *agreeable* to Kate."

"You are one to talk. You haven't been exactly hospitable," said Lydia critically.

"We all must change. In the interest of all that money."

Kate's room was small and the furniture rather battered, as children's furniture is liable to get. But it faced east, and morning sunlight warmed and cheered the room. There was no fire, but Kate was used to doing without that amenity, except in the coldest weather, and was quite hardy. She threw a woolen shawl around her shoulders and sat down at a small table to write to her father.

Absorbed in describing all that had happened in the past few days, she did not hear the first timid knock on the door. When the knock was repeated Kate called out, "Come in!" No one entered. Her curiosity aroused, Kate went to the door and looked out. The hall seemed empty, but from the corner of her vision Kate saw a white pinafore and pantaloons disappear behind a highboy.

"Cousin Adelaide?" she called. There was no answer. "I know you're there behind the chest. Come on out."

After a minute during which all was quiet, an anxious face peered around the side of the chest. Kate smiled, and with this encouragement the girl emerged and stood stiffly, staring.

"Come into my room where it's warm in the sun. I've been feeling lonely and would love to have company." Kate put out her hand and Adelaide reached for it. Her hand was cold.

"Are you sure it is all right? I won't be a nuisance?" she asked doubtfully.

"Of course it's all right. More than all right. It's a pleasure! Sit down here with your back in the sunlight and you'll soon be warm."

The girl sat down abruptly and stared at Kate wide-eyed.

"How clever of you to know where I was," said Kate.

"I peeked when the housekeeper brought you up yesterday. My room is down the hall, on the other side of the schoolroom. Why did they give you Lydia's old room? There are much better ones. I would have given you a nicer one."

"Oh, I imagine I'm not such a special guest. I'm just a poor relative."

"Aren't you supposed to get Uncle William's fortune? I heard Mama say so."

"Perhaps. It's all on condition."

"What condition?"

"I must learn to conduct myself like a lady."

The girl's face relaxed, and she gave Kate one of her radiant smiles. "*You* must learn to behave?"

"That's about it."

"Then there are two of us!"

Kate laughed. "So there are. We'll have to help each other."

A shadow crossed the girl's face. "But you are good already. I can see that. And I am bad, very bad. We are not alike."

"Whatever makes you think you are bad?"

"Everybody says so. It must be true."

"Who is everybody?"

"Mama. And Mrs. Mitchell. Lydia. Donald."

"They are not everybody. *I* don't think you are bad, for instance."

"You don't?"

"Of course not. Why do they think you are bad?"

Adelaide puckered her forehead in thought. "Because I am happy sometimes," she said finally.

At the unexpected reply, Kate looked at her carefully and said, "That's an odd reason! Give me an example."

"Well, yesterday I watched you get out of the countess's carriage. I was so happy, so happy that you had come! I ran down the stairs, although Mrs. Mitchell didn't want me to, and told them you were coming. I'm afraid that I shouted."

"I am flattered! You make me feel truly welcome! That was not bad."

"Donald said that I would have to go into an institution."

"If Cousin Donald said that, then *he* is bad."

"*Donald* is bad?" Adelaide looked shocked.

"Let's stop using the word *bad*," said Kate. "Let us say instead that Donald is mistaken."

"Oh." The girl's forehead puckered again. "Was Mama mistaken, too, last night when she sent me to bed without supper?"

"She did that?!"

"Yes, for shouting. And then I had to go to bed early because I was bad again."

"What did you do?"

"I was playing the harpsichord in the schoolroom. Papa taught me how to play when I was little. We used to have concerts, Papa and I. He sang and I played. But Mama put the instrument in the schoolroom after Papa died. She does not like music. Last night she became angry when she heard me playing. She said I was to stop and that I had to go to bed."

"You poor child! I am afraid that Aunt is not happy about my arrival and that you have been the scapegoat victim of her displeasure."

Adelaide pondered this. It was such a complicated thought. Slowly she smiled her luminous smile.

"Was that it? Oh, Cousin Kate, I don't mind suffering in your place!"

"You angel! But that must not be. Somehow I must win the affections of Aunt Harriet, so that she is in a better humour."

"She is very difficult to please. *I* never please her, but I'm sure that you can because you are so pretty and clever."

"You dear child, you say such kind things to me."

"I am not a child, Cousin Kate," said Adelaide, with dignity. "It's just that I am feebleminded and never grew very tall."

"You are *not* feebleminded! Don't believe it for a minute. Don't say it! And you must be nearly as tall as I. What is your age?"

"Sixteen."

Kate gasped. Her guess would have been ten.

"You are surprised, aren't you? You see, what happened was that I loved Papa very much, and he died when I was ten. They say the shock was too much and so I became stunted."

"Nonsense!" Kate's voice rang out, and Adelaide jumped in her chair as though jolted by lightning.

Shadows stirred in the girl's mind and began to evaporate, as the morning sun disperses mist and chill; fungi of morbid notions began to dry up in the atmosphere of that healthy denial. Adelaide felt a little dizzy, as from taking a deep breath of oxygen.

"I suppose 'they' again are Aunt Harriet, Donald, Lydia, and Mrs. Mitchell," Kate went on stormily. "Do you know what *I* think of *them?* I think they are—"

"Mistaken?" The voice was gentle.

"Very *much* mistaken! We'll show them! The very idea, setting themselves up—"

A knock at the door interrupted her tirade. Kate tried to collect herself, but her "Come in!" was angry.

The bulky Mrs. Mitchell entered, blinking her eyes in the sudden sunlight. She began without preamble, focussing on Adelaide. "You naughty girl, hiding like this. You ought to be put in stocks, you ought, the stocks on the village green, so everybody could see you. Then we'd know where to look to find you. Or sent to a house of correction—they could deal with the likes of you there. I've heard Sir Donald speak of it, don't think I haven't. Better still, *I* say, transportation down under—"

"I beg your pardon," said Kate, livid, rising from her chair. "Who are you?"

Mrs. Mitchell allowed her attention to be distracted by the person in the shabby dress. From the fact that Kate had been assigned this child's room, long ago abandoned by Miss Lydia, she had deduced that Kate was someone of small account.

"Oh," she sniffed, "you're the niece come to live." She looked around the room and noted with satisfaction that there wasn't even a fire in the grate.

"I did not ask who I was. I asked who you were."

Mrs. Mitchell was speechless at this upstart.

"You have seen fit to enter my room," Kate went on coldly. "State your business."

"I didn't mean to discommode you, I'm sure," said the woman haughtily. "I am Mrs. Mitchell and I am—I take care of Adelaide." She considered herself above the classification of nanny. "She sneaked away and I have come to fetch her."

"Miss Adelaide is my guest. I invited her to pay me a visit, and when we conclude our conversation, *perhaps* she will want to return to her room. Or we may decide to stroll in the garden."

Mrs. Mitchell stood openmouthed at this effrontery.

Kate gestured her away grandly. "You may go now."

The woman retreated to the door. "We'll see about this" was her parting shot.

"Yes, we certainly shall," replied Kate, getting in the last word.

Adelaide sat transfixed, her hands clenched together so tightly that the knuckles were white. "Oh, Cousin Kate, what if she goes to Mama?"

"Let her. We shall have to speak to Aunt Harriet about her anyhow. Do you care for Mrs. Mitchell?"

"Care for her? Oh, no, she is dreadful. I am like a prisoner. She often locks me up. And she tries to make me learn and I can't. And then she tells Mama, and I get punished."

She looked up at Kate and was surprised to find her cousin smiling. "I doubt that she could teach you much, to hear the way she speaks. And besides that," said Kate, "she is ugly. She lumbers around like a gorilla."

Kate walked around the room heavily from one foot to the other, with her shoulders hunched, in the way she imagined a gorilla would walk. She bared her teeth and pounded her chest and spread her fingers wide as though about to seize Adelaide. The girl giggled and clapped her hands with glee. It had been a long time since anyone had played with her.

"So you sneaked away, did you?" said Kate, snarling. "Don't you know what happens to people who go sneaking away from gorillas?"

"No! What?" said Adelaide breathlessly.

"They get to go walking in gardens," said Kate anticlimactically. She seized her cousin's hand. "Let's go!"

The two girls ran laughing through the hall and down the staircase. Mrs. Mitchell, hulking in the doorway of the schoolroom ready to pounce on Adelaide and drag her off to Lady Weyward, drew back into the room when she saw the two of them and heard the disconcerting sound of lighthearted laughter. She plumped herself down on the dunce's stool to sort things out.

— 7 —

KATE WALKED QUICKLY along the right-of-way to Radburn Park, her sturdy shoes accepting myriad little blows of pebbles and twigs. It was good to get away from Coulder Hall, and she took deep breaths of the air of freedom.

Odd—at breakfast that morning Lady Weyward had actually offered her the use of the coach-and-four for her call upon the countess. After the frostiness of her aunt's reception of her, Kate had not expected such kindness. In truth, Kate did not care for carriages as a whole, the countess's being an exception; it was too exhausting to be helplessly bounced around so. Now if her aunt had offered a horse that she could ride and be in control of—that would be different! But her ladyship would never think of that.

It was Lydia who had objected, saying that she needed the coach to ride into Tweedstun. Donald intervened, saying that their dear cousin and guest had priority, bestowing an indulgent smile upon Kate that revealed his teeth, both uppers and lowers. He had meticulously cleaned them that morning with chalk and orrisroot, especially so that he could smile broadly at Kate and be fascinating. Warning glances were exchanged between Lady Weyward and her daughter, and Lydia gracelessly retired from the field with "Oh, very well, let her have it!"

Kate swallowed her tea quickly and excused herself, saying, "The day is fine. I really prefer to walk and will get an early start."

It was good indeed to get away! At least Lady Weyward

appeared to have accepted her presence at Coulder Hall, and this in turn might make things easier for Adelaide.

The sun gathered strength, and Kate pushed back the hood of the blue cloak. In Radburn Park, the foliage seemed greener and less ragged. Birds exchanged calls from either side of the right-of-way. Within sight of Radburn Hall, she paused to appreciate the imposing mass. Older than Coulder Hall, and larger and plainer, still it was more inviting.

A squirrel came out to greet her, his paws with their long claws clasped across his chest with all the awareness and self-possession of a Chinese mandarin. She skirted the Hall in order to go to the stables first, and the squirrel followed, graciously stopping whenever she did.

The stable doors were open. Everything inside was in order and clean. Fantastique was in good condition but kept moving restlessly in his stall.

"Have you had any exercise, *chéri?*" asked Kate, striking his long, elegant nose. He stamped his hoofs and switched his tail. On a hook, temptingly, hung his saddle.

"Morning, miss."

Kate whirled around to find Roscoe, cap in hand. "Didn't mean to startle you, miss. Handsome colt, that."

"Yes," said Kate, "isn't he. I am grateful for the care you have taken of him. He looks fine."

"It's a pleasure, miss. Would you be leaving him here?"

"Yes, if it's all right with Lord Radburn. The stables at Coulder Hall are not quite—"

"I knows what you mean, miss. Jack Hinds knows better, but he's too heavy on the likker, that feller. And Sir Donald don't pay no attention. You can rest happy that Lord Radburn will want Fantastique here, and good care will be took. Mind, that colt needs more exercise. I took him meself around the racing track a couple of times, but he's asking for more than that."

"I agree. He seems restless."

"Miz Wilcox, she that's the housekeeper, she axed me to give you this."

He handed her a rectangular case, bound with a leather strap. Kate unfastened it at once, curious. Inside were the riding clothes she had left behind, all cleaned and brushed, and her boots had been softened and blackened and the spurs made shiny.

"How kind of Mrs. Wilcox! Will you thank her for me?"

"Yes, miss." Roscoe's face became bland. "If you was wondering what to do with that case, miss, and not wanting to carry it up to the Hall and all, there's room here." He indicated a space between Fantastique's stall and the next one. Fastening the leather tie again, he inserted the case into the space.

"You see how it just fits, and nobody the wiser?"

"That's very convenient," said Kate smoothly. "Suppose we just let it stay there."

"Just as you say, miss. Sump'n else I oughter show you, if you would foller me."

He led her outside and around to the back of the stables. "If ye look sharp, ye'll see a path through the trees. See! Here it is, miss. Almost overgrown now 'cause not many knows as it's here. Foller it, and ye comes soon to the righterway. Cross the righterway, it starts up again and takes you straight to the stables of Coulder Hall, the back of 'em, just like here."

"It's a shortcut?"

"Aye, miss. Like the path of a bird. Saves mebbe half."

"I am very grateful to you for pointing it out."

"S'nothin', miss." He looked up at the expanse of sky. "See ye how the days is gettin' longer? Sign of summer comin' in. Folks don't pay no attention, though. It's light real early, but they go on sleepin' like they allus do."

"So that," said Kate evenly, "if someone were to go out riding, say, just at dawn, nobody would notice?"

"Shouldn't think so, miss. Not likely. Not like at all."

"Mmh. I see what you mean." Kate looked up into the kind, lined, browned face. "Thank you so much, Roscoe, for the information. I appreciate it."
"S'nothin', miss. Happy to help."

Kate was announced in the morning room. To her surprise, the countess was not alone. Both of her sons rose on their long legs as Kate entered.
The countess was looking very pretty in a white dress with violet ribbons about the neckline. In her hair was entwined a matching ribbon, tied in a bow on the side of her broad forehead. The white mound beside her on the loveseat was Frou-Frou, looking even fatter because of a recent bath that had left her hair fluffy. A violet ribbon was tied around what was probably her neck. She recognised Kate as her saviour from suffocation and managed to move something that was meant to be a tail, but she was too lazy to jump down for a real welcome.
"You are just in time," said the countess. "Edward is planning a ball here at Radburn Hall. When will it be, dear?"
"What's wrong with a fortnight from today, at the summer solstice? The floors in the ballroom are not in bad condition. The servants can have them waxed and polished in a day or so, I wager."
"So soon! My dear boy, there's more to a ball than a shiny floor! What about engaging musicians and setting up card tables and preparing for tea?"
"I'll do it all myself, Mama. Don't you worry. I know what to do."
"I'm sure you do. But in a fortnight's time? What about invitations?"
"I'll write them out today and personally deliver them tomorrow."
"I'll help you," offered Lionel.
"There, you see, Mama? Practically done!"
"But shouldn't you invite the Prince Regent?"

"I'll send his invitation by mail coach today. It will reach Brighton by tomorrow afternoon."

"The Prince Regent!" gasped Kate. "You will invite the Prince Regent?"

"We'll *invite* the Prince Regent, Kate. Most likely he won't come. But he feels miffed if he doesn't at least get an invitation," said Edward in his assured way.

"Well, if you think you can arrange it, dear," consented the countess, pouring chocolate from a silver pitcher, holding the hot curved handle with a linen serviette.

"The Prince Regent!" breathed Kate, not over her astonishment.

"Don't worry, Miss Martin, you would find him most amiable," said Lionel.

"Especially amiable to pretty young women," said Edward darkly.

"*Edward!*" protested the countess. "That is not very nice." She held back his cup to punish him.

"But not unfair," insisted Edward, reaching out and taking the cup.

"Miss Martin," said the countess, changing the subject, "tell us how you find things at Coulder Hall. Are you comfortable?"

"Yes, ma'am. Quite comfortable, thank you."

"And Lady Weyward and your cousins? Are they pleasant to you?"

Kate hesitated. "Yes—"

"But?"

"But they are changeable. At first, it seemed that they were displeased with my arrival. But this morning they were quite kind."

"They have come to realise your worth," surmised Edward sententiously. He winked at her mockingly.

"Or they are up to something," said Lionel, looking to his mother for help.

The countess bit into a buttered and creamed biscuit. Frou-Frou, who had studied the layered biscuit all through the construction stage in Edward's hands, stretched out a paw and touched the countess's arm just to remind her who was sitting next to her; she was rewarded with the remainder of the extravagance.

"We must watch what develops," said the countess. "My dear, if you ever feel that you are being treated unfairly, please feel free to discuss it with me or either of my sons. We might be able to help."

"We certainly could," said Edward confidently.

"Please do, Miss Martin," affirmed Lionel. "Don't ever hesitate."

When Kate rose to leave, the countess remarked the sturdy shoes she was wearing.

"Oh, yes, I walked from Coulder Hall."

"That's a good distance. Wasn't Lady Weyward able to lend you her carriage?"

"She did offer it, but Cousin Lydia had need of it."

"I see."

"I really don't mind. I enjoy walking."

Lionel smiled. "I just happen to have my curricle with me this morning. May I drive you home, Miss Martin?"

"You are most kind."

"You just happen—" repeated Edward, it sinking in on him how many times his younger brother had got there first and cut him out with Miss Martin. Lionel taking the lead! Edward wasn't used to it; he glanced at his mother, puzzled. The countess, however, didn't meet his eyes. She absently stroked Frou-Frou.

"Well, *I*'ll be calling at Coulder Hall tomorrow to deliver invitations," asserted Edward. "Will you be at home, Kate?"

"I expect to be, Lord Radburn," said Kate formally and stiffly, "although Lady Weyward may have made other plans for me that I do not as yet have knowledge of."

Along the road, Lionel allowed his horses to dawdle, although they were strong and the curricle was light.

"Miss Martin, there is something I would like to speak to you about," he began gravely.

"Please call me Kate. Lord Radburn does."

Lionel smiled. "Yes, I noticed. That's the way my brother is. He means no harm, Miss Martin—Kate. If I may, I would rather call you Katherine. I think it better suits your special kind of beauty."

"My beauty!" Kate laughed. "Vicar, that is an outrageous compliment. I am not beautiful."

Lionel looked chagrined. "I was speaking of your comeliness of character, Katherine. Although, of course, your person, too, is far above average."

"Oh, better and better!" Kate laughed at him outright. Then, realising that he was embarrassed, added quietly, "I am afraid that while you may see the Katherine in me, Lord Radburn sees only the Kate. What is it that you had to discuss with me?"

With a forefinger, Lionel pushed spectacles up on his nose. "I am very much concerned about your young cousin Adelaide. I understand that the Weywards are thinking of having her placed in an institution for the insane."

"Monstrous!"

"You have met her, then? I regret to say that these establishments in England are abominable—dirty, overcrowded, with poor food. The mentally afflicted are lumped together with criminals, sometimes violent ones. There is no attempt at understanding or cure. Many do not survive a year in such environments. I fear Adelaide would not."

"On no, not a day!"

"The matter of reform has been taken up again and again with the Prince Regent, but he, estimable gentleman though he is, does not like to consider these ugly matters and declines to act."

"Cannot Parliament deal with it?"

"Not the present Tory government. By philosophy they

do not want to change the status quo. They are the Prince's friends, and he and they reinforce each other's thinking at those enormous banquets at Carlton House and at Brighton. They just don't *think*."

"And the Whigs? Cannot they do something?"

"The Whigs are out of favour with the Prince at the moment, for reasons I won't go into." Lionel looked embarrassed, swallowed, and went on. "I keep hoping my brother will take an active interest in politics. He is very liberal and has some good ideas on reform of different kinds. And the Prince thinks highly of him and would listen to him."

"Then why doesn't he do something?"

They had reached the gates of Coulder Hall and passed through. Lionel shook his head. "Too many interests and distractions. In many ways he is like the Prince, and that is why they get along so well. Life has been good to him, and he is content."

Kate was indignant. "And in the meantime, Cousin Adelaide's fate, indeed her life, is at stake if she is sent to one of those dreadful places."

Halfway up the entrance road, Lionel stopped the curricle. He was anxious to finish their conversation before they drew up to the door and the footmen ran out to assist.

From the second-storey window Donald watched them. He looked cross. What were they talking about, those two, so intent, so absorbed in each other's words, so serious? He put a finger down the linen at his neck, for it was choking him. Good Lord, was he putting on weight?

"What is *your* impression of Adelaide?" Lionel was asking.

"Oh, she is a darling! Rather childlike, but very acute in her responses. I believe she is not used to speaking to people and does not give the pat answers we all give—that are expected of us. The family has convinced her that she is not mentally or physically normal, and she believes them.

Being deprived of contact with Society, she has no knowledge of her own powers."

"Thank you for your opinion. It corroborates my own. I have seen her rarely—usually she is hidden away. Very cruel, I say."

"Is it true that she was deeply affected by her father's death?"

"It occurred when we were all in London, but I believe so. After that, Edward and I spent a year on the Continent and didn't see her at all. Adelaide was Sir Joseph's favourite child. Unfortunately he made it obvious, tutoring her himself and rather ignoring his other children. He taught her to play the harpsichord, and I understand she became quite proficient. His death must have been a terrible bereavement to the poor child. I do not like to say this, but I believe that Adelaide is a victim of revenge, her natural grief exaggerated by them and exploited maliciously. Yes, I am sure of it now—I shall not aid them in their present desire to be rid of her."

"Oh, no, please do not!" beseeched Kate.

Lionel took both her hands and smiled his gentle smile. "I assure you that I shall not. You have been of great assistance to me in clarifying my thinking, Katherine."

"And I shall continue to help you in this matter, Vicar. Adelaide and I have already become good friends."

"One thing more—don't call me Vicar. My name is Lionel."

"Very well, Lionel. I feel *we* have become good friends, too." They exchanged smiles.

"Something wrong with the mares?" asked a high, affected voice.

Lionel let go of Kate's hands, and, in the light of their conversation, both turned to Donald with displeasure. He interpreted this as anger that they had been interrupted at lovemaking. Never mind, he told himself, I am certainly fair competition for that skinny vicar of Tweedstun!

8

BEFORE DAWN THE next day, Kate was in the kitchen for some of Nurse Amelia's strong black tea and then outdoors to find the way to Radburn Park that Roscoe had pointed out to her. A pearly mist all but obscured the path, and she had to watch carefully not to go astray. When she reached the right-of-way, she knew that all was well, for once across that, she was close to the rear of the Radburn Park stables.

Fantastique was asleep, stretched out on the hay, and she spoke to him gently. He leapt to his feet and twitched his back to get rid of stray slips of straw. The case with the leather straps was still in the space between the stalls, and she quickly changed her clothes, adjusted Fantastique's saddle, and led him outside. In spite of the mist, her sense of direction told her where the downs would be.

They rode slowly. Only the hollows now were white with mist; the rounds of the hillocks were clear. At the top of one she paused and looked about her. The sky above was pale and limpid, and a flickering star, reluctant to leave, was still visible. In the hollows the mists were moving and heaving like a sea, and the rounds were like islands within it, uninhabited, primaeval, silent. Fantastique belonged to this ancient world, she thought. Hadn't her father told her that horses were among the earliest known animals, smaller then and with a different hoof, but their fossils still recognisable?

Even as she watched, the mists dissipated, the sky

turned blue, eons passed, and nineteenth-century England reasserted itself. With a sigh, she plucked at the reins, and she and Fantastique began to ride fast, then faster, until it seemed that Fantastique's evolved hoofs weren't touching the solid earth.

Lord Radburn was late in delivering invitations to Coulder Hall, and it was nearly time for midday dinner when he was announced. Lydia, elaborately dressed, had been waiting for hours; she had been in a fevered state ever since Kate had mentioned the ball and Edward's proposed call on them.

"Do stay and dine with us," cooed Lydia, "and tell us all your plans for this exciting event."

"Thank you, no," he said, much to the relief of Lady Weyward, who really didn't want the fuss that Lord Radburn's presence would create in the kitchen nor the expense of extra corner dishes. "I am pressed for time because of the short notice of the ball."

"But have you time for some port?" asked Donald, who had been at the drink for some thirty minutes and was looking for a drinking companion.

Edward, disappointed at not seeing Kate, was about to refuse when she appeared in the doorway.

"Good morning, Kate!" said Edward, graciously consenting to the wine.

"Lord Radburn," Kate acknowledged coolly and curtsied. She had been summoned by Lady Weyward from the schoolroom, where she had been teaching Adelaide a French song, and Adelaide had been writing down the notes to play on the harpsichord. Adelaide had not been summoned.

"As you see, I have come with invitations for you all." He looked immensely pleased with himself.

Kate flipped through the invitations and slapped them down on a table.

"For the ball at Radburn Hall. We talked about it

yesterday," he reminded her, wondering what was wrong. "You *will* come, Kate?"

"Indeed it would be a pleasure to accept, Lord Radburn," said Kate, "but I am puzzled over one thing. You say you are inviting all of us, but what about an invitation for Adelaide?"

"Adelaide?" Edward looked blank.

"Yes, Cousin Adelaide."

"But she is a child, and she—"

"She is almost as old as I am."

"Now, my dear, let us not start that," interrupted Lady Weyward. "You know very well that it is impossible to invite Adelaide."

"She would spoil *everything*," said Lydia, her voice rising.

"I had not thought," said Edward, still looking at Kate.

"Do think, milord," said Kate, with a set face.

Edward, who had never felt awkward in his life, felt so now.

"Now look here," said Donald thickly, setting down his glass. "The girl's feebleminded—" The glass missed the table and crashed to the floor.

"She is *not*," contradicted Kate. "She is simply unused to Society."

"Lord Radburn," said Lady Weyward, in a voice that said she was taking matters in hand, "please excuse my niece. She means well, of course, but, regretfully, Adelaide cannot attend your ball, any ball. Do not concern yourself. We will leave her in her room with company and with something entertaining to do. She will be well looked after. It is a difficult situation, and it is the best we can do for the present."

"Indeed, she will be attended," said Kate, "for if Adelaide must stay home, sir, so shall I to keep her company. I withdraw my acceptance."

"She doesn't mean that," said Lydia, with a curl of the lip. "She is just showing off."

"I assure you that I do mean it. Excuse me, please." Kate curtsied to the company and would have left.

"Kate!" begged Edward. "Please! Please hear me. I apologise for not inviting Adelaide. I truly never thought of it and meant no slight. I—it—has never been done."

"Quite," said Kate.

"That is not a good excuse, I know," said Edward, embarrassed, a rare state for him. "How can I make it up? Should I go upstairs and personally invite her?"

Kate smiled at last. "No," she said, "I am afraid you would overwhelm her. I shall extend to her your invitation. I am sure she will be happy to accept. And so shall I."

Edward bowed formally.

"This will all be *your* responsibility," Lady Weyward warned Kate.

"Of course. Gladly. One thing more, my lord—"

"At your service, Miss Martin."

"I am still Kate! Do you think the vicar would care to stop by with a special invitation for Adelaide? So that she will not think it secondhand somehow?"

"Vicar, vicar," muttered Donald, "all she thinks of is the vicar."

"He would do it willingly, I know."

"Thank you so much," Kate said, beaming. "I think it's going to be a lovely ball!"

Edward picked up his hat and crop and bowed to the Weywards gravely.

"Now see what you've done with your nonsense!" hissed Lydia. "You've made him angry!"

At the door Edward turned and came back to Kate. "May I engage you for the opening set, Miss Martin?"

"Miss Martin refuses," she said, "but Kate would be delighted."

She smiled after him as he left. Lydia was left open-mouthed.

"Oh, no," groaned Donald. "Oh, no, not Edward, too."

He tossed off Edward's half-empty glass of port and refilled it.

Lady Weyward said irritably, "We have held up dinner. I disapprove of being late for meals. How will the servants finish their work this afternoon?" She was red-faced with frustration. "And you, Donald, have broken a perfectly good glass!"

— 9 —

"NO," SAID LADY WEYWARD, "I have no money to pay for a gown for Adelaide. The whole idea of her going to the ball at Radburn Hall is absurd, anyway. You will simply have to abandon the plan and so inform Lord Radburn."

"Uncle William has provided funds for *my* expenses this year, has he not? I shall be happy to share with Cousin Adelaide."

"You will do nothing of the sort. You may have something of your account for a gown for yourself, although it is very early in the year to be advancing you anything."

Reluctantly Lady Weyward went to her desk, unlocking it with one of several small keys she wore on a ribbon about her neck. Except that she would be ashamed before the countess if Kate were to appear at the ball looking shabby, she would have refused the request. Unlocking an inner drawer with still another key, she took out three coins, hesitated for a second, and put one back. She locked the desk decisively and handed the two coins to Kate. "This will have to do," she said.

Kate was inexperienced in the area of clothes and their cost, so she assumed the money adequate not only for a gown for herself, but also for Adelaide. She soon found out differently.

Lydia grudgingly allowed Kate and Adelaide to share the coach with her. As they jolted along, with Adelaide cringing in a corner to avoid the notice of her sister, Lydia informed them that her dressmaker could not take on any more commissions.

"She is already making several frocks for me, besides a

new ballgown. Who you will find to make two gowns on such short notice I'm sure *I* don't know."

"We'll find some solution," said Kate.

"I do not want you insisting. I won't have her hurried with *my* gown."

"We are not insisting," pointed out Kate. Her eye for style, although untutored, informed her that Lydia's clothes were ill-made and unbecoming, and she was more than willing to find someone else.

"See that you don't," said Lydia. She smiled a mean smile; she knew exactly how much money Kate was carrying in her reticule, and also knew to the halfpenny the cost of materials and labor not only in Tweedstun but in Lewes as well.

The carriage stopped before the dressmaker's. "The draper's shop is across the green," said Lydia carelessly, not asking the coachman to take them. "I leave here at five. If you are not back, I shall leave without you."

"We will be, we will be!" promised Adelaide anxiously, jumping out of the carriage.

"If we are not," said Kate, "don't worry about us."

"I assure you I will not."

At the draper's shop, the innocent pair had to wait their turn while the florid-faced Mrs. Collins assisted her other customers. As they waited, they examined the shop like tourists. It was something like a library, with shelves up to the ceiling, but filled with bolts of cloth instead of books. On wooden uprights, prints of the latest fashions from London and Paris were fastened, and the girls studied them, pointing to a neckline here and sleeves there. Alas! When it came their turn and Mrs. Collins puffingly brought out bolt after bolt for their inspection, they learned that the price of any of them was far beyond the two little coins. Using the coarsest gauze, there might be enough for one gown. But then how to pay a dressmaker?

"Buy it for yourself," whispered Adelaide, "and I will help you make it. It don't matter about me."

"It does matter about you!" Kate whispered back. She shook her head at Mrs. Collins. "We'll have to think about it," she said proudly.

In the middle of the village green was a great old oak with a wooden bench encircling it, where they sat down to rest. Not far away some children were playing with a red ball. They both watched the children without really seeing the game.

"Please, Cousin Kate, it really don't matter if I don't go to the ball. I have never gone and nobody would miss me." Adelaide was so used to disappointment that it seemed to her that that was the way things were supposed to be.

"*I* would miss you," said Kate stoutly, "and so would the vicar." She glanced at Adelaide and saw the blush at the mention of his name. "Not only did you promise him to attend, but you promised him the first set. You can't go back on your word. It would be rude to disappoint him."

The red ball rolled to Adelaide's feet. A little boy, too timid to approach, stood a good twelve feet away. Adelaide picked up the ball and tossed it to him. "Thank'ee, miss," he called and ran away.

"Still—" said Adelaide.

"We are both going to the ball if we have to go in nature's garb!" announced Kate determinedly.

"Cousin Kate!" said Adelaide horrified, and then she giggled. "I disapprove," she continued primly, mimicking her mother. "It would not be ladylike." It was the first time Kate had ever heard Adelaide make a joke. They both laughed and felt better.

The big bell in the church steeple boomed four times, and a smaller one tolled twice.

"We should go back to the coach," said Adelaide. "We mustn't be left behind."

Kate's face had the intense look of a kitten about to spring. "Here's a conundrum! We are *not* going to be left behind, and we are *not* going back to the coach. Where are we going?"

Adelaide thought carefully. "It must have to do with the fairies."

"You're right. I know where there is a treasure trove of ballgowns fit for a duchess of the realm! Just for the asking!" She jumped up.

"Where are we going?"

Kate shook her reticule, making the coins jingle. "We are going to hire a gig and wait upon our fairy godmother who guards the treasure."

Adelaide clapped her hands in glee. "Our fairy godmother! Who is that?"

"The countess, goosey, the countess!"

"No," said Lady Weyward, "if you have come to beg for more money, the answer is *no*." She expected Kate to come back submissive—chastised after learning the value of a shilling—and grovel before her, begging for more money.

"You mistake me, Aunt. The question of our ballgowns has been—arranged."

"Arranged? For the two of you? Now look here, if you have run up any bills in the village, don't expect *me* to honour them."

"We have not, Aunt," said Kate. She put her hands behind her, crossed her fingers on both hands, took a deep breath, and plunged into a lie. "Mrs. Collins had some pieces of muslin left over from her bolts—remnants she called them—that she didn't need. They are enough—Adelaide is small and I am thin. Also Mrs. Collins knows a seamstress who will run them up cheaply. They will be plain, not stylish like Lydia's, who has commissioned a dressmaker."

Lady Weyward looked somewhat mollified. "Neither of you has Lydia's fine full figure. It is only right that she have an expert to bring out her good points. Adelaide is going, then?"

"Yes, Aunt."

"I can see that she is going to prove quite an expensive burden if she is to go out in Society."

"Aunt, it is the—burden of Adelaide's expense that brings me to you."

"You have sense enough to realise that, do you?"

"Yes, Aunt, ever since I saw that you keep a special—tutor for her. Mrs. Mitchell, I mean. It must cost a lot to pay Mrs. Mitchell!"

"Indeed it does. And her keep besides! And she isn't even honest! There is a question of candles missing!"

"Shocking! I was thinking that *I* might act as Adelaide's tutor, and then it wouldn't cost you anything!"

"You? What do *you* know?"

"Not much, Aunt, except French, and I only know that because Papa came from France. But I could teach the language to Adelaide, and besides, we could read history and poetry together and *both* learn."

"And where do you propose to get books?"

"I don't need any books to teach French. As for books on history and poetry, I thought we might ask the vicar if we could borrow from his library."

Lady Weyward was more than willing to accept the offer. To be rid of the light-fingered Mrs. Mitchell and her salary and keep was much to her satisfaction. And to have a daughter of hers, even though it was only Adelaide, with a pretext to call on one of the Radburns, even though it was only the vicar, was a social advantage. However, it would not do to show enthusiasm or she would be under obligation to Kate.

"You must know by now that Adelaide is incorrigible. Mrs. Mitchell has never been able to teach her anything."

"If you will excuse me, Aunt, I don't believe that Mrs. Mitchell has anything to teach. Adelaide *can* read but hasn't been encouraged to do so. If we read together, I think she may come to enjoy it."

"Well—" said Lady Weyward, displaying considerable doubt. "If you really think you can—"

"I know I can, Aunt."

Lady Weyward graciously submitted. "Very well then."

Lady Weyward, however, was still not satisfied. She

wanted to be rid of Adelaide by having her confined in an institution. But no doubt Lydia was right, she thought; it would be better to wait until Lydia was married, in case of any social repercussions. And, by the way, when was Donald going to make his offer to Kate? He hadn't even been quick enough to obtain the first set of dances from her for the ball. No, Lord Radburn had engaged Kate for the opening, and Lord Radburn was the one she had tagged for Lydia.

Lady Weyward was far from satisfied. No.

— 10 —

"LADY WEYWARD."

The butler's sonorous tone rang out over the music and the buzz of party conversation. Lady Weyward descended mincingly into the ballroom at Radburn Hall. Her smile, practiced beforehand, was set. She had gone to great pains with her appearance and, in her desire to appear *à la mode*, had put on everything in her possession that was fashionable, so that one expected her to jingle. It was for moments such as these that she had jilted the younger son and married the title; she was intent on making the most of it, savouring each step, nodding from side to side, and imagining herself the cynosure of admiring eyes. In fact, no one more than glanced in her direction, except deaf old Admiral Benson, who leaned over to his wife and stage-whispered, "Good Lord! Is that Lady Weyward? She looks a sight!" Mrs. Benson hastily put a warning finger across her mouth.

"Sir Donald Weyward."

Donald adjusted his monocle and superciliously surveyed the scene from the top of the steps. His entire outfit was dun-coloured, an exact copy of one worn by Beau Brummel, so his tailor had assured him. Since Donald's colouring was pale and his features, although regular, were not distinctive, the costume succeeded only in wiping him out. He believed himself the most well-appointed man in the room, and descended with hauteur.

"Miss Weyward."

Admiral Benson narrowed his eyes to get a better look, as

did a number of other gentlemen. Her gown, of heavy silk in a reddish purple, was low-cut and sleeveless and would certainly have fallen down if it had not been for her ample proportions. At the last minute she had noticed that reddish purple did not suit her sallow complexion and had liberally sprinkled cornstarch over face and arms and bosom. "She looks like a tart" was the Admiral's judgement. His wife pinched him to make him quiet, but he was too busy looking to notice.

"Miss Adelaide Weyward."

A number of people looked up in surprise. Miss *Adelaide* Weyward? Most had never heard of her or had forgotten her existence. For a moment no one appeared, then a small figure entered in a rush, as though pushed from behind. She descended the stairs shakily, her small face pale with apprehension. With eyelids lowered so as not to see the crowd, all she saw were the pink ribbons dangling from her collar, vibrating with each heavy heartbeat. Her gown was pretty, of sprigged muslin, and she was glad now that Lucy Wilcox, in her efforts to shorten the gown, had cut off the elaborate flowers around the hem. What if she had to worry about a hemful of artificial flowers whilst descending this endless staircase! As she reached the bottom, she felt that she might faint. Out of the blur of faces, the vicar's came into focus. He took her cold hands. "I have been watching for you," he said.

"Miss Martin."

Everyone in the ballroom paid attention. The news that Lady Weyward had a niece visiting her who might inherit an immense fortune had gone the rounds. Every unmarried male stopped in the middle of conversation and stared. Their mothers examined her shrewdly to see if she were a type that could be easily managed. Some of the older guests had known her parents and were curious to see the offspring. The young feminine contingent darted glances at her, pretending not to care; they were chagrined to find her appearance extremely elegant.

Elegant she was. Her muslin gown, formerly the duchess's, was the colour of nutmeg, with vertical satin stripes of the same colour. It swung slightly as she moved. At her orders Lucy Wilcox had removed the nutmeg-coloured ribbons hanging from each shoulder, and this afternoon, with Adelaide's help, she had woven those ribbons into her luxuriant auburn hair, some of the ribbons falling over her ears. The result was bewitching.

She was smiling when the butler announced her name, for she had just given Adelaide a good push. All afternoon her cousin had required her attention; Adelaide had turned fearful and was ready to cancel the whole evening. Another sagging of nerve had occurred as they were getting into the coach, and Lady Weyward was all for leaving her behind; but Kate said that *she* had need of Adelaide to get through the ordeal herself, and Adelaide was persuaded to continue. When she saw Lionel greet Adelaide at the bottom of the steps, she was relieved.

Kate had gone down only a few steps when she became aware that everyone had become silent and was staring at her. Disconcerted, she stopped. All of Adelaide's fears suddenly were her own, and she had a wild impulse to turn around and flee. Someone at the bottom of the steps held out a gloved hand to her: Edward, an unsmiling Edward. His dark eyes held hers. Looking only at him, she took a deep breath and carefully finished the descent. He took her hand and bowed over it briefly.

"Steady on, old girl," he whispered.

On the chance that the Prince Regent would honour him by attending, Edward had prepared the elaborate gold chair at the end of the ballroom. He waited a good hour before giving up hope of the royal visitor. By then, Kate and Adelaide had been introduced to everyone in the county, and their *carnets de bal* were completely filled in. Both girls were flushed with excitement and expectation.

At last, Edward signaled the musicians to prepare the

first contra-dance, and the company lined up, ladies and gentlemen facing each other. Kate was opposite Edward at the head of the line; Lionel faced Adelaide at the foot. Kate again was held by Edward's dark eyes as they awaited the opening measure. She was puzzled by how different he seemed. It must be his clothes, she thought, for he was indeed handsomely turned out. His violet velvet jacket had silver embroidery on lapels and cuffs; Venetian lace was folded at his throat and matching lace fell over his hands. At the proper time they came toward each other; Edward bowed and Kate curtsied. No, she thought, it is not his clothes. He looks different because he is not smiling.

The intricacies of the dance separated them, and she responded to other smiles as she took the hands of the various Curtis boys, the old admiral, even Donald, some others whose names she couldn't remember, and at the end, Lionel. Lionel was looking festive in grey velvet, with some discreet gold embroidery on lapels and cuffs; he was obviously feeling festive. Returning to Edward, she smiled at him too, but although his lips responded politely, his eyes remained somber. At least he isn't mocking me, she thought. Suddenly the music stopped.

"His Royal Highness, the Prince Regent!"

The Prince descended the staircase briskly. He was alone. For a portly man he moved gracefully, and his meticulously tailored clothes concealed any faults of figure. His jacket, decorated with seed pearls, was deep blue, his favorite colour.

The countess made him the most stately, perfect curtsey that Kate had ever seen. Taking her hand, the Prince led Lady Radburn through the center of the ballroom, where, as though a wind were blowing them over, the ladies curtsied and the men bowed. Hurriedly the servants lighted the candles of the chandelier near the "throne," and another chair was drawn up for the countess.

"Pray, continue," said the Prince graciously to the dancers.

The music started up, and the Prince gave his undivided

attention to his hostess. They discussed the Prince Regent's health, which he said was excellent, and the latest work of his architect, John Nash, at Brighton-by-the-Sea, who was turning the Prince's fantasies into fact in the form of an Indian pavilion with a Chinese-wallpaper-inspired interior.

"The decoration may sound exotic to you, Countess, but I assure you that in much of the structure we are using English cast iron."

"You make that sound comforting, Prince," said the countess, "if not comfortable."

The Prince leaned back and laughed. He is still handsome, thought the countess, although much of it now depends on his warmth and ease of manner and, yes, an air of majesty. She was too discreet to inquire after the neglected Princess Caroline, and, since he had arrived alone, after Mrs. Fitzherbert either.

The dancing continued vigorously until the music stopped again, this time for refreshments. So many delicacies were spread out on the long table that the Prince Regent, a gourmet, declared himself highly pleased and partook of everything offered.

Card tables were set up for those desiring to play whist or backgammon. A footman lighted candles near the harpsichord. Wilfred Curtis played a few runs on it and his brother John commenced to sing in a passable tenor. Kate slipped into a small gilded chair at the end of a row to listen, until Lionel bent over and asked if he might speak to her. She rose with a nod and they moved over near the French windows so as not to disturb the concert. A bust of the countess by Canova seemed to be looking benevolently at them.

"I want to tell you how grateful I am for all that you have done for Adelaide. She seems a new creature, really blooming!"

"It has been a pleasure! She and I have become good friends. I feel closer to her than to any of my other relatives at Coulder Hall."

She looked across the room to find Adelaide, but instead

her glance fell on Donald, seated at a card table. Over the top of his cards he was watching her. Kate looked away and shuddered, moving behind the Canova head on its marble stand to block his view.

"Sneaky," muttered Donald, interpreting her movement as meaning that she did not want to be seen talking alone with Lionel.

"Vicar—Lionel, I have a favour to ask you."

"Pray do ask."

Kate hesitated. "I know this sounds presumptuous, but I have taken over the duty of tutoring Adelaide. Mrs. Mitchell has been dismissed, to everyone's relief. Adelaide and I will have to learn together, for I am woefully lacking in the requirements of a teacher. One problem is that we don't have suitable books. The best of the library at Coulder Hall was disposed of—nobody cared for them. I—we were wondering if we might borrow from *your* library, if you—"

"Of course! I should be delighted. What kind of books did you want?"

"We thought we would read history, since we are both appallingly ignorant of the subject." She smiled ruefully and, forgetting about Donald, moved from behind the sculpture. "Then, as a reward for that labour, we thought we might read poetry, Shakespeare perhaps."

Lionel, who was a good scholar, replied ardently, "Yes! I have many books to interest you! Let's see, if you want to start with the Roman Empire, I have Gibbon—fine man, he's done a lot of research and writes very well. For more recent history I have Edmund Burke on the French Revolution—you, with your background, I am sure will find that absorbing. Now, as to poetry! There is Shakespeare, naturally, and perhaps you would enjoy reading some modern poets. Byron is much the vogue in London, although I personally prefer Wordsworth. Oh, I say! May I join your sessions? At Oxford I once played Macbeth. 'Hold on, Macduff, and cursed be he who first cries "hold enough." ' " Lionel pretended to be fighting a duel.

Across the room Donald muttered, "So he'll fight for her, he says!"

The admiral, sitting opposite him, bellowed, "Eh? Dash it all, sir, are we playing or not?" Several in the audience listening to the music turned around and hissed, "Shh!"

Kate flushed with gratitude. "Would you do that for us? That *is* good of you!"

"Katherine, it is *you* who are good. You have done—are doing—so much for your cousin!"

"It is my pleasure. No, I am not good. Not anymore." She lowered her head.

"Why do you say that?" At once Lionel was the vicar of Tweedstun.

Kate blurted out, "I have learned to lie and deceive, and I seem to be very good at it!"

"What have you lied about?"

"Many things! For example, about our ballgowns—Adelaide's and mine. I told Aunt that the goods had been given us, and then run up by a seamstress. She didn't give us enough money, you see, so I asked the countess—"

"I understand. I wouldn't worry about that, Katherine. Lady Weyward asked for it. She has a reputation for being—thrifty. And you did it for Adelaide as well as for yourself. Incidentally, I must say, you are both looking very well turned out this evening."

Kate gestured with her hand, dismissing both his excusing words and his compliment. "No. It is something false, and it twists the whole world around. I feel in my heart it is wrong." For emphasis, she put her hand over her heart.

Lionel's eyes shone behind his eyeglasses. Without any further remark, he took her hand, raised it solemnly, and kissed it.

Donald, adjusting his monocle, said, "Damme!" believing that he had seen a declaration of love and its grateful acceptance.

The old admiral squirmed around in his chair to see what was so interesting. "Ah, the little Martin. Monstrous pretty and lively, ain't she? What's he kissing her hand for? It ain't done, kissing a young girl's hand. You can kiss anything else, but not her hand." After this discourse on etiquette, he squinted his eyes to see better. "Who is that, the vicar? Hardly knew him. Well, now!" Fortunately his loud tones were covered by applause for the performers.

There was another witness to the scene behind the statuary: Edward. He was conversing with the Prince Regent but had kept brooding eyes on the couple from the moment his brother had tapped Kate on the shoulder.

"I beg your pardon," he apologised to the Prince, realising that he had been asked a question. "Promising colts? Yes, sir, I do have a new one. Not mine, really, but I'm keeping him in my stables. Prince, he's a real beauty and a born racer! He doesn't run—he flies! His name is Fantastique and he *is* fantastic!"

"Fantastique." The Prince savoured the name. "Who owns this paragon?"

"Excuse me, your Highness, I am not at liberty to say at present." Edward smiled his apology. "Let me put it this way, a mystery owner, who rides as well as Fantastique runs."

"I am intrigued! Will we see this mysterious pair at next year's race meeting?"

"It is my hope, sir."

"And mine, too, now."

Lydia Weyward was enjoying herself. Men were buzzing round her like bees seeking honey. True, the old admiral had made an improper suggestion in a loud voice and Wilfred Curtis had squeezed her waist as he passed during the quadrille, but it was all very heady, and she kept giggling. True, too, Edward had danced with her only once so far, but he had danced only once with Kate; in fact, after the opening set he had gone nowhere near Kate! She tugged at her gown, bringing the décolletage down to a dangerous level, and rolled her eyes flirtatiously at Wilfred Curtis, who was approaching gingerly bearing in each hand a full glass of Madeira.

Waiting until the audience had dispersed, Adelaide rose and took the opportunity to examine the harpsichord. Edward had had it made by the firm of Burkhard Tschudi in London, and it was much larger and heavier strung than the one in the schoolroom. With one finger she pushed down a key and jumped at its power. Then, stretching her fingers over the keyboard, she pretended to play.

"Do you play?" asked a voice behind her. Startled, she withdrew her hands and turned to find Edward. "Please try it. Practice some runs first."

Adelaide looked out at the company, but everyone was busy talking or flirting or drinking.

"No one will notice," he said kindly, realising her shyness.

Raising her hands, she began to play in a tentative way and was surprised at how the instrument responded. Edward showed her how she could make a muting effect—a sound like a lute—by plucking the strings close to the bridge. Soon scales turned into music by Haendel, a German who had settled in the country and had changed the spelling of his name to Handel because it seemed more English. When she finished, she looked at Edward for his opinion, and when he applauded, gave him her sweet smile. His applause was amplified by an audience that had silently gathered. Frightened, she looked out on the fashionable crowd and the royal visitor and would have fled but for the reassuring faces of Kate and Lionel in the first file of chairs. Edward took her hand, and she rose and curtsied prettily.

"Encore!" some voices shouted, and Edward looked at her questioningly. She shook her head no, but added, "Not unless Cousin Kate will sing."

Edward looked inquiringly at Kate, seated next to his brother. "Kate, will you sing?"

She hesitated, but Adelaide would not continue without her. Shakily she joined her cousin at the harpsichord, and they had a nervous whispered conference as to what they would do. Edward sat down in the place vacated by Kate, and he and Lionel applauded encouragingly. Everyone settled down to attend the two young girls with identical red hair.

"Charming, charming!" said the Prince Regent to the countess, looking appreciatively from one girl to the other. "Are they sisters?"

"No, Prince. Miss Adelaide Weyward, playing the harpsichord, is the daughter of a neighbour of mine, Lady Harriet Weyward. The singer is Miss Katherine Martin, her cousin. Her father is an émigré, le Vicomte Guy de Saint Martin. I knew her parents well."

"Ah!" The Prince passed his hand over his fine forehead. He had a special sensitivity concerning émigrés and beheaded kings. Just the other day, a mob in London had not only thrown vegetables at his carriage but had shouted obscenities, denouncing his abandonment of the Princess Caroline. If only the woman would bathe, he thought, I might find her less revolting. He had agreed to his father's choice of bride; he had performed his conjugal duties and a daughter had been born. What more did they expect of him? And the child was becoming as giddy as the mother; if only he could get the girl away! But the populace sympathised with Caroline, and he wondered how far they would go in expressing their displeasure. Well, never mind, here's delight! A pair of fillies with marvelous red manes. Which one? Mmmh. Sugar or spice, it looks like, and both very nice.

In the front row, Lionel turned to his brother ecstatically. "It is a miracle! Imagine Adelaide actually playing before an audience! It is extraordinary how Kate has drawn her out! And in such a short time, too! The angels in Heaven must be joyous!"

"Yes," said Edward, regarding his brother's rapturous face.

Adelaide played some opening runs, and Kate began to sing in French. Her voice was light and clear, but at first rather tremulous. Adelaide looked up anxiously, and Kate took heart. It was a song she knew well, one her father used to sing, about a shepherdess who had been happy with her flock until a troupe of strolling players arrived. The shepherdess had fallen in love with the Harlequin in his particoloured tights and spangles. Harlequin's voice sang that he loved her, but he was wearing a mask and she could not see his eyes. The time came for the players to move on, and the shepherdess was deserted. Watching only for Harlequin's return, she neglected her sheep.

"Prince!" whispered the countess, when Kate began singing. She seized his arm, and he looked at her in surprise.

"What is it, Countess?"

"Listen!" was all she said, leaning forward so as not to miss a note. When the song was over and the audience was applauding, she leaned back in her seat and closed her eyes.

"Countess?" said the Prince, rather alarmed. The song had seemed harmless enough.

"The song of the shepherdess," said the countess dreamily. "The last time I heard it, many years ago in France, it was sung by a queen, a beautiful, tragic, doomed queen." Behind her closed eyelids, the scene came back to her, a ballroom lined with mirrors and candlelit by rows of chandeliers. The mirrors multiplied the candles and the figure of Marie Antoinette in her shepherdess costume, holding a make-believe crook with a satin bow.

Without a word, the Prince took the countess's hands in both of his and bowed his head over them.

The musicians on the balcony tuned their instruments, as the dancing was to resume. Edward stood by as Kate and

Adelaide were presented to the Prince. They both flushed and smiled and made deep curtsies as they received his compliments. Lionel came up to claim Adelaide as his partner, and Edward watched as the Prince asked Kate to stand up with him. Kate, uncertain what to do, looked in Edward's direction, for his name was on her *carnet de bal.* He nodded that she was to accept the royal request. The Prince was clearly pleased with his bright-haired partner, and he proved to be an accomplished dancer.

Edward retired to the sidelines. He stood next to his mother, who was in conversation with Lady Weyward.

"You seem *distrait*," observed the countess.

"No, no," denied Edward, "it is a most successful ball."

"Lovely," said Lady Weyward mechanically, watching Lydia whirl by in the arms of Wilfred Curtis, who was simpering. She would have to speak to Lydia about those Curtis boys; they had not an apanage between them! The countess followed the direction of Edward's contemplation.

"She is a real aristocrat, you know," she murmured, "a genuine lady."

Lady Weyward preened, thinking that the countess was referring to Lydia. She opened her mouth to acknowledge this civility, then realised that they were looking at Kate. She clamped her lips together grimly. Just because the Prince Regent had selected her as a partner! She searched the ballroom for her other offspring. Donald was just getting up from the card table and pocketing the guineas he had won from the old admiral. I hope he hasn't been cheating, worried Lady Weyward; fortunately Admiral Benson is nearly as blind as he is deaf.

Lady Weyward circled the dancers, her furbelows agitating. Donald had just accepted a glass of Madeira from a servant and was looking self-satisfied.

"What are you doing about Kate?" she demanded without preamble. Donald choked on the wine and stepped back as some of it spilled.

"I heard the countess call her 'an aristocrat, a genuine

lady.' If we're not careful, she will slip through our fingers, money and all."

The Prince Regent danced by with Kate in his arms.

"You expect me to compete with the Prince Regent?" He wiped off the glass with his handkerchief so that the wine would not spot his clothes. His vanity prevented him from saying that it was only a vicar who was his rival, not a prince.

"It isn't the Prince Regent I'm worried about." *She* was thinking of Edward, and the countess's words of approbation.

"Perhaps you should be," said Donald, gulping his drink. The Prince and Kate were now separated, but the Prince was following her with his large grey eyes. "He doesn't act like a married man."

"Don't change the subject," rasped Lady Weyward. "Kate has had a big success tonight, although I'm sure I don't know why. No doubt it will go to her head. And you haven't even stood up with her."

"She was completely booked."

"There you are! You're not even trying. And you have more opportunity than anyone else! It isn't as if you still had the money your father left you."

She had touched a raw nerve, and Donald finished off his wine. A servant went by with a tray of drinks, and Donald put down his empty glass and picked up a full one.

"What do you want me to do?"

"Propose to the girl, you fool! *Tonight*, before it is too late."

Kate slipped out into the garden to cool off and collect herself before the next set. Had she really sung before the whole county and danced with the Prince Regent? She put her hands to her burning cheeks. Never in her life had there been such a thrilling evening! She paced the garden path and, finding a bench, sat down and fanned herself with her *carnet*. Tomorrow she would write Papa and tell him all about it. How he would enjoy hearing how she had gone out in the "world"! Her other letters describing life at Coulder Hall had not been enthusiastic. This one would cheer him up.

Donald Weyward appeared from around a row of boxwood. She stopped fanning herself.

"Kate! Well met." Donald sat down beside her unasked. He crossed his legs in the approved Beau Brummel manner, the ankle of one leg on the knee of the other. Kate could smell the wine he had been imbibing and leaned back against the boxwood away from him. She wondered when she could decently leave.

"Cousin Donald, are you enjoying the ball?"

"*Cousin* Donald! How that appellative stabs my heart. You think of me only as a relative. I assure you that *I* do not think of *you* as merely *cousin*. To answer your question, no, I am *not* enjoying the ball. That is, not until this moment. All evening long I have watched you surrounded by admirers. And *I* have had to remain sadly on the sidelines. After the first set, I danced with no one since it could not be you. In my disappointment at finding your *carnet* complete, I had to resort to card playing to pass the long, painful evening."

"Did you win?" asked Kate airily.

"What?" Donald's leg slipped from its precarious position. "Oh, yes."

Kate tried to rise, but he pushed her down. "Listen to me!" he said irritably. He resumed his fashionable position. "Lucky at cards, unlucky at love! How true the old adage is, and how bitter! What does it matter if a man is as lucky as Croesus, if he does not have the lady whose image is imprinted on his heart! What can he do?"

"Drink?" asked Kate pertly.

"What?" exclaimed Donald again, wishing he had one. "Kate!" He seized her hands to keep her in place. "You caused me such anguish this night when I observed you with your lover exchanging words of passion, nay, perhaps vows—"

"My *lover!* Who on earth is that?"
"The vicar, of course!"
"The *vicar?* You mean Lionel?"
"Do not deny it!"
"Are you mad?"

In her agitation Kate stood up, but Donald pushed her back on the bench and went down on one knee. His posture was made untenable by a pebble just exactly under this knee. He made an adjustment with his leg, and the rough edge of the offending pebble put a tear in his pants. "Damme!" he said.

"My love," he said, recovering himself. "I see that you are embarrassed that your flirtation with Lionel has been uncovered. I forgive you. Let us forget that it ever existed. Only say that you will be mine, and we will never speak of it again. Marry me, Kate!"

"This is the silliest thing I have ever listened to! Good God, get up, Cousin Donald." She rose brusquely and he lost his balance. Reaching out with his hand to stop his fall, he placed it on that same unfriendly pebble, and it promptly cut his palm.

"Why don't you go find yourself a nice hot cup of tea?" Kate called over her shoulder, running up the path, ribbons flying.

Edward was leaning against the door jamb, his arms folded across his chest. She rushed past him, too perturbed to acknowledge his presence. As she flew through the door, Lionel claimed her. "There you are! We must hurry! They are beginning the last set."

Donald limped to the door in time to see Kate and Lionel cross the room together. Edward took in his guest's wild-eyed expression, bleeding hand, and torn trousers. He raised his eyes to the stars.

"Fine evening, Weyward," he said. "Summer solstice, you know."

The ladies from Coulder Hall settled in their coach for the return home. In the east, the sky was beginning to lighten after the shortest night of the year. If everyone had been quiet, if the carriage had not been making so much noise, they might have heard the chant of the Druids at Stonehenge.

Donald, pulling on the reins of his roan, shouted, "I am not riding home with you!" He flicked his crop savagely, and the horse reared up. Kate flinched as though she herself had been struck, which, by proxy in Donald's heart, she had been. He galloped off.

"Where is he going?" asked Lady Weyward. "I wanted to talk to him." She looked accusingly at Kate, who couldn't say because she didn't know, and cared only that he was going in the opposite direction.

Lydia laughed crudely. "He's bound for the coast, probably to his favourite sailor's inn in Portsmouth. We won't be seeing him for a few days or maybe weeks!"

"Don't talk like that," whispered Lady Weyward, nudging her with her elbow, nodding in the direction of Kate. The carriage, however, was bouncing them so much that this subtlety was lost on Lydia.

"What's set him off this time? Gambling losses or failed seduction?"

"Lydia! I'm really worried."

"Don't be. When he runs out of credit, he'll come home," Lydia sneered. "Why doesn't he get married anyway?" This time the nudge was so damaging that Lydia was forced to recall the presence of Kate.

They jolted along without conversation for a while, until Adelaide spoke up. "Why so quiet, Cousin Kate? Are you dreaming of dancing with the Prince Regent?"

"No," said Kate. "I was thinking of Edward."

"Edward!" snorted Lydia. "Why are you thinking of him? He stood up with you only once all evening!"

"*And* with you!" Lady Weyward reminded her bitterly. "All that flirting of eyes at Wilfred Curtis, and he won't inherit a cabbage patch!"

"Edward did not dance very much at all," said Adelaide

thoughtfully. "He was kind, but seemed—" she searched for a word she had learned recently, "aloof."

"What do you know about it, simpleton?" said Lydia loudly.

"Cousin Adelaide," said Kate, "you observe well. That is precisely why I was thinking of him. Until now, he teased me so much, but tonight he did not. He was polite, but serious." She laughed. "Mind you, when he did poke fun at me, he got in return as good as he gave. Perhaps he's backing off."

"Perhaps," said Adelaide slowly, "perhaps he does not feel like a brother to you anymore."

The carriage gave such a jolt that the ladies were carried to the roof and back again to the hard seats.

"Simpleton, simpleton!" screamed Lydia, rubbing her head. "Oh-h-h!"

"Good God!" said Kate. This may have been in response to the thrashing that the springless carriage was giving them. Or it may have been in response to the thrashing Lydia's tongue was giving Adelaide. Or neither.

In the east, the sky turned from grey to white to silver to gold as the puissant sun prepared to rise between the gigantic monoliths on Salisbury Plain.

—11—

Donald groaned and turned over on his back. Turning over wasn't any better. He opened one eye and saw grey light filtering through oak leaves. Was it dawn or twilight? Trying to remember put an additional strain on his head, and as there was an anvil inside on which some infernal farrier was pounding, he let the question go and closed the eye. But the relentless smithy with his hammer and anvil prevented him from returning to oblivion. He pushed himself up on his elbows and opened both eyes. A forest of trees swam around in a sickening fashion. He turned abruptly and vomited.

Circling the oak with his arms, he got purchase and rose a few inches; slowly he was able to stand up. Where was he? This could be any forest in England. He staggered for a few feet, fell to his knees, and was sick again. To escape the stench, he dragged himself away. His bloodshot eyes focused on something that seemed familiar. Was it the right-of-way through Radburn Park? To be sure, he crawled on hands and knees toward the road.

Recent memories came back, and with them a rage. His roan had thrown him, and not for the first time, either. In the middle of a rainstorm, the beast had tossed him, left him on the right-of-way, and galloped off home. He, Sir Donald Weyward of Coulder Hall, had had to find protection from the rain under the trees. He'd show that beast who was boss—he would shoot him!

No, he needed money; better to sell the nag. Money!

Frantically he dug into his pockets, but not even the leather pouch remained. He fell back on the ground.

An ant appeared a few inches from his eyes. He raised a hand to kill it, but eyes and hand were not coordinated. With great concentration, he put his thumb in the path of the ant and rolled his demoniac nail over the insect when it arrived at the place of its fatal destiny. Thus satisfied, he looked around to see what else required his lethal attention, but sank back nauseous.

What day was it; indeed, what week? Portsmouth he was sure of—was he? Paddy's Duck was vague, except that he recalled a rough wooden table with a bottle of gin on it, a series of bottles of gin, and a female of the species in a bed with torn hangings. He rolled his head on the ground to clear it, back and forth, and the motion made him retch, fruitlessly. He lost consciousness.

A beetle came across the mound that was Sir Donald Weyward of Coulder Hall, and not caring for the look of it, made a detour.

Someone humming a tune brought Donald round, and he raised his head. Kate emerged from the woods opposite, crossed the right-of-way, and entered the trees again on his side. In her hand was a small bunch of buttercups. She passed so close to him that he could have reached out and touched the hem of her dress, stained dark blue from the damp in the undergrowth. Instead, he remained absolutely still to avoid detection.

When the vision was past—had he seen Kate?—he pulled himself to his feet with the aid of a fallen log and a stripling tree that broke in half under his weight. There were footprints in the moist earth; if this was an apparition, it was wearing sturdy boots and had a firm tread. Apparently she was following a footpath, barely discernible, that he knew nothing about. It led in the direction of Radburn Hall.

He lunged after her.

In a few moments, he crashed into the side of a building. What was this? Looked like Radburn's stables. Where was the girl? In the *stables?*

Groping the wall for support, he circled the building. The doors were open, but hearing the clip-clop of a horse emerging from the stables, he made a ragged retreat around the side of the building. A stablehand with a tricorn hat pulled down over his ears was leading out a dark brown colt.

The boy walked around the horse, surveying him carefully, checking the shoes on each hoof, patting the animal lovingly. Squatting down, he made an inspection of a knee. "*Bon,*" he said, rising. Reaching up, he put a little bunch of buttercups under the leather near the horse's ear and stood back to enjoy his handiwork.

"*Tu es joli,* Fantastique, *très, très joli!*" The colt lifted his head up and down and from side to side, showing off the golden bouquet.

Donald squeezed his eyes tight to stop his sight from whirling, then opened them wide.

The stablehand deftly slipped a booted foot into a stirrup and, with a little hop, swung over the other leg. Turning the horse around, he headed for the downs.

"It's muddy today, love, but you don't mind," said the stablehand with Kate's face and voice.

Donald slid down the side of the building and sank into the soggy earth. He put his elbows on his knees and held his head.

"Mus'n forge'. Ver' impor'an."

He hit his head with his knuckles to keep it awake and with an effort rose and staggered away, one arm swinging like a door loose on its hinges.

— 12 —

RAIN WASHED DOWN the great window of the library of the Vicarage, and lightning periodically forked the sky. Lionel and his two female guests retreated from the window seats, and Lionel lit the fire that had been laid in case the afternoon should turn chilly. His housekeeper came in bearing tea and scones on a large silver tray, and they put down their copies of *Julius Caesar.*

"Shakespeare will understand if we interrupt his work for some refreshment. He knew the value of a pause," said Lionel. "Adelaide, will you pour?"

Adelaide sat behind the tray, and her small dimpled hands deftly managed the array of Chinese porcelain: the pots for the tea and the hot water, a pitcher for milk and a jar for sugar, handleless cups, and a variety of small plates. Her brow puckered with concentration. She handed the cups and plates and offered the scones.

"Mmmh. Such good tea," said Kate appreciatively.

"And the scones are delicious, too," said Adelaide, biting into one daintily.

"You ladies make me very happy," said Lionel, "and I'll pass on your compliments to the housekeeper." He leaned back in his chair, holding his cup high, and an old cat, one Captain Cook, took advantage of the space on his lap and leapt up. Lionel accommodated the animal with the injunction "Well, settle down then!"

The rumble of a deep voice was heard in the hall. "Never mind, I'll just go right in."

"But Lord Radburn—" weakly protested the housekeeper.

Edward strode into the library but stopped short when he saw the cosy group at the fireplace. He removed his hat and stood there, his clothes dripping, observing.

"Neddie boy," said Lionel, "you are sopped! Come here by the fire. Cap, why don't you curl up on your favourite mat?" He placed the cat on a circle of wool crocheted for him by the housekeeper. Captain Cook gave him a resentful look and lashed out with his tail. "No sabre rattling, sailor, just enjoy the fire."

Lionel offered his chair to his brother, finding another for himself, but Edward refused with a wave of the hand.

"Please have a cup of tea," said Adelaide. "It's especially good, and nice and hot."

Edward accepted the cup from her with a trace of his old smile, but he took it over to the wide window and stood watching the rivulets racing swiftly down the long panes.

"What brings you out in this tempest?" asked Lionel.

"Did you know, have you heard, of the plight of the chimney sweep?" Edward turned and looked at his brother with drawn brows.

"Have I heard—" repeated Lionel in astonishment. "Of course I've heard!"

"What chimney sweep?" asked Kate.

"All chimney sweeps!" answered Edward wrathfully.

"Who have you been talking to?" asked Lionel.

"Roscoe. His brother-in-law's boy has been kidnapped, they think into that trade. The family has searched all London for him, but he could be anywhere from Land's End to John O'Groat's. Gone without a trace! As a sweep, his life will last only about two years, when he will develop a growth—" He looked at the girls. "Excuse me, it is too awful to describe."

"Those unfortunate boys!" exclaimed Kate. "Aren't there any laws to protect them?"

"No laws. No regulations." Edward paced up and down. "To think of this happening in England!"

"What are you going to do?" asked Lionel quietly.

"The Prince must be apprised of this. He's probably at Brighton. I plan to go there immediately. *He* will do something."

"With all due respect, Brother, he will do nothing. Many have appealed to him."

"You mean he *knows* about the sweeps?"

"Unfortunately, yes. It is not a new problem."

"Good Lord!" Edward was aghast. "But why does he do nothing?"

Lionel searched for the correct words. "He has other important matters occupying his attention. His domestic situation is an issue at the moment."

"His father must be a worry to him," said Adelaide. "Because of his madness, I mean," she added, fumbling with a fold of her skirt.

"As I understand it, he never goes near his father unless he wants him to intercede with Parliament for more money for more palaces." Lionel was becoming agitated. "And Parliament does not care to give him any more after settling his debts upon his marriage. He goes nowhere near his princess, either, and the people of England don't like it at all."

"He speaks so fair," said Kate, remembering her pleasant dance partner. "Yet, it seems he has antagonised his father, his wife, Parliament, the populace, and even the good vicar!"

"Above all, the *people*," said Lionel. " 'Tis a poor record, and to my mind, potentially dangerous."

"In what way, Brother?"

"Violence. Revolution."

"Surely not! This is England, after all, not France."

"Charles the First was beheaded in sixteen hundred and forty-nine," said Adelaide, quoting from a text they had recently read, "from the Banqueting House in Whitehall."

Edward jerked around and looked at her angrily but could not gainsay the history lesson. He strode to the window and stared at the relentless rain. A streak of lightning jabbed the sky, and a growl of thunder followed.

"The lightning is close," said Lionel.

Kate felt restless and too warm. She moved away from the fire and joined Edward at the window.

"Surely something can be done to ameliorate the situation?" she asked.

"We must face facts," said Lionel. "Fact one, we have a weak, selfish regent, and if nothing intervenes, we will soon have a weak, selfish king. Second, we do have a strong army with an excellent commander in charge of it—Wellington. His victories on the Continent please the people and make them proud to be Englishmen. Third, Parliament. How can I best describe Parliament? Stagnant?"

"Granted that those are the facts, what shall we do with them?" asked Edward.

"I would say—leave Wellington alone, don't worry about him. He knows what to do and does it, decisively. Let him stay on the Continent. His successful exploits may keep discontent from spreading. The king, king-to-be I mean, should *not* be left alone, for the reason that I fear that he is not going to improve by himself and must be protected *from* himself by a strong Parliament. His reign must be got through with as much grace as possible, curbed and guided by the House of Lords and the House of Commons." He faced Edward and said emphatically, "The key to the problem is Parliament—an effective Parliament. There is no other way out, short of violence. We need some good men, forceful men, to carry through the reforms crying out to be made. It means a lot more than legislation concerning chimney sweeps, although that is a worthy beginning."

"You speak well, Brother."

"This is what I *think*. But all I can do is think. It's your county, Lord Radburn, and it's time you took charge. Hie thee to London and start *talking*. Shouting, if necessary."

"Yes," agreed Edward, "I must be off." He picked up his hat and crop. "Ladies."

"Good Lord, man, I didn't mean this moment, in a storm. One afternoon will make no difference."

"I must go," insisted Edward, making for the door. He turned, remembering something. "What means of transportation do you ladies have in this weather?"

"Lady Weyward kindly let us have her coach," said Kate. In truth, Lady Weyward lent her carriage for these visits to the Vicarage because of the impression it might make on the countess, should she hear, and over the angry protestations of Lydia, who wanted the coach at her own disposal.

Edward nodded and would have left.

"Neddie, do come back here and help us finish *Julius Caesar*," coaxed Lionel. "Our problem is that most of the parts are for men. I did Caesar and then I was reincarnated as Mark Antony. Kate was Portia and Adelaide was Calpurnia, and there are no other female parts. I can't do Brutus and *all* the others. Would you play Brutus, Brother?"

"No, I would not! Never!"

Lionel smiled, pleased, and read the "Dramatis Personae." "Well, there are two other triumvirs besides Mark Antony, four senators, one, two, let's see, *eight* conspirators, servants, a soothsayer—"

"Not today. Time is slipping by and there is much to be done. I am at fault—I have procrastinated too long. I am growing old—"

"If you go out in this weather, you won't live to grow old," said Kate. "I wish you would stay, Edward."

She was still standing at the window, against the grey light; all he could see of her was a slim silhouette with a warm glow about the head.

"If I leave now there will be time to wait upon the Curtises. There are eight of them there together."

"Conspirators?" asked Kate.

"Constituents," said Edward. He went out and closed the double oak doors of the library firmly behind him.

Lady Weyward sent for Donald and Lydia to wait upon her in the library.

"This must be serious," said Lydia, by way of greeting. "You've ordered a fire." She flounced into a chair.

Donald came in, adjusting his monocle and looking down his nose. For weeks he had been avoiding his mother's anger and putting up with his sister's smirks; today he was determined to stand up to them. This resolve he furthered by remaining standing. With his weight on one foot and an elbow resting on a shelf, he believed that his attitude was one of superior nonchalance. A forgotten book in the corner of the shelf fell over on his arm. He threw the book into the fire and brushed his sleeve to remove any contamination.

"Where is our esteemed cousin this afternoon?" asked Lydia. "At the Vicarage imbibing learning?"

"Kate and Adelaide are using the library there, as usual."

"*And* have taken the coach? Not that I care in this rain. I'll go to the milliner's tomorrow afternoon. Do *not* allow them to have it tomorrow!" ordered Lydia.

"We shall see," said Lady Weyward, juggling priorities. She unfolded a letter and held it at arm's length but could not read it. Donald handed her a magnifying glass with disdain.

"This is a letter from the firm of Pierce, Price, and Sharpe, your Uncle William's solicitors. They beg to remind me that the time is approaching for their first visit to Coulder Hall. Naturally, we must receive them."

"How can we refuse without destroying all our hopes of the inheritance?" asked Donald.

"You can refuse as far as I am concerned. *I* haven't gone through *my* money!" Lydia raised her chin in disdain.

"At the rate you are buying outfits of every kind, you'll soon enough have nothing left," said her mother. "You aren't the duchess of Conroyallan!"

"Remember, *she* didn't snare Lord Radburn, either!" Donald reminded her.

"She did not, I agree," conceded Lydia. "But neither has anyone else. He avoids Kate like the plague. In spite of all she does!"

"What does she do?" asked Donald guardedly.

"Well—she talks to him and looks at him."

"Is that all?" snorted Donald. "She does that to everyone."

"Except you, Brother!" snapped Lydia.

"Kate was overcome by my proposal, that's all, and will come round when she gets used to the idea," replied Donald sententiously.

"Of course she will," soothed Lady Weyward. "In the meantime, I shall reply to these gentlemen, inviting them to a ball I shall give here at Coulder Hall, a coming-out ball for Kate and Adelaide together."

"Adelaide! Why Adelaide? It's bad enough to be obliged to have a ball to honour Kate, but why bother with that other ninny?"

"You had your coming-out two years ago. Don't begrudge your sister hers."

"Imagine! It was two years ago, and she isn't married yet!" taunted Donald. "Whatever can be the matter?"

"Mind your own business," shouted Lydia. "Sordid though it is!"

"Stop bickering, you two! I intend to display to these solicitors how well we are treating our ward-for-a-year." She was feeling self-satisfied with her decision, anticipating how the countess, too, would be impressed. "Besides, to include Adelaide will save the expense of a separate coming-out ball."

—13—

Jack Hinds led the roan from the dank stables of Coulder Hall and assisted his master in mounting him. Behind Donald's back he grinned sardonically, knowing why his lord moved so cautiously. It was a habit now for the roan to return to the stables alone, with Sir Donald staggering along some hours later, drunk and swearing. That roan was strict as a Methodist, thought Jack. And he didn't need no pulpit, neither, to make his message clear.

The roan turned his head around to see who his rider was, whinnied, and reared up. "There, there, laddie," soothed Jack, "it ain't that bad."

"This is my last ride on this vicious nag!" announced Donald, desperately holding on. "I'm trading him in at Tattersall's." He wished he could afford the gesture of shooting him. Gingerly he turned the despised animal in the direction of London.

Tattersall's, the horse auction mart, was located near Hyde Park Corner, just outside the city. To his surprise, Donald got a better bargain than he had hoped for. What did Tatt see in that roan? Donald wasn't about to argue. Tatt handed him some guineas in addition to an old mare, Daisy, inured to hardship and philosophical even after being led away by some insensitive jerks on her reins.

Donald tied up the drooping horse before the Subscription Rooms. When he entered, the rooms were, as usual, smoky, crowded, and boisterous. The members of the Jockey Club were a hard-riding, hard-drinking lot, given to loud discussions of the various race meetings, conditions of turf, studs, the latest favourites, and betting.

The noise abated at the appearance of Donald. Men peered at him over their shoulders and returned to their drinks without a word of greeting or camaraderie. Theirs was a strict code: he had not paid his betting debts, so-called debts of honour, and Donald was now persona non grata. No one was his friend. Donald made his way to the bar and loudly demanded a drink. The bartender, taking the cue from his betters, did not hear, polishing a glass with minute care, holding it up to the light, breathing on it, and polishing it some more. Donald stomped out of the room, a shout of laughter following him.

"Blast their eyes!" he muttered, snapping his crop furiously against the patient animal awaiting him. "They made that clear enough! I've got to get some money. Lots of it!" Roughly he turned his new equine victim in the direction of London.

In the West End, the thoroughfares were broad, and Donald found himself in the company of fine equipages with well-dressed occupants and postillions wearing colourful uniforms. Past palaces and parks he forced old Daisy, until they reached Whitechapel, where he had to slow his pace. Here the streets were narrow and crowded with people, shabby people, none too clean, who used their own two legs for locomotion. Dwellings were mean, and for a long stretch, high anonymous walls extended on either side, hiding who knew what. Further on, the door of a music hall opened and raucous sounds were heard, immediately cut off again when the door slammed shut. From a gin palace, a drunk wearing a top hat was tossed into the street, the aproned proprietor standing with hands on hips to see if the fellow would try to return—which he did. This time the proprietor seized him by the collar and seat of the pants and carried him to a mudpuddle into which he dropped him. Throughout all this commotion, the bent hat remained firmly in place.

Donald directed his animal into the district called Bluegate Fields, stopping at a house whose street door had long since been taken away for firewood. Three women in cheap finery lounged against the wall, and as Donald jumped down from his horse, one of them, with feathers stuck in dishevelled hair, sidled up to him. He examined her through his monocle. Unfortunately the woman had a turned-up nose that reminded him of his cousin. He cuffed her to the ground. She swore at him, using words even he had never heard before, and the other two women laughed. He tossed a coin at them, saying, "Mind the nag!" The coin rolled into the mud and the women fought over it like alleycats over suet.

Inside, the building was dark and odoriferous. The stairs creaked under his step; mice scuttled away. On the first landing a door opened and then closed. On the second landing a door was ajar. Lying on a mattress, dressed only in a shift, an aging woman with a face heavy with gin crooked a finger at Donald. He kept climbing. On the third floor, at a door onto which a piece of paper was held with a nail, Donald stopped and took a deep breath. One had to squint to read the word *Solicitor* written in cursive. Donald straightened his shoulders and knocked sharply.

"Who's that?" growled a deep voice.

"Open up," demanded Donald. "Business."

The door was unlocked and opened a crack. "Oh, it's you," said the voice. Grudgingly, the door was opened just far enough to admit Donald.

The voice belonged to a short man with a potbelly, a high balding forehead, and a shrewd, evil face. He was not a solicitor but knew more about the law than many a barrister of the Inns of Court, his specialty being those regulations concerning crime.

He was a product of the slums, parents unknown, who had had the good fortune to be taken in by an Anglican minister as a servant boy. By pretending piety, he had been looked on favourably by the pastor and his family. They taught him to read and write and do his sums and eventually obtained for him a job as a clerk in a law office. With his quick wits, he saw opportunities for advancement beyond his previous dreams and powers of resistance to temptation. At first, he was cocksure and wound up for a term at Newgate, that school for criminals, where he learned the rest of what was needful for him to know of the English legal and penal system.

In the East End he was known simply as the Solicitor. No one knew his real name. Rumour had it that he kept a fine house on the other side of town, complete with a respectable wife, children, and servants; that he attended church with his family every Sunday, where his booming voice led the hymn singing.

"Well?" he demanded.

"Don't you remember my problem?"

"I remember *you*," he replied with a curl of half of his upper lip, this expression used on titled clients to unnerve them. "Your documents are here somewhere," he added carelessly. Indolently lifting papers and dropping them, knowing very well that they were in the second drawer on the left, he searched through the debris on top of his cluttered desk. In his own good time he located them.

"Winton, that's the name, ain't it?" he asked, untying the string, knowing that the name was false. "Umh! I suggested that you overturn your uncle's will on the grounds of mental incapacity. Prove your sister mad, the cousin mad, the streak extends backward to the uncle. Well?"

"It won't work. My other sister resists the idea of having to prove madness in the family, says it would ruin her prospects. Besides, no one would ever believe that Kate—that my cousin was mentally deficient. Never! Even my younger sister is improving, too, it seems. They say sometimes she makes sense, although I, for one, don't see it."

"Hmmh!" The Solicitor pretended to be reading the

cramped handwriting with difficulty, although he already knew what it said. "Well, then, what about marrying this cousin, getting the money that way?"

"She won't have me."

"You have tried?"

"I have asked."

"Hrmph!" He was disgusted with his aristocratic client. "Well, there are other ways to get her to marry you."

"What do you mean?"

"What do you think I mean? Force matters—she grows a belly, with it grows gratitude for the offer of marriage." His hooded eyes watched his client; a dull dog indeed, but then he, the Solicitor, would not be so rich were it not for almost universal stupidity.

"Force Ka—my cousin? How could I do that?"

"Good God, man, do I have to spell it out?"

"She would call for help! There would be a devil of a row!"

"Is she never beyond calling distance?"

Donald remembered a scene in a forest, with a solitary Kate striding along singing. "Yes, sometimes."

"Well?"

"How could I? She's my rank, my family!"

The Solicitor felt only disgust for this snob. "As you say," he sneered. He got to his feet in a gesture of dismissal.

"Is there nothing else I can do?" asked Donald desperately.

"Yes, there is."

"What then?"

"Do her in. A nice clean job."

Donald's jaw sagged as he stared at the lawyer. Nervously he reached for his hat and made for the door.

The Solicitor's reptilian eyes followed him. He knew that this coxcomb, ready enough to skirt the edges of crime, would draw back at the notion of a real plunge. "I can arrange it for you. You can be far away."

Donald fumbled with the doorknob. "But then the money would go to his partner," he said.

"Arguable. You need it. Partner already rich. Partner not even English. Blood and patriotism thicker than the Caribbean."

Donald pulled a big handkerchief from his pocket and mopped his brow. He shook his head in an ambiguous way.

"Just one minute," said the Solicitor, "you forgot something."

Fear enlarged Donald's eyes.

"My fee."

"Put it on my account."

"You have no account."

Donald searched in his pocket for one of Tatt's guineas and handed it to him. The Solicitor kept his palm open. Donald found another and left hurriedly before more could be demanded.

On the second landing the door was still ajar, but the woman had fallen into a stupour. Donald entered abruptly and kicked the door closed with his heel.

— 14 —

Nurse Amelia lifted the big black teapot from the grate and poured the steaming liquid into two bowls. Some tea spilled on the wide-planked table. Kate reached to guide the old veined hands.

"It ain't me hands, it's me eyes, Miss Meg. And it ain't me eyes, neither, it's just old age working on me eyes. I ain't complaining, mind you. I ain't had such a bad life. My husband was a good 'un, God rest his soul, and my children grew up good, and my grandchildren, and—" Nurse Amelia stopped. She tried to remember whether she had any great-grandchildren, but all her offspring, alive and dead, were mixed up in her mind. Her husband was clear enough. "Ben Hanscomb was a good man, thanks be to God," she finished securely.

Kate encircled her bowl of tea with both hands to warm her fingers. "Do you notice it more chill in the mornings now?" she asked absently.

Nurse Amelia gulped the scalding tea, as was her custom. It didn't seem to do her any harm. "A–ahh!" she said, feeling brighter. "Ay, that it is, and the days is getting short. Almost equal to the nights now." She drained the big bowl.

"And it's only the beginning of September," said Kate.

"Ay."

Nurse Amelia refilled her own cup. "Best not leave 'til it's light. Let me hot up your tay."

Kate held out her bowl obediently.

With the second cup, Nurse Amelia remembered what it was she wanted to say. "Speaking of husbands, now that you're having a coming-out ball and all, you ought to be thinking of getting married." She paused, then added, "Lord Radburn's back."

It was Kate's turn to spill tea. "Oh? When did he arrive?"

"Two days gone. Looks peekid, says Mamie Wilcox. Working too hard for the *ree*forms. Ain't called round, has he?"

"No."

"Never did find the little feller was took for a chimney sweep. Feels real bad about that, does Lord Radburn, says Mamie Wilcox. 'Twas her brother's boy, from London."

"When does he return to London?"

"Who? Lord Radburn? Mamie says that the countess wants him to stay for your ball, yours and Miss Adelaide's, that is. He usually does what his mama says. A good son, Lord Radburn, very good." Nurse nodded her head approvingly.

Kate stood up and finished her tea. "That's good," she said agreeably, swinging a shawl around her shoulders. She wanted only to get to the stables and saddle Fantastique and ride and ride and ride.

On top of a knoll Kate reined Fantastique and looked up at the sky. With a sigh, she realised that it was time to go back. From that height the stable yard of Radburn Hall was visible, and with alarm she noticed two figures standing in the yard by the sawed-off tree trunk that was used to help people mount. One figure was Roscoe's; sometimes she met him on her return. The other figure, in shiny black boots, was undoubtedly Edward.

Kate looked back at the sky, but it offered no help. The sun was rising ever higher, and her choice was either to return now and run into Edward or to tarry until he had gone and face Lady Weyward's wrath at being late for breakfast. Selecting the lesser of the evils, Kate turned Fantastique in the direction of the stables.

Edward had his back to her, one long booted leg on the tree stump. Roscoe caught sight of her and pulled off his cap. Edward turned around.

"Kate!" he said, with immediate delight, his surprised face breaking into a smile of genuine pleasure. For a moment he looked the same as he had on that first day last spring on the right-of-way. As he came towards her to take the reins, his face straightened again with second thoughts, and stiffly he helped her alight. She noticed how pale he was, with circles under his dark eyes. He did indeed look "peekid."

"I hope you don't mind," she said, "my coming here to ride Fantastique."

"Certainly not. He *is* your horse. I might have known you would. Do you come every day?"

"Every morning, early. I get back to Coulder Hall in time for breakfast. L—Lady Weyward does not know that I come here."

"Quite. And quite right, too. I see that."

"You won't tell her?"

"Of course not!" he said stoutly. "Your secret is safe with me. And with Roscoe."

"Please do not put any blame on Roscoe for my riding Fantastique."

"I do not. There is no blame anywhere."

"Thank'ee, miss," said Roscoe, taking the horse from Edward. "Best let me wash him down today, afore you're late. The sun is summat high."

"Thank *you*, Roscoe. You are very kind. You are both very kind."

She disappeared into the stables to change her clothes. When she came outdoors, Edward was still there.

"Have you tried out Fantastique on the racecourse yet?" he asked.

"No, at least not here. I have raced him at Newmarket, however. He loved it, and he won, I assure you! He was born to be raced, Papa says."

They exchanged glances of mutual interest. Then Edward's smile waned and he said formally, "How is your father's health?"

"He writes that he is well. But I do worry. He pays no attention when he doesn't feel right and keeps going on with his work anyway. It's been so long since I have seen him last!" She turned away, distressed.

"Nearly six months, isn't it?" asked Edward softly, looking at the tendrils of bright hair loosened against her neck.

She looked at him, surprised that he should have kept track of the time. "Yes. My year is half gone."

"I wish you success in winning your inheritance," said Edward, very much the lord of Radburn Park. "And in all endeavors."

"Thank you," said Kate, "very much." She started toward the path to Coulder Hall.

"Kate!" Edward ran to catch up. "I meant to tell you. Please feel free to run Fantastique over on the course."

"Thank you. I will do that."

"I hope you plan to enter him in the spring race meeting here?"

"Yes, if you like. Fantastique would enjoy that." She walked away determinedly.

"I'll ask Roscoe to leave the gates of the course open," he called after her.

She waved her hand in recognition that she had heard him. A few seconds later it was Kate running back to Edward.

"Will you attend our ball next week?" she asked. "Adelaide's and mine?"

"It will be my pleasure," said Edward with a bow, "and my family's. The countess will be happy to attend. And, of course, the vicar."

Donald, lying on his stomach on a blanket of pine needles near the right-of-way, kept dozing off. Blast her eyes, he grumbled to himself, why does she have to get up so early? He was sleepy and uncomfortable and had a hangover. Besides that, he was hungry. It was time for his breakfast.

But Kate had become an obsession with him; he thought of little else. He wanted the fortune that would most likely go with her, but also now, blindly, he wanted Kate herself. Her scorn and disregard of him only whetted his desire, and so he waited for her.

He was jealously aware that half the county wanted to marry her. Coulder Hall was under siege with invitations and callers. Lady Weyward, in her pride, imagined that she at last had taken her Rightful Place in Society, although the financial cost of entertaining preoccupied her, and she nagged him constantly about Uncle William's money. Lydia, in her vanity, believed that she was the one being sought after, and thought only of new clothes.

Donald snorted. Only he, Donald, was acute enough to see that Kate was the magnet, drawing every eligible—and ineligible—man in the county. And only he knew that it was Lionel who had captured her affections. Hiding it, too, she was, pretending that she went to the Vicarage several times a week for education! Huh! He saw through that! Worse, she sneaked over here every morning to ride out on the downs, and he was sure that it was for the purpose of an assignation. Why else would she disguise herself in those boy's clothes? Sly, sly!

What an achievement it would be for him, to take this prize away, not only from Lionel, but from everyone. What ignominy it would be to let her escape, and she under his own roof by the very terms of their uncle's will!

The scuffle of leaves riveted his attention to the path. Kate appeared, running fast from the direction of the Radburn stables, her hair falling down, tears on a flushed and agitated face. He rose quickly to follow, but the question occurred to him, whatever is she running *from?* Could Lionel be chasing her? He did not feel like facing the vicar, so he hid behind a tree and watched the path. No vicar appeared, only a brown-and-grey squirrel, alarmed by the disturbance in the autumnal quiet.

Donald felt like a fool and threw a stone at the squirrel, who evaded it by running up a tree. He ground his teeth in frustration. Blast Lionel! Blast Kate! His quarry not two feet away and he had let her go. After rising so early, too. Next time, he would have her, willy-nilly!

—15—

"FANTASTIQUE, *tu es formidable!*"

Kate had taken him several times around Edward's racecourse, walking him at first so that he would grow accustomed to the turf and the conformations of landscape and architecture. Gradually she built up speed, and today was beyond her expectations. He loved riding fast as much as she did, and the last time round had let loose a speed greater than any he had ever displayed. He showed power, a magic, and Kate was a part of it.

Finally she began to slow him down. In the cold morning air, his breath came from his nostrils in two white parallel streams. She stopped him and jumped off, tearfully enthusiastic, and searched in the pocket of her shabby jacket for a reward. Fantastique savoured the honey lump, his long jaw moving from side to side. He swallowed and nudged her for more. Obligingly, Kate explored her other pockets and found another sweet.

She remounted, and Fantastique thought they were ready to run again.

"*Non*, *chéri*, that is enough for today. I must get back early. Tonight is the ball, and Cousin Adelaide will be nervous and looking for reassurance. How *I* am to remain calm, I don't know."

The stable yard was just as she had left it, with the big doors open. She had returned too early to meet Roscoe.

"And Lord Radburn isn't here, of course. He hasn't been here since that accidental meeting last week. He really *is* avoiding me," she confided in Fantastique's ear, which twitched in sympathy.

She hung up the saddle, rubbed him down with big brushes, gave him oats for breakfast and lots of fresh water. He was a thirsty colt.

Her petticoats and old blue-and-white dress had been thrown over the wooden partitions. She went into the stall next to Fantastique's, removed each of her boots with a little grunt, and then took off the riding clothes, shaking out each garment and folding it into the case on top of the boots. The battered tricorn was pressed down, the case closed and placed between the partitions. Just as she reached up for the petticoats, she saw him. Donald was standing in the doorway of the stall, leering. She stared at him in disbelief.

"What a nice little filly! Already in deshabille, ready for lovemaking. How fortunate I am." He looked her up and down. Although she had on a white cotton shift and pantaloons, she felt naked. Instinctively she placed her arms across her body.

"*Venus Surprised at Her Toilette.* Exactly like that statue they dug up in Italy."

Kate looked about her.

"Don't bother. No one is anywhere near. I have been watching the stables for some time. I have been watching *you.*" He entered the stall. "Now I am tired of just looking."

Kate retreated. "I shall scream," she said between stiff lips. The words came from a mouth that seemed frozen, and she wondered whether she *could* scream.

"It would do no good. No one would hear."

Her back was now pressed against the cold stone wall of the stables. He reached out and took her by her bare arms. "Relax, Kate. The worst that can happen is that you will have to marry me." He pulled her against him.

"Fantastique!" she cried out wildly.

In the next stall the colt reared up at the cry and began to buck and kick the intervening wall. Astonished, Donald let her go. She took the opportunity to squeeze herself between the outside wall and the end of the partition and got through to Fantastique's stall. With frantic strength she threw herself up onto his saddleless back like an acrobat, leaned over, and opened the gate.

"Oh no you don't!" Donald shouted and ran around the partitions to stop them. There were no reins to catch, so he threw his arms around the neck of the animal and held on. The colt reared up again and swept Donald off his feet. Kate reached for Fantastique's mane, but the shiny hair slipped between her fingers, and she fell off behind him. As she landed on the ground, left shoulder first, something cracked. The animal, enraged at Donald's holding on to his neck, swung his head, and Donald was thrown against a post. Fantastique, the whites of his eyes showing in fury and saliva dropping from his mouth, went after him.

"Fantastique, no!" cried out Kate, getting to her feet. The animal paused. "Come here!" He looked at each of them in turn, then quietly returned to his stall. Donald, freed but terrified, ran for the door.

He shouted back savagely, "If you say one word of this, I'll inform the whole county how you go riding every day, and your aunt not knowing about it. From the *Radburn* stables! They'll soon figure out the reason for that—everybody is talking about you and the vicar. I'll tell them how you disguise yourself as a boy and ride astride, huzzy that you are!"

He brushed at his clothes and patted down his hair. "Try to get Uncle's fortune then!"

Coulder Hall reverberated with preparations for the ball. All morning Lady Weyward was loud and emphatic but confusing in her orders, which changed every minute. The harassed servants muttered but kept working. Donald had disappeared, which annoyed Lady Weyward, for she felt that he should be helping her. Lydia was in her room, feverishly trying the effects of various furbelows and coiffures, determined to take the attention from the two girls in whose honour the ball was being given. As the colour of her gown was acid green, it was difficult to find scarf, slippers, jewelry, and ribbons that did not clash. Then too, disconcertingly, her face had erupted in disagreeable blemishes due to an overindulgence in tansy pudding.

Adelaide, admonished by her mother to stay out of the way of the preprations, ran to Kate's room for encouragement and found it locked.

"Cousin Kate! Are you there?" She heard Kate pull back the bolt. "Did you go back to bed? I'm so sorry I troubled you. I'll come back later."

"No, please come in. Do, do. I want your judgment as to how to fix my hair. Would you do it for me?"

"I say, you do look pale."

"I'm all right," said Kate, determined to ignore the pain that shot through her shoulder when she moved her arm. "It's the excitement."

"I'm being a pest. I think I should leave you alone."

"No! You are not a pest! Do stay. After all, one doesn't 'come out' every day."

"Just think, Cousin Kate, it means that it's time for us to get married!" Adelaide sounded awed.

"It means that we are old enough to get married, but it doesn't mean that we *have* to."

Adelaide laughed. "It isn't as though we are being threatened!"

"No," Kate said, and put a hand over her throbbing collarbone.

At midday, the name representatives of Pierce, Price, and Sharpe arrived and were taken to their rooms, the finest in Coulder Hall, which the servants had just cleaned and made comfortable. Kate was introduced to the gentlemen in the dining hall. Pierce and Price were rotund, middle-aged, and cheerful-looking, with long side-whiskers. Sharpe was younger, clean-shaven, tall, lean, lowering. Kate curtsied nervously, and they all sat down at the long table. At the last minute Donald came in, smelling of whiskey. He darted a swift glance at his cousin, who abruptly turned away. Pierce was seen to whisper to Price, who whispered to Sharpe.

The house became quiet in the afternoon, all the principals except Kate settling down for a nap. She slipped downstairs to find Nurse Amelia, who was dozing outside in the sunshine, her white-capped head on her chest and her gnarled hands with their big brown age spots folded on her ample stomach. Kate shook her with her right hand.

"Eh? Miss Kate, is it? Why ain't you upstairs snoozing like everyone else?"

"Nanny! Please wake up. I need something urgently."

"What do you want, a nice cup of tay? Here, help me up then."

Kate extended her other hand without thinking, then jerked it back at the searing pain.

"Something wrong with you arm, is it?"

"My collarbone. I think it is broken."

"Broken! How did you manage to do that, child?"

"I fell from a horse."

"Fell from a horse? Ye?"

"It was an accident. Oh, Nanny, do you have any laudanum? The pain is intense and the ball is tonight."

Nurse Amelia leaned her weight on the chair and hoisted herself up.

"Let's go inside and I'll take a look at that there arm."

A slight swelling over the area of the break was all that was visible, but Kate flinched at Nurse Amelia's gentlest touch.

"Best tell Lady Weyward and get Dr. Gilford over. Ye can't go to no ball like that."

"No! Don't tell her! I'll get through it all right. Just give me something to stop the pain."

Nurse Amelia regarded her dubiously. "But you are hurt, child!"

"Please, Nanny, in the name of my mother, just give me some laudanum."

Nurse Amelia sighed and, squinting to see, drew forward a small bottle from the back of a shelf.

"I ain't doing right," she said, fetching a glass of water. "I feel it in me old bones."

The countess, quietly resplendent in dove grey velvet and rows of pearls, and flanked by her two sons, was among the early arrivals at the ball.

"How lovely you both look!" she said, regarding the two young girls in the receiving line and knowing very well where their gowns came from. "Don't you think so?" she asked, turning to her sons.

"They always do," said Lionel gallantly. "But tonight exceptionally so."

"Extraordinary!" said Edward, his dark eyes drinking in the vision of Kate. She was dressed in the duchess's gown of shell-pink mull-mull, and Lucy Wilcox's nimble fingers had removed some of the heavy satin roses that decorated it, using the material to make a scarf, which Kate wore in a way to hide the swollen collarbone. Her slippers were of bright red velvet with flat heels, and Adelaide had arranged in her hair a chaplet of scarlet sage from the garden. Her face, usually healthy-looking and vibrant, was pale and withdrawn; her luminous eyes with enlarged pupils didn't focus on anything. From a healthy, athletic girl she had changed into a fragile-looking, mysterious one; she was absolutely stunning. Edward had trouble taking his attention elsewhere.

Once the guests had gathered, the dancing began. In the days before the ball, Kate had refused all offers for the first set, hoping for one special invitation, which never came. Now she overheard Edward petitioning her cousin Lydia, who had the week before allowed Wilfred Curtis to write his name at the top of her *carnet;* in view of this more gilded opportunity, Lydia turned her back on poor Wilfred and proudly took Edward's arm. Wilfred was left looking foolish and angry. He blindly sought out the nearest available partner, who happened to be Adelaide. She accepted him readily. Kate leaned her head against the wall and closed her eyes, relieved to be out of it. The pain in her collarbone had dulled, but the laudanum was making her drowsy. Everything seemed unreal and far away.

"Look at Kate," said Lydia loudly. "She has no one to dance with at her own ball!"

Lionel immediately replied, "You are wrong. *I* am her partner. I was delayed by Lady Weyward."

Taking Kate's hand, he drew her to the line of dancers.

"Lionel, I am surprised at you, telling such a fabrication. It's un-vicarlike," said Kate, trying to sound merry.

"Not at all," he said. "I *intended* to ask you." In his correct way, as the music indicated, he handed her on to the next gentleman, who happened to be Donald. Lionel smiled as he let her go. "My intentions are as good as accomplishments, you know."

Donald, hearing the last remark, imagined that it was intended for him as mockery; imagined that Kate had confided in the vicar, who knew all about Donald's failure of purpose that morning and thought it funny. He repressed his rage, his temples throbbing.

Kate danced every set until it was time for refreshments. She felt in a dream; one person meant no more to her than another. She danced automatically, like a wound-up doll. Perched on frail little chairs along the wall of the ballroom, the three solicitors observed her and occasionally remarked to each other.

When the music stopped, Donald called for quiet and made a speech whilst raising his glass.

"Ladies and gentlemen, your attention, please. I wish to

toast the two youngest adornments of my household, in whose honour this ball is being given—my beloved little sister Adelaide, and our dearest cousin, Katherine Martin. May their lives be long, happy, and prosperous—and by their sides, the best of husbands."

"Hear! Hear!" cried the company.

Adelaide blushed and nervously smiled, twisting the colourful ribbons that decorated her flowered satin gown. Kate, as duly noted by Messrs. Pierce, Price, and Sharpe, remained pale and remote, as though she had not heard. The effect of the laudanum was wearing off, and the pain in her shoulder made any other sensation of small importance.

During the next set, which began with a minuet, Donald noticed something interesting: Kate winced whenever someone took her arm, and once when her scarf fell back, he saw that her neck was swollen and red at the collarbone. The minuet was slow and measured, and Kate got through it; however, the gavotte that followed was lively and hence more painful. Donald seized his opportunity. When he came to her in the course of the dance, he gave her a rough turn. She looked up at him in alarm, and he smiled malevolently and skipped by, enjoying his game. At the next turn, she refused him her hand. He frowned in frustration and, moving on to the following lady, who was Adelaide, he vented his spite by turning her with unnecessary force. He came to Kate a third time and swiftly seized her left hand and raised it above her head, held it there, then twisted the arm. Unable to stop herself, Kate screamed out in agony and fell unconscious on the floor.

Confusion followed, and the musicians faltered. Voices were heard asking, "What happened?" "Is it a joke?" "Who screamed?"

The company milled about, bewildered, while Donald edged to the door. Edward was the first to bend over the inert figure on the floor.

"Katie!" he exclaimed in dismay and turned her over on

her back. Blood had stained the pink satin scarf where it covered her shoulder. Gently he lifted the satin and saw that the broken bone had torn through the flesh.

"Pray hurry, go fetch Dr. Gilford," he said to Lionel, who had joined them and, seeing the gored shoulder, ran to follow out the request.

"Stay back, please!" Edward said to the company, who had gathered around in horror.

"Is she dead?"

"Who did it?"

"Everyone, please!" said Edward. "I believe Miss Martin has fainted. She seems to have broken her collarbone—how, I do not know. It is best not to move her until Dr. Gilford arrives. Will you all step back to give her air?"

"Fainted?"

"Broken collarbone!"

"Whilst dancing?"

Lady Weyward rushed up, officiously proffering a bottle of smelling salts. "What has she done? Spoiling the party like this!"

Edward took the bottle and moved it back and forth under Kate's nostrils. Her eyelids fluttered.

"Does anyone know what happened? Who was dancing with her?" Edward looked out over the crowd.

The guests questioned each other in whispers, trying to remember.

Adelaide, stiff and white with fear, cried out, "Donald! Donald did it, I saw him! He grabbed her hand and raised it over her head and turned it!" She pointed to Donald, ready to go out the door.

"Don't pay any attention to her!" said Lady Weyward.

"She's mad!" shouted Lydia. "Everyone knows that!"

Donald, who had at first thought that he had killed Kate and was running for it, now realised that he had not and came forward with bravura.

"Yes, I was dancing with her," he admitted, "but how can you hurt a person dancing a gavotte? If that were true, all the ladies here would be lying on the floor bleeding." He looked at the three solicitors, who were standing at the front of the crowd. "Oh, no, my friends, ask *her* how she broke her collarbone!" He was gambling again, gambling that Kate would not denounce him.

Kate opened her eyes and tried to rise.

"No, Kate," said Edward gently. "Stay on your back until Dr. Gilford arrives." He placed his big white handkerchief with lace trim over the wound to stanch the bleeding.

Kate's eyes flickered from Edward to Donald to Lady Weyward to Pierce, Price, and Sharpe.

"I broke my collarbone this morning," she said. "I fell from a horse."

"How could that have happened?" asked Edward.

"From a *horse?*" gasped Lady Weyward. "Why were you on a horse?"

"What horse?" asked Lydia, jealously watching Edward take Kate's hand tenderly.

"It was my own horse. I rode him from Newmarket. Papa gave him to me. I left him at the Radburn stables, as I did not want to arrive at Coulder Hall in riding clothes."

"She wears boys' clothes when she rides," gloated Donald. "I have seen her. Pants, boots, and jacket!"

Edward picked up the remark. "You have seen her?"

Donald ignored him. He was busy thinking up an answer in case Kate accused him of attempting to seduce her. He had it: he would say that Kate had tried to seduce *him*, had thrown herself at him, to win his silence.

Kate went on, speaking in a voice barely above a whisper. "I love horses," she said simply. "They have always been a part of my life. I have been riding my horse every morning ever since I came here to Coulder Hall."

"Without my knowledge!" accused Lady Weyward.

"Yes," whispered Kate.

"Astride!" shouted Lydia, so that all could hear.

"Yes."

"You see what she is," said Donald, gesturing to the

solicitors. "Sneaky and untrustworthy!" It seemed almost too easy, and he was beginning to enjoy himself. He wished now that Kate would accuse him, so that he could accuse her back.

"A shameless huzzy, I'd say!" said Lady Weyward, realising what Donald was about.

"Is it true, Cousin Kate?" asked Adelaide, anguished. "Do you really go riding every morning in *pants?*"

"Yes, dear Cousin Adelaide, it is true."

Pierce looked at Price. "Bold," he said.

"Brassy," said Price, turning to Sharpe.

"Brash" was Sharpe's opinion.

Edward said coldly, "Weyward, I think you should dismiss your guests."

"I'll dismiss them when I please and not before," said Donald petulantly. Edward half rose.

The countess stepped forward and said clearly to Lady Weyward, "My dear, how disagreeable this must be for you! It is too bad the ball had to end this way. But it's very late. As soon as Lionel returns with the doctor, we must leave."

Taking their cue from the countess, the guests began to leave. Shawls were found, coaches called for, and farewells made. The ballroom emptied with many a backward look, leaving Kate in the middle of the floor with Edward kneeling beside her. Her eyes were closed, and he forced back the questions he wanted to ask. Edward could smell the hot melted wax as it ran down the white candles and spattered on the polished ballroom floor, and he watched as hot tears rolled down Kate's pale face.

"This is Kate's room?" questioned the countess, following Adelaide, who led the procession carrying a candelabra.

"Yes. It's Lydia's old room. My room is just across the hall, next after the schoolroom." She saw the countess's disapproval. "At least we are near each other."

"Yours is like it?"

"Yes. They aren't much, but as Kate says, since they are small and low-ceilinged, they are warmer."

"I see."

"You've let the fire go out!" Lady Weyward accused the maid, Nettie, one of Nurse Amelia's grandchildren. The grate obviously hadn't been used for years, but the maid, who knew her mistress well, wrinkled her nose at the lie and went to fetch some firewood.

"Lay her flat, without a pillow!" said old Dr. Gilford as Edward entered with his burden of pink mull-mull and satin roses, incongruously shawled with yards and yards of surgical cloth.

Tenderly Edward placed her on the narrow bed.

"Good, good," said the doctor. "Now, ladies, let's get this finery off, and then I'll give her something to make her sleep."

Edward joined Lionel and his mother in the hall.

"Thank God it was only a broken clavicle," said Lionel. "She might have been killed. Fell from a horse, I understand?"

"Yes. I find it hard to believe. There must be more to the story." Edward frowned.

Nettie came down the hall, leading a line of her little brothers, who were staggering under loads of wood. Nettie curtsied as she passed the group at the door.

"Nettie," said the countess, "has Lady Weyward asked you to stay with Miss Martin this night?"

"No, ma'am, not Lady Weyward. 'Twas Grandmama. She's says I'm to sleep against the door."

"Wise old Amelia," approved the countess.

The procession passed on into the bedroom. Lionel picked up a piece of wood that had fallen from the arms of the littlest and restored it to the bundle.

The countess turned her attention to the three solicitors, who were standing at the end of the hall arguing. Each held a single candle and gesticulated with it. Price and Pierce moved theirs from side to side while Sharpe moved his vertically.

"I fear she may have lost her inheritance," said the countess.

"What a pity!" said Lionel. "She would have used it well!"

"It isn't fair!" protested Edward.

The countess watched the solicitors meditatively. "Perhaps I'll ask these gentlemen to tea," she said.

She approached them carrying a small candle; their candles poised in midair, and soon four candles were seen to burn quietly at the end of the hall.

— 16 —

THE COUNTESS REMOVED to the spa at Bath, where she had a compact but comfortable row house on the Royal Crescent. With her as guests she took several members of the family of Coulder Hall. The way it came about was thus:

The Messrs. Pierce, Price, and Sharpe were most pleased to take tea with the countess, and in the course of civilities, she extracted the following information from them: One, no, they had not reached any decision concerning the eligibility of Miss Katherine Martin to inherit her uncle's fortune. In fact, the terms of the will decreed that they wait until a full year was up, which would not be until next spring, some six months hence. Two, yes, Miss Martin must remain at Lady Weyward's side. The terms of the will were emphatic on this point; Miss Martin was to remain under Lady Weyward's constant tutelage and influence for one year.

"If I should invite Miss Martin to Bath *along* with Lady Weyward, and the Misses Weyward, of course, would that be in accord with the meaning of the will? Sir Donald naturally would have to remain at Coulder Hall to take care of the affairs of his estate."

"Would Lady Weyward accept your invitation?"

"I believe she might," said the countess, scratching Frou-Frou behind an ear.

"Well, then—" said Pierce, lifting heavy eyebrows at his partners for assent. Price and Sharpe nodded. "That would be agreeable."

Kate had expected to be sent back to Newmarket in disgrace. From her first day at Coulder Hall, she had berated herself for her lies and deceit; to lose her inheritance seemed to her a just punishment. If she had not deceived Lady Weyward about Fantastique, Donald would not have been able to attempt what he did at the stables. Yes, she had brought it all on herself. But, oh, that her father should have to suffer on account of her willfulness!

But now, it seemed, she had a reprieve. They all were invited, except for Donald, to Bath. I will be so good, she promised herself, exactly what Lady Weyward would want. Of course, she did slip away to say farewell to Fantastique.

"My brave, brave Fantastique! How can I ever repay you? I must go away for a while—but I'll come back. Be very good, learn the course well—every blade of grass and every undulation. Roscoe will take you. And next spring you will race!"

Her eyes were shiny with tears as she bade farewell to him. She tried to put her arms about his neck, but the sticking plaster and bandages on her shoulder prevented it. At the sound of her breaking voice, Fantastique twitched his ears and blinked his intelligent eyes.

"And then, if I am very good and can inherit, we'll go back to Papa! He will get well again, and we will be happy and ride every day, every single day! Think of that, Fantastique!" Fantastique nodded his elegant head.

"*Sois sage, mon petit*. Do what Roscoe tells you. You will be in good hands, and I'll be back one day."

Fantastique felt the change that was coming, and as Kate left the stables, he neighed in discontent.

Lady Weyward had graciously allowed herself to be persuaded to accept the countess's invitation, after a show of reluctance to cover her jumping at the chance. To be a guest in the countess's house in Bath would certainly affirm her position in the Highest Society! Of course, it would condone what Kate had done, but never mind, there was more than one way to skin a cat!

Adelaide was delighted to accompany her dearest friend to Bath. All was forgiven; in fact, the more she thought about it, the less fault she could find. Her mother and brother and sister were just mistaken, that was all. Then, too, the vicar had promised to spend as much time in Bath as his parish duties permitted and to continue his tutoring of the young ladies. He planned to bring books with him each time he came, and told them of a circulating library at Bath from which they could withdraw the very latest publications from the London and foreign presses.

Edward would not join his mother at Bath. Pressing matters concerning an election, he said; he had promised to support a candidate who entertained his own ideas on reform. He planned to canvass for him vigorously and would, therefore, remain at Radburn Hall.

Lydia, upon learning that Lord Radburn was to stay behind, announced that Sir Donald could not possibly run Coulder Hall by himself, unfortunately. "He is such a dreamer," she said plaintively, "that upon our return we would find sheep and chickens in the downstairs hall and the servants ungovernable. No, I must remain here. You three go and enjoy yourselves. Don't think about me." Her look of martyrdom would have been complete had it not been for her eyes, alert with expectation. With Kate disgraced, or at least in a kind of limbo with regard to her reputation, Lydia, with all her fine new clothes, was sure she could bring things to the point with the indifferent Lord Radburn.

Before the party left, Donald and Lady Weyward closeted themselves in their bookless library for more than an hour, and both emerged therefrom smiling smugly. Lady Weyward's campaign to discredit Kate had been thoroughly revised.

Due to her natural good health and the care provided on the Royal Crescent, Kate recovered quickly. Every morning she slept until she wakened, and she had only to touch an embroidered pull at her bedstead to have Mrs. Wilcox arrive with a tray laden with a full breakfast. In a pretty white cotton morning robe (inherited from the duchess), she breakfasted at a small table facing the rear garden, watching and listening to the birds in the trees. Lucy Wilcox helped her bathe and dress and arrange her hair, so that she would not have to lift her arms.

"She is being spoiled," said Lady Weyward to her gullible neighbour from the county, Lady Curtis, now also removed to Bath. "And Heaven knows she is hard to handle already."

Lady Curtis nodded absently and slapped the hand of her youngest, still a baby, who had put his fingers in the jam pot. Before her marriage and many children, she had been a pretty, thoughtless girl. Her face was still smooth and bland, free from wrinkles, but her figure was matronly, at the point of slovenly, and she had not a single thought in her head that was not planted there by her husband or her friends. She believed everything Lady Weyward told her, and repeated it later with an air of certainty, as though she herself had come to these conclusions.

Kate and Adelaide rarely went out with Lady Weyward; they were relieved that she arranged it thus, so that they did not have to watch their every remark, which Lady Weyward would be bound to find fault with. Often the two girls went into a large park near the Crescent and read to each other or conversed in French. If they walked into town they were accompanied by Lucy or Mrs. Wilcox. It was the custom in Bath to visit the Pump Room every morning, ostensibly to take the waters, but actually to see friends and to be introduced to newcomers. As an invalid, Kate was required actually to drink the water, but as it was immediately followed by tea and biscuits, she did not mind.

Kate's reception by Society at Bath was confused and mixed at first but deteriorated as Lady Weyward circulated about. The story of Kate's deception was repeated to all who would listen. "She kept a horse at the Radburn stables, and I knew nothing about it. At the least, it was a breach of confidence and trust in me. As to what else went on in the Radburn stables, I leave that to your own good judgement." As to Kate's riding astride, Lady Weyward would say, "Yes, and you know, not even the most wanton doxie would do that!"

The fact that the countess, whose social position was impeccable, sponsored Kate, brought her to the Assemblies, and introduced her to everyone in the most gracious of terms only served to make Kate a *cause célèbre*. Lady Weyward counteracted this beneficent influence with the remark, "What else can the countess do? She is simply putting a good face on things. From what I hear went on in her own stables, her son will have to marry Kate. Yes, the good vicar!" She would give her listener a knowing look and reduce her voice to a whisper. "The countess's doctor visits Kate every few days. I am in the house. *I* know."

"But didn't she break her collarbone?" would come as a weak objection. "Isn't that why the doctor comes?"

"So they are putting out. That is what they want people to believe."

"Oh, how wicked!"

"Yes, isn't it!"

"But won't she lose her inheritance if a scandal breaks out?"

"I should say so! That is what they are trying to prevent. You see, Lionel is only a second son and has few resources; better to marry an heiress than a penniless girl."

"Imagine his marrying for money!"

"Imagine!"

"Oh, Lady Weyward, you must tell the solicitors everything!"

"Don't think I won't, when the time comes!"

Kate's own outspoken demeanour was not in her favour. Old Admiral Benson, in Bath for his health, hearing from his wife that Kate "was no better than she should be," one day leaned over and, in what he thought was a whisper, asked Kate to meet him in the park. "Just us two," he bellowed.

"You old roué!" laughed Kate. "What would Mrs. Benson say?" She lightly slapped his face with her scarf and walked away from him.

Mrs. Benson was not amused, and what she said to the admiral we shall be excused from learning here. The admiral's defence to his wife was that Kate had led him on, and his excuse to himself was that Kate must really be besotted with the vicar to refuse him, the handsome and heroic admiral.

When the vicar came to Bath, as he often did, all eyes watched Kate and him for signs of guilt. Adelaide was always with them. The three could be seen riding in his curricle or walking along the street, a girl on each side of him, each clinging to an arm. The general opinion was that the lovers were being careful, nay, sly and deceptive, using Adelaide as a companion so that everything seemed innocent.

Bath Society had its thirst for gossip assuaged one day, appropriately enough in the Grand Pump Room. Lionel was witnessed by all handing Kate a glass of the waters, repeating in Greek the motto from Pindar which was written on the architrave just above Lady Weyward's head, "Water, best of elements." It was said in the tone of a father encouraging a child to take her medicine but, as it was in Greek, was instantly misconstrued.

"Did you hear that?" demanded Lady Weyward of her neighbour. "They have a secret language so that no one else can understand. Not even Adelaide! But then it is easy to fool Adelaide, poor thing."

But Adelaide did understand, for she and Lionel and Kate had been reading of the origin of the spa in connection with their study of Roman history. Adelaide could have informed her mother that Bath was discovered by the invading Romans in A.D. 54, and that they built a whole system of baths here, calling it *Aquae Sulis*, the water of Sul, who was a goddess. The legend of Prince Bladud, cast out from his court because he had leprosy and was miraculously cured by these waters, which Adelaide might have told her mother, was probably apocryphal.

Thus did Kate's reputation sink like lead in Bath's water. The women were the worst, whispering behind fans or uplifted hands. The younger ladies, seeking surcease from a formidable rival, helped eagerly to spread the stories. Mothers warned their eligible sons that in a few months the girl would be either married to Lionel or denounced by the solicitors and left without a farthing, and that they should leave her alone. The result was that she was not spoken to or asked to dance publicly but was relentlessly pursued in a covert way as fair game.

Kate suffered from the change in attitude and assumed that it was because of her riding Fantastique. Deception and lies are wicked, she thought, and it is just that I be punished. Yet it didn't seem to her that riding Fantastique was wicked, and as the weeks passed and her shoulder healed, she longed to ride again. She stroked the noses of the countess's handsome four, fed sweets to Lionel's greys, and wondered wistfully how Fantastique was doing. If only Edward would pay a visit, she could ask him in detail, but he resolutely refused to come to Bath. The countess, hurt by his absence, wrote to him constantly, begging him to come. It's my fault, Kate told herself; he doesn't like me and won't even come to visit his mother as long as I am here.

Often the thought of returning to her father tempted her, of just giving up the struggle of being thought a lady and the whole inheritance. But the countess would speak to her of responsibility to her father, to herself, of doing good with the money once it was hers. So she hung on.

Kate saw that the countess was distressed in another way that was her fault: having Lady Weyward in the house. As long as Kate was there, Lady Weyward would have to be, too. Lady Weyward was an obnoxious guest, faultfinding and overriding, believing that she was in control of the destiny of those around her. The countess could, of course, at any time send all of her guests packing, but that would mean that Kate would be under the same roof again as Donald, and although they had never discussed Donald's behaviour, the countess was aware of it.

At night, Kate tossed back and forth in her bed, trying to find a way out of her dilemma. If the attitude of Society was any indication, it was evident that she was not going to inherit, no matter how perfect her behaviour. To suffer until spring and make the countess suffer with her, only to be told that she was not qualified, seemed a useless penance for both.

As Kate's prospects declined, Adelaide's improved. In the countess's household she was, as might be expected, well treated and well cared for, and she had developed becomingly. She was less shy now about joining in the conversation, and her opinions were listened to and respected. Lady Weyward still made acid remarks about her: "childish," "backward," "the cross I have to bear," but actually Adelaide's comments were not ill-received by the *haut ton* of Bath who happened to be in the market for a wife, or by their parents. A docile wife or daughter-in-law, easily handled, accompanied by a medium fortune, was not by any means undesirable. Lady Weyward's judgements on her daughter served to obscure the fact that she had a first-rate mind and bookish tendencies, which might otherwise have been to her detriment. Adelaide's suitors were many.

It was the vicar who was hardest hit by Adelaide, quite suddenly so, it seemed to him. The epiphany occurred in the overheated, crowded Pump Room when Adelaide let her scarf fall. Her back was to Lionel; her sleeves were in the style called "puffed," high up on her arm. The scarf fell, and a plump arm was revealed, with an elbow faintly pink and with delicious curves and, yes! a dimple. It was the prettiest and most desirable elbow that Lionel had ever seen. Without taking thought (for the first time in his life), he was drawn to it as by a magnet and placed his hand on the tantalizing object.

Adelaide turned around. "Yes?" She smiled, seeing who it was. Lionel stared at her without reply, intently, wonderingly, and her smiled faded. Then, understanding, the smile returned at its sweetest and most luminous.

"Yes," said Adelaide, nodding her red curls.

— 17 —

In the county, Lydia was not faring so well with Lionel's brother. Weeks went by before she saw Edward, although she entertained on a scale the expense of which would have made Lady Weyward, had she known, scream in horror. Edward, however, sent his regrets to her invitations and sometimes forgot even to do that.

"He's out getting votes," said Wilfred Curtis, recently returned from Bath. He had forgiven Lydia for her treatment of him.

"Oh, votes!" said Lydia petulantly. "Is that all!"

"It is very important to get support for the reforms," said Wilfred, assuming Edward's stance and frown. "The slave trade, for instance—"

"The slave trade is a bore!" snapped Lydia. "Is reform all he cares about?"

"It appears so," said Wilfred reflectively. "Nothing else seems to matter to him."

"Umph!" was Lydia's response, and she turned her attention angrily to her other guests.

"Lord Radburn is a fool" was Donald's judgement. "Not only is he wasting his time, he is making enemies by advocating that this lucrative, useful business be prohibited. He is ruining his career for a quixotic ideal. It will come to nothing, believe me."

"If you say so," said Wilfred dubiously. He was as impressionable as his mother, but Lord Radburn had always been his mentor and model for behaviour. Now he was confused.

Lydia accepted every invitation that came her way, stylishly riding about the county in Lady Weyward's coach-and-four, with not only a coachman but also two servants in livery riding behind; she never, however, met the object of her hopes. Lord Radburn had become unsociable, in a complete turnabout, declining invitations to teas and dinners and balls, although she heard from others that he would wait upon them at odd times and discuss his projects for hours.

One Sunday morning it occurred to her to go to services in the village church. It was a brilliant idea, she assured herself, for there he was in the first pew, absorbed in listening to his brother's sermon, though how he could find it of interest was beyond her. Unfortunately he left immediately after service, without a glance in her direction, bowing to a few people in his path, placing his hat securely on his head, and riding off, a man with a purpose.

Lydia's only consolation was that he was courting no one else. Her greatest relief came from the information relayed by her mother that in all this time he had not paid a visit to Bath. The field was open—if only she could get his attention!

One afternoon she achieved that. Returning to Coulder Hall in her mother's coach after attending a tea, she saw Edward approaching on horseback. She stuck her head out of the window and hailed him, whereupon he removed his hat, nodded to her soberly, and would have passed on, but Lydia had waited too long for this opportunity to allow him to escape.

"Lord Radburn!" she shouted. "I must speak to you urgently!" She ordered her coachman to stop, and Edward drew up. "Edward," she continued in a softer tone, "excuse me for shouting like that." She fluttered her eyelashes and hoped that he was noticing her new bonnet with feathers. "I have had news from Bath that I find most distressing."

"From Bath? But I had a letter just yesterday from Mama, and all seemed well."

"Naturally she would not tell you!"

"Tell me what?" demanded Edward.

Lydia turned her head aside, as though overcome by embarrassment, shaking her head to make the plumes on her bonnet wave.

"Look, Lydia, out with it, stop hedging."

"I am not hedging! I stopped you, didn't I? The fact of the matter is that my cousin Kate and your brother Lionel have created such a scandal that poor Mama doesn't know what to do! Naturally she is concerned that Kate will lose her inheritance—"

"Kate and Lionel are fond of each other, always have been. However, I should think it is too soon for them to be thinking of matrimony." Edward's frown deepened.

"Too soon, you say! Not soon enough, *I* say!"

"What *are* you trying to say, Lydia?"

"It isn't just what *I* say, it's what all Bath is saying. Mama is trying to scotch the rumors, but it is hard. Everyone is watching to see—when it will begin to show. Wilfred Curtis was saying to me just yesterday—he was in Bath until a few days ago —that since Kate is not likely now to become an heiress, your brother doesn't want to do the decent thing. Oh, it is quite a scandal, I do assure you!"

Edward abruptly turned his horse around and, leaving the main road, sped off across the fields, the shortest way to the Vicarage.

"Well, I never!" said Lydia to the empty air. Then she ordered the coachman to drive on, a self-congratulatory smile on her face. After all, he had noticed her.

Edward burst into the library, where Lionel was trying to prepare Sunday's sermon, but the good vicar kept looking out of the window with an expression on his face that alternated between joy and wonder. At his brother's abrupt entrance he jumped up, threw his arms about him, and kissed him on both cheeks.

"Neddie boy, where have you been? I have been looking for you everywhere! I am happy, so happy!" Lionel's eyes were moist with emotion, and his glasses steamed up.

Edward let out a long breath. "So you are going to marry her," he said flatly.

"How did you know? We've only just decided!"

"I met Lydia Weyward on the road."

"How could she have known so quickly? Well, good news travels fast, they say. Have a brandy with me, Neddie, we'll toast my betrothed." He turned two glasses upright and poured from a cut glass bottle.

"I might have known you would do the correct thing," said Edward.

"Correct thing! You mean the *only* thing!"

"Good. I would have married her myself, if you had backed down."

"Backed down!" Lionel laughed. "You are mocking me, Brother. I suppose a man in love is a bit of a fool and not to be taken seriously. Thank God, *she* did! In these past few weeks in Bath, she has really come into her own. Any number of swains would be happy to jump into my place if I had backed down, as you put it."

"I believe you."

"Mama is delighted. *Everyone* is taken with her, young and old alike. She will make an exemplary vicar's wife, exemplary! So sweet, so —loving."

"Just so," said Edward miserably. He sighed and raised his glass. "To Kate, then."

Lionel, who was about to drink, paused. "You are jesting again. Did you think to trick me? To Adelaide!" He raised his glass and finished the draught.

Edward stared at him, the glass poised in midair. "You are not going to marry Kate?"

"Kate? No, I told you—I am going to marry Adelaide."

"But the scandal!"

"What scandal?"

Edward opened his mouth and closed it again in the face of his brother's amazement. He tried again. "You mean you have not been courting Kate these many months?"

"*Me?* Courting *Kate?* Oh, no, you are mistaken. Mind you, I have the greatest admiration and respect for Katherine Martin. I would say of her that she is the most truly *moral* person I have ever known. I am a man of the cloth and I say it. It was silly of everyone to make such a fuss about riding a horse astride. She is a fine person. Never will I forget what she has done for Adelaide. Never!"

Edward began to laugh, a real laugh from the depths, such as had not happened to him in months. He slapped his thighs and laughed, and bent over and laughed.

"Are you all right?" asked Lionel, unable to resist joining in the laughter.

"No!" gasped Edward. "I am not all right. You said yourself that a man in love is a bit of a fool. I'm the entire clown from cap and bells to sock and buskin! Kate is free! For me! And has been all along!"

He took his brother's arms and forced him into a dance around the library, singing:

"Oh, the vicar takes a wife,
The vicar takes a wife,
Heigh-ho, the chapel O
The vicar takes a wife!"

Lionel took up the song:

"Lord Radburn takes a wife,
Lord Radburn takes a wife,
Heigh-ho, the county O
Lord Radburn takes a wife!"

The dancers knocked over a table and chair and fell against Lionel's desk, causing Sunday's sermon to fly through the air. Captain Cook, who had been thinking for some time now that this was no household for a venerable feline to end his days in—the vicar was definitely no longer himself, ever since those females started to visit—sought doubtful refuge under the sofa. Still, there were tidbits of mutton from the housekeeper to be considered (and sometimes game or fish), and his own special crocheted rug by the fire. The dance became a hornpipe, then a reel, and the dancers leaped and turned until stopped at the door by the stolid appearance of the housekeeper.

"Will Lord Radburn be staying for supper?" she asked as though nothing unusual were happening.

"Lord Radburn will not!" said Edward, whirling about alone. "Lord Radburn is riding to Bath this night, where a goddess awaits him!" He leapt over the sofa, scaring Captain Cook out of hiding and out of his wits. The cat streaked across the room to the protection of the housekeeper's feet and, fearing that this was not sufficient, ran around her feet and out into the hall, away from this chaos.

Lionel said practically, "Pack him some supper for the road, anyway. He may get hungry later."

"Certainly, Vicar," said the housekeeper, politely curtseying as though Lord Radburn had not just lunged into the bookcase and fallen down under a load of books.

During the night, Edward paused at a stream to water his horse.

"*Joie de vivre!*" he shouted at the full moon.

In a cottage nearby a farmer woke up and shook his wife. "The Frogs have landed!" he whispered hoarsely. "I always told you they would. I hear them shouting in that foreign tongue of theirs!"

His wife, who was braver than he was, crept to the window and peeked out from behind the curtain. "*Go* on!

It's just a single feller baying at the moon. One of those gypsies, most like, drinking again."

"Just one?" asked the farmer, gathering courage. "Best get my rifle."

"Don't be daft. He ain't doing no harm. Come back to bed and let him be."

Downstream another rider, no more than a boy by all appearances, heard the shout and decided against meeting any strangers by night. He led his horse down under the bridge. "Shh!" he said, stroking the horse's nose to keep him quiet. In a few moments the horseman galloped over the bridge like thunder, shaking its foundations.

When the sound of hoofs receded in the distance, the youth swung lithely on his horse and turned him in the opposite direction from Lord Radburn's. The full moon lighted clearly the road to Coulder Hall.

—18—

"SHE ISN'T HERE," said the countess. "Kate isn't here."

"Not here? Where is she?"

"Two days ago she received a letter from Richard Tattersall. He is that man who trades horses."

"Yes, yes! I know Tattersall. So?"

"Don't be so impatient, Edward. It's rude. Mr. Tattersall is a good friend of her father's. His letter stated that Guy Martin had taken a turn for the worse, had had a haemorrhage, and was confined to bed. Guy was against Kate's being told, but Mr. Tattersall and his good wife felt that she should know."

"I see. So she has gone to Newmarket. Did Lady Weyward accompany her?"

"No. Lady Weyward was disinclined to go. I sent Kate in my coach with Mrs. Wilcox. Theoretically, of course, Kate should not leave Lady Weyward's side, but I suppose it will be all right, considering that it is an emergency."

"When do you expect her back?"

"Soon, I should think. Considering the terms of her uncle's will, she should not stay long away from Lady Weyward. Such a complicated business—I am really angry with William Weyward for creating this uncomfortable situation."

"William Weyward is dead, Mama."

"Dead or alive, I am really put out with him. His work lives after him, as you see. What was his purpose?"

"He did own a tremendous fortune, Mama, and I suppose he felt the responsibility for its being well used."

The sound of a coach-and-four drew Edward running to the window, but it passed on up the street. He sighed heavily and sat down, suddenly fatigued from lack of sleep and from disappointment.

"I love the girl, Mama," he said. "I am mad about her."

"You have a fine way of showing it. You didn't let her know, did you? You weren't even very polite."

"There was Lionel between us. Or so I thought."

"Lionel? How can that story have got about? For some time I have believed and hoped that Lionel would wed Adelaide. She is perfect for him. And now it is going to happen. You did hear about the engagement?"

"Indeed, and am most pleased. More than I can ever tell you or anybody. Except Kate."

The countess began to scratch Frou-Frou behind an ear, her custom when she was deep in thought. Frou-Frou bent her ear to the side for full enjoyment.

"It was, I am sure, Lady Weyward's doing. Some items of her nonsense have come back to me. Not very nice of Lady Weyward, spreading such wickedness whilst living under my roof."

"She is, indeed, a mischievous woman. But I don't blame her for my own blind stupidity and pigheadedness."

"Well, all is not lost, is it? Kate will return momentarily." She changed her scratching to Frou-Frou's other ear, and Frou-Frou bent in that direction. "You should know, however, that Lady Weyward's machinations may have a deleterious effect on Kate's prospects of inheritance. If the solicitors come to believe even half of what is being spread about, I don't believe that there is a prayer for her chances. Would you take a penniless Kate?"

"I'll take her in her shift if she'll have me."

"Edward!"

"Sorry, Mama. But I don't care about her Uncle William's involved legacy. I have enough for us both, certainly."

The countess stopped scratching Frou-Frou and looked at Edward with love in her eyes. "My son!" she said.

Frou-Frou jumped down, shook herself so that her disturbed hair would fall back into place, waddled over to Edward, and although until now there had always been bad blood between them, began to lick his hand.

"What are you doing here?" asked Lydia ungraciously. "And in that regalia?"

"I have not come to see you, I don't want to see you, and I certainly no longer care about your or anyone else's opinion of my riding clothes. Where is Donald?"

"I haven't the faintest idea," said Lydia loftily. Actually she was afraid of Kate in this mood.

"Send him to me, and also Nurse Amelia and her granddaughter Nettie," ordered Kate.

"Umph!" Lydia grunted and flounced out of the room.

"Disgraceful!" she said to the empty corridor. She hated the idea of obliging Kate but knew that something extraordinary was in the wind, and so she hurried along to her brother's room and shook him awake. With some difficulty, since he had thrown himself down just a few hours before, she got him to listen to her. It took some emphatic repetition to get the information through that Kate was downstairs awaiting him. In all the world it was the only message that could make him stagger across the room and douse his head with a pitcher of cold water.

"To what do I owe this unexpected visit?"

Donald entered the room with the air of a man of pressing affairs who was being delayed by some irritating trifle. There were three people in the room. The ample figure of Nurse Amelia was seated on a sofa, and curled up beside her with her head in the nurse's lap, sound asleep, was Kate. Nettie was standing next to them, looking pale and frightened, and she curtsied when Donald entered. Before them was a table with a piece of folded paper, an inkwell, and a plumed pen on it. Nurse Amelia shook Kate, and Donald watched her face, soft and relaxed in sleep, turn hard as she opened her eyes.

"Cousin Donald," she said, as though the name were distasteful on her tongue.

"Cousin Kate," he replied mockingly.

"Nettie, would you please stand outside the door and keep anyone from entering or listening."

"Yes, miss," said Nettie. Her first job was to dislodge Lydia from the keyhole.

"What is your pleasure?" Donald adjusted his unnecessary monocle.

"No pleasure. It is a business proposition that I have to make."

"Business proposition?" Donald stroked the side of his nose, scenting money. "What business proposition?"

"A marriage between us."

Donald sat down, his knees, shaky from dissipation, finally giving way. "That is not a business proposition."

"The way I intend it, it is."

"Ho! So the story is true. The vicar has had his way and now won't marry you."

"Don't be an ass! Lionel is engaged to your sister Adelaide." Kate was so enraged that she wondered if she could carry through her resolution.

Donald's mouth sagged open. If only my head didn't pound so, he thought, I could see my advantage better. "He should have asked my permission first!" he protested.

"He asked Lady Harriet, who agreed two days ago."

"And now suddenly you want to marry me!"

"It may be sudden, but it has nothing to do with Lionel's engagement to Adelaide. I assure you that I have not been jilted." Her lip curled in scorn of him.

"Then why do you want to marry me?"

"I don't *want* to marry you. I am suggesting a marriage which will be a business arrangement only. The marriage will never be consummated—you are never to be in my presence without a third party."

"And why should I agree to this?"

"For half of my legacy."

Donald put one hand on his knee to quell the quivering of his leg and another to his temple to allay the throbbing.

"You don't like me very much, do you?"

"I detest you."

Donald swallowed. "What makes you think I'd go through with such a charade?"

"You know and I know that at this moment I am not likely to inherit. You and Lady Weyward have seen to that, and my own thoughtless behaviour has assisted you."

"Now Cousin Kate—"

"Don't Cousin Kate me. I have been an ignorant and trusting fool. A fool I still may be, but ignorant and trusting—no. I am now quite aware that if you thought I would inherit and you would be cut out, you would kill me for it." She rubbed her shoulder, which had reached a point in its mending where it was itchy.

"Don't be absurd."

"I'm not. I know that the only way I can still inherit and stay alive—with my reputation intact—is to marry you. That was your original plan, wasn't it? Why do you hesitate? Because you would only get half?"

"You are imagining—"

"Would that I were! But think, cutting me off from my inheritance, one way or another, is only half your battle. As the will reads, and I have recently confirmed this, if I do not inherit, everything is left to Uncle William's partner in the West Indies, and there is no provision that *he* has to prove himself a *gentleman* first. Do you have a plan to get around that?"

"I have legal counsel—"

"I am sure you do, but the outcome is uncertain at best,

isn't it? It would be a long fight, and you could well lose. No, Cousin Donald, it would be easier for you to marry me and at least be sure of half."

"When do you want the marriage to take place?"

"Today. I have seen the notary in the village, and he has drawn up this contract—here it is on the table—which we are to sign with Nurse Amelia as witness. We will then ride into Tweedstun to deposit this paper and to have the notary marry us. Sign here."

"You think of everything, don't you?"

"Sign it!"

"I don't know what Mama will say—"

"You're a grown man, aren't you?"

Donald picked up the pen and signed with a flourish, wishing his fingers were steadier. Kate signed and helped Nurse Amelia to make a cross next to her name.

"Now we will ride into Tweedstun and finish the business." She jammed the shapeless hat on her head.

"You are going to get married in those clothes?"

"I suppose you would prefer a formal wedding in church with the vicar officiating and a crowd of people."

"Yes, I would."

"You are not going to have it."

Donald hesitated. Kate looked at him with ice in her eyes.

"Are you coming or not? The contract is not valid until we are married."

"Just a minute." Donald poured a whiskey, gulped it in one swallow, grimaced, and followed her out.

"Congratulations on this happiest of occasions, Katherine, Lady Weyward!" said the bewildered notary, after the briefest of ceremonies, trying to put the best face on these unusual proceedings.

"Katherine, Lady Weyward!" repeated Kate. "Lady!" She burst into wild laughter, hysterical laughter, and wiped away the tears with her ragged gloves. "Lady, lady, *lady!*"

She ran out of the office, leaped on her horse, and disappeared down the road, leaving clouds of dust behind her.

It was twilight before the countess's carriage returned to the Royal Crescent. Before it stopped, Edward was down the steps and opening the door. Mrs. Wilcox was alone in it.

"Where is Miss Martin? Still in Newmarket?"

"No, milord. She is, I believe, at Coulder Hall."

Edward assisted her from the carriage. "Coulder Hall!" he repeated, a foreboding of disaster creeping about his heart. "Come in and tell us what happened."

Seated before Edward and his mother and with a cup of tea in her hands, Mrs. Wilcox related the history of the visit to Newmarket.

"He is right sick, is Guy Martin, and that's a fact, if I know anything. So thin I wouldn't have known him, and with hollows-like in his face. Still it's been nigh twenty years since I seed him last. When Miss Kate leaves the room, she cries like a baby. Mr. Tattersall, he offers to pay for a London physician to come, only Guy Martin wouldn't hear of it. Said he'd be all right and got all excited and started coughing something awful. Nice feller, Mr. Tattersall. Big feller, like this." She held out her arms wide.

"Go on!" said Edward. "What happened next?"

"Next morning Mr. Tattersall goes back to London, and Miss Kate ax if she could ride with him and he says yes and off she goes saying to me how she would be back by night in the public coach. Good as her word she was, but all riled up. Said she had been to talk to those solicitor fellers to ax for some money ahead of time, as it were, but they wouldn't give her nothing, her year not being up and it not atall clear that she *would* inherit. Not nasty but tight-mouthed, and tightfisted too, you might say. So Miss Kate puts on some old clothes, boys' clothes, like she wore when she first comes to Radburn Hall. She tells me to take the carriage back to Bath tomorrow—today, that is—and off she goes on one of her father's horses. 'Where are you going, miss?' I calls. 'To Coulder Hall and hell!' she shouts back. Excuse me, ma'am, but those was her words."

Mrs. Wilcox leaned back and drank her tea. The countess looked distressed, and Edward, standing by his mother's chair, squeezed the knobs until his knuckles were white.

The silence was broken by a pounding on the door, and soon after, Lucy Wilcox, with a scared look at her mother, came in to announce that an urgent message had come for Lady Weyward.

"Then go fetch it, girl!" said Mrs. Wilcox, and Lucy ran out to obey.

Lady Weyward looked up from the letter, dazed. "Donald and Kate were married this day," she said. "That this should happen now!" She, who considered herself a mistress of intrigue, had been outmaneuvered.

"That this should happen now," Edward repeated and put a hand on his heart, then bent over, as though the pain were unendurable. "Now."

—19—

KATE FOUND HERSELF mistress of Coulder Hall.

Her plan had been made and executed so swiftly that she had not thought out all the consequences; it was with surprise and chagrin that she found the servants coming to her with domestic questions to be answered, menus to be planned, permissions to be given for afternoons off, and personal problems to solve. It took much of her time and thought. After a while, though, she noticed that the problems repeated themselves, and she was able to come to immediate decisions based on precedent.

Finances were her biggest worry, for Donald was deeply in debt. Every day she learned of some new bill. Adelaide was not yet of age to receive her father's legacy. Lydia had money but would use it only for display. This was of some help in keeping the servants outfitted and the coach in repair.

Lady Weyward, returned from Bath, still held the purse strings and held them tightly. However, Kate had obtained from the solicitors exact information as to how much Lady Weyward had received for her niece's keep for the year and was able to extract from time to time sums to pay wages and the various bills that came from the village. Kate learned the price of everything and became expert in stretching farthings; she was far from the ignorant girl who first came to Coulder Hall and did not know the cost of a muslin dress. And most especially, she said to herself bitterly, did I learn the price of obtaining my own inheritance.

The precipitous marriage astounded everyone, and at first there were no callers at Coulder Hall. The ramifications of the marriage were unknown; there had been no customary long engagement in which to discuss them. No one could figure out the situation. The vicar's betrothal to Adelaide had been announced; how could that have come about? What should their postures be in the face of these strange events? Fearing to make a social blunder, no one did anything, and the new bride and groom were left severely alone.

Lady Weyward had returned from Bath in a fury. Donald had got the full blast of it—how dare he act without her permission! Everything had been going so smoothly, according to their *mutual* plan! Lady Weyward had enjoyed her position at Bath, her address on the Royal Crescent, and the flattering silences that fell whenever she spoke in Society. Then Donald had spoiled it all by marrying the girl! The countess had said forthwith that Lady Weyward's place was back in Coulder Hall—to fulfill the terms of the will, the countess had said—but Lady Weyward had smarted under the dismissal. Well, at least the countess's younger son was going to marry Adelaide, so Lady Radburn wouldn't be able to ignore her for long. Too bad it wasn't the elder son with the title. But if only Lydia could catch that one, then the countess couldn't send Lady Weyward packing!

"It's done, Mama," Donald had said defensively, "and the fortune will be divided between us when she inherits. Half a loaf is better than none."

"Now I suppose I have to reverse myself and restore her character!"

"It would certainly be wise."

"Wise! It would make me out a fool, or worse! I won't do it!"

So everyone in the county stayed uneasily away, uncertain how to act, and because the countess remained at Bath, they were unable to obtain from her an indication of proper behaviour. Edward had returned to London.

It was Lydia who rebelled at the social stagnation.

"How am I ever going to get married if I never see anyone? Kate is two years younger than I and married already. Adelaide is three years younger and engaged. What is going to happen to *me?*" wailed Lydia.

Lady Weyward relented; it wouldn't do at all to allow Lydia to become a spinster just because Lord Radburn was interested only in his career. She called on the vicar first, who she knew would have to receive her as the mother of his intended. She smiled over tea at the other guests, declaring her approbation of the match, leaving the impression in their minds that they must have been mistaken if they had ever thought she had ever said anything derogatory about the countess's younger son. Why, she said, one only had to look at him and listen to him to know what a fine upstanding person he was, which indeed was true.

Redeeming Kate was harder. As she circulated about the county, Lady Weyward met with resistance in this regard, the man easily excused, the woman still under suspicion. Lady Curtis was almost wrathful.

"Lady Weyward," she said petulantly, "when we were in Bath you said that Kate was so low you wondered how you could allow her to remain by your side. You even implied that she was—" Lady Curtis placed her hands over her own middle, which was, alas, enlarging yet again.

"*I* said! *I* implied!" retorted Lady Weyward. "I did no such thing! Just because *you* are forever having babies, you think the whole world is!"

"You did too say that!"

"I did *not!*" shouted Lady Weyward, glaring at her in a manner quite intimidating. Poor Lady Curtis was no match for this ferocious denial and subsided into pouting acquiescence, the whole thing driven out of her mind by the arrival of five of her younger children, noisily demanding her attention to settle some juvenile argument.

With the return of the countess to Radburn Hall, the matter was settled. The very day after her return, the countess invited Kate to tea, sending her own coach to fetch her. The other guests duly noted the countess's affection and respect for the newlywed. It was remarked that Lady Weyward had not been invited and that Kate, instead of enlarging, had become even thinner.

With the exception of calling on the countess, Kate dreaded her social obligations, for now invitations began to pour in. It made her ill to have Donald hovering or to feel the touch of his hand removing her cloak or guiding her down steps. Although she sternly performed all the duties required of her and was pleasant to everyone, even those who had snubbed her in Bath, she was now criticized for being too cold and formal.

Chaperoning Lionel and Adelaide was bittersweet. The two girls still spent long afternoons in his library continuing their studies. Until tea came in, the trio would read and discuss history or poetry, and Kate still found this enjoyable. After tea, however, Kate would take a book to an overstuffed chair by the huge window and sit with her back to them, ostensibly to get the waning daylight but in reality to give the lovers a measure of privacy in which to hold hands and look into each other's eyes. The book would lay open on Kate's lap unread while her thoughts tortured her. She told herself that the happiness that the couple behind her were enjoying would now never be hers. Teardrops would fall on the printed page, and she would resolutely wipe them away, only to have them fall anew a minute later.

She heard news of Edward, of the kind Lionel did not report, one evening at dinner with the Curtises. All the

Weywards had been invited, but Adelaide had to send her regrets as she was dining with the countess and Lionel at Radburn Hall.

"Now I don't mean to say that Edward doesn't work hard," said Wilfred Curtis, helping himself generously to the wine, "urging forward his ideas on reform in the House of Lords, but in his leisure hours he does go tearing after that duchess of Conroyallan. She's leading him on a merry chase, I can tell you, piqued because of his long neglect of her. Jolly good-natured she is at bottom, though, so no doubt she'll forgive him. Maybe the chase this time will end up at the altar!"

"Don't presume to guess at something you know nothing about," snapped Lydia. "The countess will have something to say about it, I wager. She didn't like it at all when the duchess stayed at Radburn Hall so long."

"The countess looks forward to grandchildren," said Lady Weyward knowingly, "and the duchess is getting on. No, the countess prefers someone young and healthy and *county*." She nodded her head at Lydia, leaving the impression that her daughter was the likely choice.

Lady Curtis, in a moment of clarity, saw through this. She had been seeking a way to get her own back from Lady Weyward and decided to do some fabricating of her own.

"I heard, from friends in London who *know*, that the real lady in Lord Radburn's life—behind the scenes at present—is the Princess Charlotte! Naturally, this is all confidential until final approval by the Prince Regent."

"Princess Charlotte *herself?*"

"Yes! The Regent's daughter—heiress to the throne!"

"Do you think the Prince Regent will agree to the match?"

"He has been heard to say that he has had enough of princes from the Continent and would favor an Englishman."

"Certainly we have had enough of foreigners!"

"Just think," mused Wilfred Curtis, "of the political power he would wield as the son-in-law of the Prince Regent!"

"I hear that the princess is a silly, giddy thing!" protested Lady Weyward. Lady Curtis had spoiled her appetite and her evening.

"She is young and healthy," pursued Lady Curtis, "and although not *county*, I think the countess might make an exception for *royalty!*"

Donald had been studying Kate across the candlelit table. She was silent and pale. "What do you think, Kate?" he asked, envy of Edward vying with sudden fires of jealousy.

"I should think Edward will make the right choice when the time comes," she said noncommittally.

"As his brother did?" asked Donald loudly.

The whole table looked at Kate. "As his brother did," she agreed quietly. "Lionel could not have selected a more suitable wife."

"Here, here!" said Wilfred, breaking the tension. "Soon I'll be the only bachelor left in the county! Then watch the ladies flock 'round."

He smiled fatuously at Lydia. This time she did not contradict him and even managed a faint smile, wondering if, after all, it was going to have to be Wilfred Curtis.

— 20 —

KATE'S ONLY MOMENTS of happiness were in riding Fantastique, which she did now openly and astride.

"At least that much good has come out of Donald's having caught me out riding you," she said to the colt. "I no longer have to endorse *that* particular hypocrisy."

It was to Fantastique that she opened the secrets of her heart, and like a true friend, he listened sympathetically and never assayed to give unwanted advice.

"I am a prisoner, Fantastique, at Coulder Hall. If only I could be with Papa! But there is no leaving Lady Weyward until next May, and she refuses to go to Newmarket. I am sentenced by the terms of the legacy to stay at her side. As soon as I inherit—oh, let us hope and pray I can, amour—we shall ride to Newmarket and send for the best doctors in the universe."

She galloped Fantastique to the top of a rise, paused, and took some deep draughts of air, looking along the road that led to London and beyond to Newmarket. The countryside looked brown and tired. The temptation to abandon everything and fly to the side of her father suddenly overwhelmed her, and she turned Fantastique along the road. After a mile she stopped, remembering.

"I must hold back, I must! And I do have good friends here, Adelaide and Lionel, Nurse Amelia, the countess, and"—she lowered her voice—"then there is Edward. Don't tell anyone about that, Fantastique. It is so painful. He doesn't care a button for me."

Sighing, she directed Fantastique back toward Radburn Park. "He will be here at Christmas, the countess says. Parliament isn't in session then, and he will have to come home. Perhaps his engagement will be announced then. Christmas is often the time chosen for those announcements. Will it be the duchess? How can I bear it if he looks at her with eyes of love, the way Lionel looks at Adelaide?"

Leaning over, she put her arms about Fantastique's neck and hid her face in the shiny black mane.

In order to have Fantastique nearer to hand, she brought up the subject of cleaning the stables of Coulder Hall. It met with prompt objections, as she knew it would be.

"Leave the stables alone!" ordered Donald. "I am in charge there, and they are good enough."

"They are not," contradicted Kate. "They are disgracefully filthy. I would not insult a horse of mine by housing him there."

"Then keep him over at Radburn Park and out of my stables. The less bother the better!"

"Donald just wants a place out of the rain to sleep it off," his sister said, unexpectedly on Kate's side, "when he can't make the steps." Lydia had once heard Edward laughingly criticise the condition of their stables and was worried lest this might reflect on her.

"Lydia, don't say things like that!" said Lady Weyward. "The main objection, of course, is the expense. We haven't any money for refurbishing stables."

"It isn't a question of *re*furbishing, Aunt," said Kate. "It's more a problem of *un*furbishing, of just plain cleaning them out. Water will do the job, and there is a well just a few feet outside the stables. Diverting a river would be better, but there it is."

Adelaide giggled delightedly at the classical reference.

"What are *you* laughing at?" snapped Lady Weyward, fearing that she was the butt of a joke.

"Hercules, Mama, in the Greek legends. One of his

labours was to clean out the Augean stables, and he did it by diverting a river."

"Very funny, indeed," said Lydia, who felt uneasy at the way Adelaide and Kate knew more than she did.

"Now that you've had your little joke, the answer is still no," Donald said decisively. "Jack Hinds is doing a good job at the stables, and I don't want him disturbed in any way."

"Like you, Brother, he does a good job of sleeping in the hay 'til noon."

"What is this?" questioned Lady Weyward. The idea of a lazy, drunken servant deepened the line between her eyes. "Sleeps 'til noon, does he?"

"Or after," said Lydia. "Sometimes when I want the carriage, I have to get the footman to set up the horses in their traces."

"Donald, did you know this?"

"She is exaggerating!"

"Take a look for yourself some morning, Mama, if you have the stomach for it."

Lady Weyward had no intention of lowering herself by entering the stables, but the very suggestion that a servant of hers could be taking wages for doing nothing made her switch allegiances on the spot.

"Kate, I find I go along with you on this question of cleaning the stables. And Jack Hinds will do it."

"No, Mama, I forbid it!" said Donald, in a last grasp at authority.

His mother ignored him. "Send for Jack Hinds immediately. I'll enjoy telling him to get to work. Pull the cord on the way out, Donald."

His face flushed with anger, Donald stalked out of the room, neglecting to pull the cord.

"You might tell Jack Hinds that Kate will assist him—that seems to be her idea of pleasure," said Lydia contemptuously, pulling at the cord as she swept out with a disdainful lift of her skirts as though to protect them from filth.

"I'll help you, Kate," said Adelaide, "if you tell me what to do."

Kate was able to recruit a number of Nurse Amelia's grandchildren to help in her project when they returned in the afternoons from the village school. Brooms were made by tying brambles onto sticks, and once Jack Hinds had shovelled the heavier of the muck onto a barrow and wheeled it out (taking well over a week to perform this chore, even with the assistance of his eldest, Bert), the children set to work with their brooms, attacking the next layers of dirt, their labour sweetened by the promise of treats with their tea in the kitchen.

After the sweeping came the cleansing with water. Wooden buckets were found (Kate discovered that Nurse Amelia could commandeer anything). Two lines of children were lined up, back to back, from the well to the stables. Kate and Adelaide, nearest to the well, took turns drawing up the water and handing the full buckets to the larger of the children, who passed them along the line, which ended with Jack. He hurled the water wherever it would reach and handed the empty buckets back to the line of smaller children, who then passed them back to Kate and Adelaide.

"What's going on here?" demanded a baritone voice. "A fire?"

Kate, who had been pulling on the rope, let the bucket drop back down into the water. She straightened slowly and looked up into the dark eyes of Edward. With all the noise and movement, she had neither seen nor heard him ride up.

"Kate!" He was as astonished as she. "Lady Weyward," he said, recovering quickly.

"Good afternoon, Lord Radburn," said Kate quietly. "No, there has been no disaster, much as it may look like it. We have been cleaning the stables and have reached the water stage now."

"And well organised you are, I can see that," he said, looking at the lines of children, bashful before him.

"Adelaide!" He jumped down from his horse when he saw her, taking her hands and kissing her. "You who are to be my sister. How delighted I am!"

"I am happy that you approve, Edward."

The children, with nothing to do, clustered around Kate, plucking at her skirt and whispering to her.

"I am afraid I have interrupted your labours," apologised Edward.

"Please stay and visit," said Kate, motioning toward Adelaide. "The children have been promised apple tarts with their tea and are more than ready for them." She turned to the eager faces. "Go get your tea, children, we'll call it a day. But don't forget to come back tomorrow!"

The children scampered off to the kitchen, gleeful at their escape. Edward's attention was centered on Adelaide exclusively, and Kate felt awkward and unwanted.

"If you will excuse me, I will join them. Nurse Amelia will need a hand," she said.

Kate, who usually did not care, was painfully aware of her appearance: the water-spattered dress, the sleeves rolled up, a faded handkerchief holding back her hair. Even more painful was the discrepancy between Edward's attitude toward Adelaide and herself. Except for calling her by her title, he might not have known that she had married. Since he had such disregard for her, it was best not to burden him with her presence. She turned away.

The kitchen was noisy with shouting, hungry children. The tarts weren't quite ready, and Nurse Amelia's face was flushed from constantly looking in the oven.

"Get ye away from that there stove, it be red hot and ye get burnt, young'un." Nurse Amelia called all her grandchildren "young'un," this covering both sexes, singular and plural, and any age up to fourteen. That way she didn't have to worry about names.

Kate found a heavy cloth and poured tea from the huge metal pot. The children seated themselves on benches on either side of the wooden table and kicked their feet back and forth impatiently. The smell of apples baking in the oven was mouthwatering. At last Nurse Amelia pulled a great tray of tarts from the oven to the accompaniment of clapping and whistling. Kate helped to distribute the tarts with the warning, "Pick them up carefully! Don't burn your mouths!" Obedient, the children plucked at them gingerly and blew on them.

"May I have one, too?" said a familiar baritone.

"Please do, Lord Radburn," said Kate, proffering the tray, glad that the heat and commotion in the kitchen would cover her embarrassment. "The tarts at this end are more cooked, if you prefer them that way."

"Young'un, fetch Lord Radburn a chair," ordered Nurse Amelia.

"Nonsense, I'll sit on the bench with the rest!"

The children obligingly squirmed together to make room for him. Kate found a cup for him and for herself, willing her hands to be steady as she poured the tea. She sat down on the bench opposite him. Somehow she had become hostess and searched for a topic of conversation.

"We did not expect you until Christmastide," she said politely.

"I say, this is delicious, Nurse Amelia!" Edward said delightedly, like a boy, regarding the tart.

"Thank'ee, milord. Take another," she coaxed. "Straight from the oven. Have a care, now!"

He finished a second tart, drank the tea, then looked at Kate as though suddenly remembering her.

"I beg your pardon! You were saying—"

"Only that I believed you were not expected until Christmas."

"Oh, yes, I'll be here at Christmas, all right. This is just a brief trip to clear up some business matters. I return to London tomorrow."

"I see."

Nurse Amelia brought around still another tray of tarts, which he refused with a wave of the hand, but the children seized them greedily. He stretched out his legs and crossed them comfortably.

"You look well, Lady Weyward," he said in a leisurely fashion.

"I am quite well, Lord Radburn."

"I believe I forgot to send congratulations on your marriage. Pressure of affairs kept me occupied there for a bit. May I amend that oversight now by wishing you every happiness."

"Thank you."

The children, after third helpings and with their pockets bulging with extras, began to leave, crawling under the bench or sliding down to the other end so as not to disturb their elders, who were so carefully unabsorbed in each other. When the children were finally all gone, Nurse Amelia settled down in her favourite chair and within a second of closing her eyes was fast asleep. The kitchen was warm and redolent of apples and cinnamon and sugar.

"Have you heard from your father?"

"I had a letter just this day. A note I should say, not a letter—it was very brief."

"He is well?"

"He always says he is improving. Thank you for asking."

Silence fell. Daylight faded and the grate now was only embers. With the children gone, thought Kate, it is so quiet in the kitchen. I wonder why *he* doesn't go? He has said all that manners require.

The clock on the mantle swung its pendulum serenely back and forth. The big stove, cooling, made occasional grunts as the metal contracted. The two people at the table were so still they might have been statues. The clock chimed the quarter to the hour, but still Edward did not move.

Kate's eyes lifted from her empty teacup and looked at Edward's left hand resting on the table. The back of the hand was square and strong; the fingers, like the rest of him, were long, graceful now in relaxation, the tips touching the table. Her eyes lifted, one brown button at a time, along his jacket, up to the white linen draped about his neck, on to the long straight mouth, and in a final jump, to his eyes, black and brooding and watching. His eyes held hers, supported them, kept them from falling once when they fluttered. So they remained joined in a spell, until the patter of running footsteps in the passageway returned them to reality.

Nettie burst into the kitchen.

"Here you are, milord! I feared you had left," she said breathlessly. "Miss Adelaide, she says for you to accept her apologies for taking so long to write her letter to the vicar. She also asked if you will take this book along to him, too. She has put in little slips of paper showing the pages he is to read. If you would be so kind, milord."

Edward got up and accepted the burdens. "It is no trouble, tell your mistress."

Nettie curtsied and skipped away.

"I am having supper with Lionel," explained Edward. "Adelaide asked me to deliver a note to him."

"I see." Kate found herself taking deep breaths, as though to force life back into her body. Life as it is, she told herself, brutal. She had thought—how could she have? What must he think—

Edward stood at the door with his back to her, one hand on the knob.

Why don't you just go? she felt like screaming at him. And never come back!

He turned. "Kate."

"Yes?" she said angrily.

He took her eyes for a second time. "I wish you well."

"Thank you, Edward."

He left quietly. Kate crumpled to the floor at the feet of Nurse Amelia and buried her face in the voluminous lap.

Lydia burst into the kitchen, a smile of greeting on her expectant face. It dissolved as she looked about the darkening and cooling room.

"Where is he?" she demanded. "Where is Edward?"

"Gone," said Kate, her voice faint and muffled.

"Gone! Why wasn't I informed that he was here? Why

do I have to learn everything through the servants? What was he doing in the kitchen anyway?"

Kate said something unintelligible; it may have been a groan.

"When is he coming back? Answer me!" persisted Lydia.

Kate turned her head to the side. "Christmas."

"Christmas!" Lydia snorted and slammed the door on the way out.

Nurse Amelia slept on peacefully.

Kate brought Fantastique to Coulder Hall in ceremony.

The stables were not only clean but repaired. Jack Hinds, with a new pride in the stables, found some whitewash to paint the inside walls and slate to mend the roof. On the day of Fantastique's arrival, Kate decorated his stall with ivy and pine branches. Fresh fodder and water were set out for him. Jack's son Bert produced from somewhere a newly washed blanket as a special gift.

As Kate and Fantastique approached the stables, Jack and Bert awaited them on either side of the door, caps doffed. Fantastique moved slowly and majestically, nodding his head from side to side like royalty. Wonder shone in the face of Bert.

Kate had had her eye on Bert as the jockey for Fantastique in the races. He was fourteen, small and wiry, and she had noticed the sure way he handled the horses during the renovations when the animals were put out under the trees.

Bert took the reins as Kate jumped down. "Oh, my lady, he's a beautiful colt! I never did see such a one before." He reached out hesitantly and stroked Fantastique with awe.

"Would you like to try him?"

"Ride him, my lady? Me?"

"Please do."

Bert climbed up on the saddle and slowly guided Fantastique about the yard in front of the stables. Kate watched critically, a hand shielding her eyes against the sun.

"Trot him a bit."

Fantastique responded to the boy's touch, his long muscles moving rhythmically.

"Gallop!"

Round they went, earth flying into the air in the wake of powerful hoofs. Kate observed the mutual trust that made their riding easy.

She nodded. "Whoa!"

Bert stopped the colt and jumped down.

"Let's try it this way." Kate shortened the stirrups.

"Excuse me, my lady, they be too high, to my reckoning. I ain't that short."

"Just try it. I have my reasons. Can you make it up?"

"Yes, my lady. I don't need no stirrups nor nothing." He leapt up and bent his knees high to get his feet into the stirrups.

"Now gallop him, leaning forward as far as you can. Take heed that you don't fall. It will feel awkward at first, but you'll get used to it."

The boy galloped Fantastique round and round the yard, gradually circling faster.

At last Kate stopped them. "Well?"

"Oh, my lady, that were a treat!" Bert stroked the colt's nose, elated. "I ain't never rid so fast in me life."

"You see what happens when you position yourself like that?"

"Yes, my lady, it makes a difference. It sure does. And this colt's fast! He goes like he's magic."

"Do you think he could win the Silver Bell?"

"Yes, my lady, I do. I be going to the race meetings every year, helping out in the stables. I ain't never seed anything like him."

"Would you like to ride him?"

"You mean—at the race meeting?"

Kate nodded, expecting him to be overjoyed.

The boy considered, then shook his head. "No, my lady. I ain't good enough. A real trained jockey would be better, like the kind that comes from Newmarket. Otherwise it wouldn't be fair to the colt. Not that colt."

"I come from Newmarket, Bert, and know a little about jockeys. And I want *you.*"

The boy looked at her doubtfully.

"It'll take a lot of work. Working out daily, both here and on the course. Lord Radburn has given me permission to practice over there."

"Practice on the Radburn racetrack! Oh, my lady!"

"Do you want to do it, Bert?"

"Want to! Oh, yes, my lady, that is, if you thinks I can. I promise I'll work very hard. It won't seem like work, neither!"

"Good boy! Now, let's take Fantastique to his stall and I'll show you how to rub him down."

"I knows how to do that, my lady."

"Not the way *I* want it done."

"No, my lady."

Early every morning Kate and a sleepy-eyed Bert rode over to the Radburn course to work out Fantastique. Bert and the colt seemed to come to life at the same time, and Kate would then simulate racing conditions, lowering a white handkerchief to start them and measuring the time with the chronometer that her father had given her. Bert improved daily, and Kate was pleased with her choice.

As they were setting out one morning, they met Donald returning from nocturnal festivities down on the coast. He lifted his hat elaborately as they passed, not recognising his wife. Bert sniggered behind his hand.

"I want to tell you something, Bert, in confidence."

"Of course, my lady. Me ears is open but me lips is sealed."

"I would prefer that Sir Donald go nowhere near Fantastique. Do you think you could manage that?"

"Easy as pie, my lady, 'cause Sir Donald, he don't come no more inside the stables. Take a look, my lady."

She turned in the saddle and watched. Faithful Daisy stopped before the doors, and Donald drooped there for a moment, then fell off, landing on his knees. He got up on his feet and gave the horse a shove, thinking it had thrown him. Next, he groped for the reins and attempted to tie them about the post but could not locate it. Angered, he took a swing at the post; unfortunately, this time his fist struck home. Swearing and shaking his hand, he staggered toward Coulder Hall.

"You see, my lady, he din't go in." The boy grinned widely. "He allus leaves Daisy outside. She's a good nag, she'll stay put."

The boy saw Kate's serious face and straightened his. "I know how it is, my lady. Me Pa drinks too," he said sympathetically.

"You say Sir Donald never goes inside the stables now?"

"No, my lady. No more he don't, since you keeps Fantastique there. Onc't he did." The boy was churning with held-back laughter. "He comes in, my lady, he looks around, and right away Fantastique smells him or something and gets all riled up. Never seed him like that afore, he rears up and hits the stall with his hoofs, 'til I think sure it's going to bust apart. Sir Donald, he goes running out of the stables like Old Nick is after him. You shoulda seen him, my lady! And he ain't been back since, neither."

He could no longer control his laughter and doubled up.

Kate smiled. "Just keep Fantastique safe."

"Oh, yes, my lady. You don't need to tell me that!" gasped the boy, holding his sides.

— 21 —

"LYDIA," SAID DONALD, watching Kate's face as she played bezique with Adelaide, "did you know that Edward came home today for the holidays?"

Kate, about to play, paused and studied the card carefully, as though doubtful about the move.

"Alone? Was he alone?" asked Lydia importunely.

"No, he was not alone," Donald said and, tantalisingly, did not go on. Kate tapped the card against her teeth.

"Was the duchess with him—or the Princess Charlotte?" Lydia's novel fell to the floor.

"Do you think the Princess would be permitted to journey around the countryside with a man, even if he be the estimable Lord Radburn?"

"It was the duchess, then. She's back!"

"No, it was not the duchess."

"Stop being childish. Who was it?" Lydia was becoming frantic.

"Wilfred Curtis accompanied him."

"Is that all?" said Lydia, relieved. She picked up her book and quickly turned the pages.

Adelaide looked up. "Play, Coz, I beseech you."

"The two most eligible bachelors in the county returned, and you don't care?" Donald went on, baiting her.

"It will be pleasant to have extra dancing partners at the balls," said Lydia loftily.

"Pleasant, is that all it is?" He steadily watched Kate.

His mother intervened. "Donald, stop ragging Lydia."

"Cousin Kate, I am going to gain more points if you keep playing like this."

"Wilfred says he hardly had room to sit. The carriage was full of Christmas presents for everyone."

"Edward was always generous." Lady Weyward gave her son a significant look.

"When is the party to be?" asked Lydia, mentally going over her wardrobe.

"In three days' time. Winter solstice."

"*Mariage*," cried out Adelaide, spreading out her cards. "I've won again."

Kate rose. "I am very tired. If you will excuse me, I will retire."

Nettie, nodding in a corner, woke up and followed her out, carrying a candle.

"No wonder she's tired. Riding all day!" said Lydia. "Some wife you have, Brother. She wears herself out and then goes to bed early, with a maid stretched across the threshold as sentry."

"Shut up!"

"That isn't fair, Lydia," said Adelaide. "She manages Coulder Hall and does it very well. That in itself is full-time work."

"*I* ran it very well, too," said Lady Weyward resentfully, "if you remember."

"Of course you did, Mama. I only meant, considering her age and inexperience, she is remarkable."

"She is spoiling the servants. Far too lenient."

"But still everything gets done, Mama. I only hope that when I become mistress of the Vicarage I can handle servants so easily."

"Oh, the servants!" said Lydia crossly. "Who cares about them?"

"You won't have the opportunity to care about servants," said Donald, "if you don't get married pretty soon."

This time his mother did not reprimand him. She thought the point well taken.

On the morning after the Christmas party at Radburn Hall, Lydia demanded a family parley. Fury was in her face.

"This is between my mother and my brother and myself, if you don't mind. You two are not concerned in it." She dismissed Kate and Adelaide with an abrupt wave of the hand. The air vibrated with trouble, and they were happy to be released.

"Mama," began Lydia, when the three had gathered in the barren library, "you have got to do something about Donald. He is ruining my chances!"

"I? What have I done?" said Donald blusteringly.

"Mama, you should have been there last night, you might have stopped it."

"Stopped what?" Donald was worried. Had the admiral noticed those cards in his sleeve?

"Now, Lydia, you know I had a bad headache and had to send my regrets to the countess." The truth was that Lady Weyward had hoped to slight the countess by turning down the invitation to the party; she had reasoned that the whole county would notice. In fact, no one missed her except for Lydia, who needed her help. "Donald's a grown man. Must I still look after him?"

"Yes! Apparently so. He's made a bad marriage, and he tries to get even with Kate in public. Don't deny it, you! It's clear enough. But I'm the one who really gets hurt."

"I might have known that Kate was at the bottom of this," said Lady Weyward.

"After supper—Mama, listen to this—the dancing was informal, there were no programmes. Lord Radburn signalled for the music to begin and then sat down beside the countess. *Your son*, Mama, brings his wife into the ballroom, then conspicuously abandons her. There she is, standing all alone. The countess whispers to Edward and he gets up and leads Kate to the first set! Edward and Kate opened the dancing! It should have been *me!*" Lydia's voice was close to hysteria. "I saw it all. Edward did not want to start the ball with her. His mother told him to!"

"Edward is an obedient son," said Lady Weyward, glaring at Donald, who only sulked.

"So it went the whole evening. *Your* son, Madam, goes off to a card game—the one nearest to the punch bowl, of course—leaving Kate high and dry. Lionel helped her out, of course, he always does, and Wilfred and Admiral Benson and some others partnered her. They all felt sorry for her, but it was Edward who had to carry the burden."

"But Edward danced with you?"

"No, Mama, not once!" wailed Lydia. "Why do you think I'm upset? There were no princesses or duchesses there, but my stupid brother and his wife managed to spoil it all. My life is being ruined!"

"*I* get the blame because Edward doesn't dance with her? What will she think of next?" Donald was on his dignity.

"Next, Mama, when Edward was giving out the Christmas presents, Edward calls out 'Sir Donald,' and *your son*, Madam, doesn't even come forward. 'Hand it to me,' he says to the admiral."

"That wasn't nice, Donald. What was the gift?"

"Just some old snuff."

"It was Spanish snuff. The kind that the Prince Regent uses. And Donald didn't even thank him!"

Lady Weyward considered. "Of course, Edward is very arrogant. The whole family is. I don't entirely blame Donald. What did Edward give the countess?"

"A doghouse. Yes, a doghouse! For that miserable Frou-Frou. Of course, it was very pretty, especially made, with a carved walnut frame, all lined inside and out with blue velvet."

"Expensive, no doubt." Lady Weyward was feeling regret that she had not gone to the party and claimed a gift. "What was your present, Lydia?"

"Oh, a bolt of wool goods. Plaid!" Lydia wrinkled her nose.

"What's wrong with that?"

"Nothing, except that he gave Adelaide the same thing. Different colours. Mine are prettier."

"What did he give Kate?"

"Not much. A brass star. You know, one of those things that fasten onto bridles. And the way she thanks him! 'Oh, Edward!' she says."

"That wasn't a major speech."

"It was the *way* she said it, tears in her eyes and lower lip trembling. You'd think it was encrusted with diamonds."

"Brass, eh?" said Lady Weyward. "Couldn't have cost very much."

"Then he says, 'For the star in your life. And mine.' "

"What's that?" asked Donald sharply. "What did he say?"

"If you had been with your wife, you would have heard! He said, 'For the star in your life. And mine.' Quiet-like."

"Whatever did he mean by that?" asked Lady Weyward.

"Well, the star in her life is that horse of hers. It certainly is not her husband!"

Lady Weyward frowned. "But what did he mean by 'and mine'?"

"Don't you see? The same thing. Everybody expects her horse to win in the Radburn race meeting. They're talking bets already."

"Won't she be puffed up then!"

"Oh, I'm not worried about her." Lydia, remembering something, tittered. "You should have seen what happened under the mistletoe."

"What happened?" asked Donald anxiously.

Lydia gave him a venomous smile. "Oho, Brother, now you care. I'm not going to tell you."

Donald seized her by the shoulders and shook her. "*What happened under the mistletoe?*"

"Let me be!" shouted Lydia, breaking loose. "You see, Mama, you see what he's like!"

"Donald, behave yourself!"

He threw himself down into a chair and pounded the arms.

"Now, Lydia dear, tell me what happened. I am quite curious."

"Well," said Lydia, rubbing her shoulder and glaring at Donald, "in the middle of the ballroom, a bunch of mistletoe was hung from a chandelier. When the music stopped, the couple under the mistletoe would have to kiss."

"Were you kissed?"

"Of course, Mama."

"She probably arranged it, elbowing all the other ladies out of the way," muttered Donald.

Lydia ignored him. "Once, when the music stopped, Edward and Kate were under the mistletoe. Everybody looked to see who had been caught. Edward and Kate just gazed at each other. Then Edward takes her hand and very elaborately bends over it. I don't think his lips touched her."

"You don't have to worry about her" was Lady Weyward's opinion.

"Of course not, Mama. She's no rival. That's not my argument. My point is that it should have been *me* there with Edward under the mistletoe. And probably would have been if this oaf had been attending to his wife."

"Mind your own business," snarled Donald.

"That's what I'm trying to do!" Lydia howled her old refrain, "I want to get married!"

— 22 —

THE WINTER WAS bitterly cold. Rime stiffened the bare branches of the trees, causing them to creak like arthritic bones when gusts of wind bore down on them from the north. The earth was frozen hard. People stayed indoors if they could, huddled about fires with woollen mitts on. Small animals remained secure in their burrows, except now and again a restless squirrel who would come out, run around curiously, stop suddenly and sniff the air, then run back home again.

Despite the weather, it was a rare day that Kate and Bert did not ride over to Radburn Park to put Fantastique through his paces. Fantastique was the hardiest of them all, not only enduring but enjoying all kinds of weather—frost, wind, rain, snow flurries. He was game to go out in anything.

When they returned, Bert would take care of him, even before he had his own tea, washing him down, making him comfortable with his blanket, and feeding him. Fantastique's hide glistened like satin. With her father's instinct for perfection, Kate watched over everything constantly. Often during the day, she would throw a heavy shawl over her head, dash out to the stables to check on some point, and have long conversations with Bert and Jack, and with Fantastique himself.

"He has to win," she said to herself fiercely. Somehow his winning the race for three-year-olds was mixed up in her mind with winning her inheritance. If he won, then she would get her uncle's bequest, she convinced herself. There was nothing she could do now about the inheritance but wait and hope, but the race she could prepare for, and with her whole might she did.

Edward sent word that the race meeting would be held the last week in April. Since the solicitors wrote that they would need to visit Coulder Hall for a last time, Lady Weyward replied, inviting them to have their stay coincide with the Radburn race meeting.

In March the ice began to melt and the streams swelled. They were clear, cold, and noisy, and sweet to the taste. Pussy willows shyly appeared and fields of snowdrops daintily dotted the downs. Kate and Bert were no longer alone at the track. Other families in the county had been given permission to use Radburn Park, and with the more amenable weather, Kate had sight of some of her competition.

Wilfred Curtis appeared with a new bay, Pasha, smaller than Fantastique, with a short, thick neck, but muscular and fast. Wilfred was proud of his acquisition, which had cost him more than he could afford. He felt he was entitled to make disparaging remarks about Fantastique. "Rather thin, isn't he?" "He has a good disposition, certainly, but this will be against him in a race." "Handsome, of course, but no real spirit."

Bert was troubled by these criticisms. "Be it true, my lady? Be Fantastique too nice to win?" he asked one day as they were riding back to the Coulder stables.

"Don't you believe it. Fantastique doesn't run for the satisfaction of beating the others. He runs for the sheer joy of running."

"Ye don't think we oughter be harder on him like? Peter, he that be Mr. Curtis's jockey, leathers 'im with his whip and digs his heel awful hard, and Pasha do go fast."

"Never! That is the wrong way to spur a horse! As my father says, *'Il faut être avare des coups et prodigue des caresses.'* "

Bert grinned. "I understood 'caress,' my lady."

"Good, Bert. It means, 'Go easy on blows, but give lots of caresses.' That's the way to handle a horse."
"Yes, my lady."

It was through Wilfred that Kate learned that Edward would be home at the end of March. "He's got to fix up the old place, I expect," he said, jerking his head in the direction of the fine grandstand, which had been erected just a few years before. "Prinny is coming."
"With the Princess Charlotte?" asked Kate offhandedly.
"Don't know. Don't think so. She's fishing in other waters, I hear. Across the water, if you take my meaning. Why they have to marry foreigners, I'm sure I don't know. Oh, I say, I beg your pardon. Your father—"
"It's all right, Wilfred. Papa is English now."
"And *you* have married English," he said, as though this made everything all right.
"Yes, I have, haven't I?" said Kate. She never thought of herself as married.

Early in April, she led Fantastique into the weighing room below the grandstand and came face to face with Edward.
Edward caught his breath. "As beautiful as ever," he said quietly. Realising that his guest, Lord Easton, was staring at them, he patted the horse's rump as though he had been talking about Fantastique and made the necessary introductions.
"Perhaps he's too thin?" asked Kate, for something to say, her heart thumping. She took an excessive interest in the weighing.
"Just about right, I'd say," said Edward, the corners of his mouth twitching mischievously. Kate blushed and was furious with herself for her lack of self-possession.
"I believe it's his nature to be lean," she said to Lord Easton, trying to cover her confusion. "Certainly he eats heartily enough."

She hastily excused herself and led Fantastique outside.

"Ah, so that's the little one from Newmarket, who rides *à calefourchon*," said Lord Easton. He considered himself a connoisseur of horses and women and watched interestedly as Kate lithely swung herself up on Fantastique.

"You have heard of her, then?"

"We hear of things sometimes up in Lancashire, you know. They say she is starting something of a new fashion in riding for women." He stepped outside, the better to see her canter away. "Somehow I thought she'd be more worldly looking, don't you know. This one looks so innocent. Positively chaste! Deucedly good-looking with those dark blue eyes and that voluminous red hair, just a bit wild!" He savoured her appearance.

"The horse looks promising, don't you think?" said Edward sharply.

"The horse? Fine animal, fine animal. Will make a fair showing. She married Coulder, eh? Too good for him, I'd say. They ran off, was that it?"

"I don't know the circumstances. Shall we go to the paddock? I have something to show you."

Lord Easton was not to be distracted. "Wasted on him, wasted on him. He isn't worthy of her." He winked. "I hope I'm around when she realises it."

"This way!" said Edward, seizing his guest roughly by the arm and pulling him in the opposite direction.

"Have a care!" said Lord Easton, jerking his arm away and straightening out his sleeve.

— 23 —

The Prince Regent and his entourage arrived at Radburn Hall the day before the meeting was to begin. No ladies accompanied His Royal Highness, only his secretary and some servants. The countess, who had prepared for every contingency, breathed a sigh of relief. Mrs. Fitzherbert or the young Princess Charlotte she would have been happy to receive, but the duchess of Conroyallan, from all the rumours, still had designs on her elder son, and she feared that Edward might succumb in a foolish moment of recklessness. She welcomed the Prince wholeheartedly. It struck her that, in spite of all, he was a lonely man.

The Prince, on his part, was delighted to be there. The countess had always seemed to him the most charming and understanding of women, never chiding him, even playfully, with regard to his fickleness toward the fair sex or his propensity to corpulence. She did not nag him about Princess Caroline nor rag him about Mrs. Fitzherbert. Lord Radburn, now, did have a way of criticising what he called the Prince's lack of initiative in the matter of reform—did the fellow have to be so earnest in these matters? Never used to be that way. What had got into him? But at least he did it to his face, not in some covert, dark way that smelt of treason. No, Edward was loyal to the throne; he was sure of that. This quirk about reforms aside, he was a jolly fellow, good company, and did he know horses! The Prince had had to sell his own extensive stables to Tattersall to pay some tiresome debts, and he relished attending the

Radburn race meeting to see what horses were currently running.

"There, gentlemen!" he said as an aide unwrapped a parcel and ceremoniously placed the newly minted Bell on the mantlepiece.

Edward and Lord Easton examined the heavy object sparkling in the light from the fire. In relief across the front of the Bell was a depiction of Radburn Hall.

"It is beautiful," breathed Edward. "I am deeply touched."

"Handsome bit of silversmithing" was Lord Easton's judgement. "Fine craftsmanship."

The Prince beamed his pleasure. "Any favourites among the three-year-olds, Radburn?"

"Thank you, sir, for the Bell. I am overwhelmed. It is, indeed, a marvelous object, and it is an honour to have it offered. As to favourites, there are three. Wilfred Curtis has a bay, a compact kind of beast, very strong. Lord Easton here has a grey, who belies his name of Trappist by the glare in his eye and his evil temper!"

The Prince turned to Easton. "A grey? You are not superstitious about greys, Easton?"

"Not at all, sir. I consider it a stroke of *good* luck, for I am relying on everyone else's superstition to avoid betting on Trappist, and I shall mop up when he comes in first."

"I have always suspected you of being astute, Easton!"

"Perhaps it would be better not to so label me, sir, until Trappist does earn the Bell," said Easton superstitiously.

"You mentioned three favourites, Radburn. What is the third?"

"The colt I mentioned to your Highness before this. Sable, with the name of Fantastique."

"Yes, I recall the name. There was some mystery concerning the ownership?"

"Only because the owner was a young girl, a Miss Martin. She is now a year older and a married woman besides, having become Lady Weyward of Coulder Hall."

"By marriage to —?"

"Sir Donald Weyward, a neighbour of mine."

"Can't say I recall him."

"You will meet them both tomorrow, sir."

"Married her for her colt, did he?" said the Prince, smiling. He held up his brandy glass to look at the colour.

"I believe there were—other considerations," said Edward hesitantly.

Lord Easton chortled. "Her trim figger and disordered red hair, more like."

Tentatively the Prince took a sip of brandy, then smacked his lips appreciatively. "Red hair? I seem to recall two girls with bright hair in this county, lovely young ladies, one played and one sang, very musically. Cousins, I believe."

"You have a good memory, sir. One was indeed Miss Martin, now the Lady Weyward. The other, Miss Adelaide Coulder, is betrothed to my brother."

"Ah me, how things can change in a short year!" said the Prince, sipping moodily.

"Overnight!" said Edward fervently.

The Prince looked at him in surprise. "And you, Edward, when are you going to marry?"

"You should stop dawdling, Radburn. Your brother is beating you to the halter!" Lord Easton quipped.

"I am in no hurry," said Edward.

"No, no, don't be in a hurry," advised the Prince, draining his glass. "Let him alone, Easton. A mésalliance can be disastrous." He nodded and the glass was refilled.

The Messrs. Pierce, Price, and Sharpe had arrived at Coulder Hall, and Kate was having private conversations with them daily. Her manner with them was subdued, which was, in fact, her usual demeanour now, unless she had to make a special point or was alone with Adelaide, when she might be herself. She had found that in this way she avoided friction if not outright argument. So these conversations with the solicitors consisted of questions by them and answers by Kate. They left her exhausted. So much depended on making the right impression. Mr. Pierce asked her many questions about Fantastique and riding, and as the week of the meetings continued, she realised that it was because he took a real interest in racing. Her replies were forthright.

"Yes, Mr. Pierce, I know my way of riding astride is controversial, but it is the way my father taught me at Newmarket. It is far more practical, believe me, and safer than sidesaddle. I do not do it to be bold or to attract attention."

Mr. Sharpe, the tall, lean, youngish one, kept returning to the question of her marriage. Here her lids would lower, and she would reply evasively.

"Your marriage was precipitous, was it not, Lady Weyward?"

"I realise that many think so."

"Has it been successful, would you say?"

"It has been—all that I thought it would be."

"Are you happy?"

"I am full of hope. That is happiness."

"I see." He clamped his lips together.

The solicitors closeted themselves with Lady Harriet several times, and with Donald and Adelaide. Once they spoke with Lydia, but only briefly, much to her annoyance, as she considered her testimony invaluable.

"How is it going?" asked Adelaide, poking her head in Kate's room one evening before supper.

"I really feel that there is nothing about me that they have not perceived or cannot intuit. I can only hope that my conduct appears to them as sufficiently ladylike."

"Oh, it is, it is, Cousin Kate! You are as great a lady as the countess!"

Kate smiled. "In *your* prejudiced opinion, dear girl, but what about theirs?"

With the Prince Regent installed at Radburn Hall and races every day in the Park, social events in the county reached an excited pitch. Every house had guests, and the inn at Tweedstun overflowed. The villagers rented their bedrooms, while they themselves slept rolled up in blankets in the kitchen. All went to the track every day, and it was hard to say which was more entertaining, the races with their sometimes reckless betting or the crowd itself, adorned in its colourful best, mingling, eating, observing, and periodically drawn to the fence, shouting, when a race was on. The Prince, high up and remote in his box away from the jostling crowd, observed everything, his telescope ranging from the horses to the crowd to the grandstand.

Hampers filled with fresh, delicious country food and wines from Spain and France were provisioned for the royal party and others in the grandstand. Down below vendors shouted their wares of fried tripe and onions cooking away on little stoves set up on drays. Others did a brisk business with kegs of ale drawn on dogcarts.

In the evenings, the Prince suppered formally and sumptuously at the countess's long table, with not only the menu but the guests chosen by her for his pleasure. Course followed course, and those individuals who tried to keep up with the Prince soon found themselves exceedingly uncomfortable, loosening their clothes and having a tendency thereafter to fall asleep just when the Prince was ready for cards or music or dancing.

One evening the Prince had his violoncello brought in. His old friend Josef Haydn had written a trio especially for him, which he tremendously liked to play. Adelaide was recruited to play the harpsichord, and Wilfred Curtis the violin. With his ample form and the large instrument before him, the Prince had difficulty turning the pages. When he seemed in imminent danger of knocking over stand and all, Kate approached and stood near, turning the pages for him. At the end of the movement, he looked up, perspiring, and smiled at her. "I don't know why Haydn had to use such long sheets of paper to write his music on. It's awkward." The Prince mopped his forehead, nodded to the other players, and the trio continued.

The music was delightful. Adelaide acquitted herself well, although at first her fingers shook with trepidation at playing with the reigning Prince. Wilfred had enormous self-confidence, even when playing with royalty, but his scraping left something to be desired. From time to time the Prince looked at him warningly, but Wilfred was oblivious. The exquisite music saw them all through, and the audience applauded enthusiastically.

Kate receded into the company, but the Prince caught up with her.

"You were kind, Lady Weyward, to rescue me from those infernal pages."

"It was a pleasure, sir."

The Prince looked down into Kate's piquant face. He was troubled and interested. A year ago she had been a pretty girl, excited and animated. Now the face was serious, with sad shadows, and under strict control. Her movements were slow and deliberate, as though guided by some severe discipline. Has marriage made her so unhappy? thought the Prince. Marriage, bah! It makes wretches of us all.

Kate curtsied with a small rustle of taffeta, lowered her head gracefully, rose, and would have withdrawn.

"Stay!"

It was a command and spoken more loudly than the Prince had intended. The company looked up in their direction and then away quickly, smiling knowingly. Even deaf old Admiral Benson had heard it, but he only winked, much to his wife's relief, who feared he might bellow something indiscreet.

The Prince led Kate to a small sofa, just big enough for the two of them. He settled himself comfortably, crossing his legs and stretching one arm along the ridge of the back behind Kate. She waited for him to begin.

Across the room, Lady Curtis sniffed to Lady Harriet, "He always did take to 'em married!"

This annoyed Lady Harriet, because Mr. Price was standing nearby, taking everything in, rocking back and forth on his toes and heels. This was not the time for derogatory inferences to be made about Kate. The stakes were too high, and half was to go to her son. "You speak from experience, no doubt!" replied Lady Harriet.

Lady Curtis, who although foolish, was virtuous, turned away angrily and said to her son, "Wilfred, circulate over there and find what is the topic of their tête-à-tête."

The eavesdropper returned by a circuitous path. "First they were discussing music and then the conversation turned to horses," reported Wilfred.

"Satisfied?" Lady Harriet said to Lady Curtis and turned to Mr. Price. "You see how easy it is to misconstrue?"

Mr. Price continued rocking on his toes and heels.

The Prince requested that Kate be invited to his box the next day.

"With Sir Donald?" asked the countess.

"Oh, I suppose so," said the Prince.

"Try this." The Prince adjusted his telescope and handed it to Kate. As she roved the crowd with the instrument, he examined her. The fresh air had brought colour into her cheeks, and her hair was held down charmingly by *coquelicot* ribbons. She is like a banked fire, he thought, on the edge of bursting into riotous flame. He was enchanted.

The telescope stopped moving. The Prince followed its direction, which was centered on Edward down below on the track, holding up a flag, waiting for the horses to line up and the jockeys to ready them. With a swish, the flag was lowered, and the horses were off. The telescope, however, did not move with the race but remained fixed on the starter. The Prince felt a stab of jealousy and shook his head at his own vulnerability.

Kate politely handed the telescope back to the Prince that he might see the finish of the race.

"Bad luck!" he said, as his favourite failed to win. He handed the glass back to Kate and added wistfully, "But then, one can't win all the time, can one?"

Again she sought out Edward, but he had disappeared into the crowd that was leading the triumphant winner away. However, the glass riveted on another person, a figure as massive as the Prince Regent's, but the clothes he was wearing were nondescript and the hat dusty. Everyone showed respect for him by getting out of his way as though he were the Prince. The weighty person was Richard Tattersall.

"Oh, sir, would you excuse me?" begged Kate. "I see Mr. Tattersall in the crowd, and he may have news of my father."

"Of course, my dear, but only on the promise that you come right back."

He picked up the discarded telescope and followed her with it, gasping with dismay as he saw her jostled by the crowd and the ribbons torn from her hair. But she managed to reach the great man of the turf, who greeted her kindly. Through the glass the Prince observed her anxious questioning and saw Tattersall's face assume a deceptively bland look, familiar to all who had horse-trades with him. Whatever he said seemed to reassure her, although the Prince could wager that Tatt had not committed himself. Edward came into the focus as he joined them, and it was he who protectively led Kate back through the crowd. At the steps of the grandstand, he bowed and left, and Kate ascended the steps alone.

Why doesn't her husband look after her? thought the Prince irritably. He looked angrily over at Donald, who didn't see him, as his head was tipped back, the better to drink from a flask. His hand was unsteady and whiskey dribbled down his chin.

— 24 —

THE FINAL DAY of the races dawned grey and windy, but the weather did not dampen the general excitement. The race for three-year-olds was set for five o'clock, the last of all, with other races scheduled for the early afternoon.

In the Prince Regent's canopied box, the Silver Bell reposed shining in the middle of a portable table, ready to be presented to the victor. Kate's expression altered when she saw it, and the Prince smiled.

"I hope it may be yours this day, my dear," he said graciously. The Prince was resplendent in a green jacket, white hat, and tight nankeen pantaloons.

During an interval, the Regent suggested that they go take a look at Fantastique, knowing how much Kate wanted to. The party included a reluctant Donald, who could not think up any reason to be excused.

The Prince walked along with Kate, the crowd making way for them. "How did you come to call him Fantastique?" he asked. "You could not have seen on the day he was born that he would develop into so fine an animal."

"Oh, but we did, sir. At least, Papa did. Papa gets a feeling, even about newly born foals. But that isn't the reason that he was so named." Kate looked embarrassed.

"What was the reason, then?"

"I am afraid you might be offended if I tell you, sir."

"I? Do I have something to do with it? Come, you can tell me," he said, intrigued, and Kate had to answer.

"Well, sir, it happened that the day he was foaled, we

had some carpenters in to do some work on the stands at Newmarket. They had just arrived from working at your Highness's pavilion in Brighton."

"Oh?"

"They described the pavilion as very beautiful—and fantastic."

The Prince stopped and stared at her for a few seconds, then his heavy chest began to heave with laughter. Many a head turned curiously to see what had put their regent in such a merry mood.

"Oh ho, that is good! To name a horse after a description of my pavilion!" The Prince roared, delighted. "I must tell this to my architects!"

They reached Fantastique's stall, and the Prince admired him from all angles. He stroked the colt's smooth neck. "With such a name, Fantastique, how can you lose?"

Kate's expert eye quickly looked the colt over and saw that all was well. She patted the brass star hanging from his bridle for luck. Then she looked around for Bert. He was behind some partitions further along the aisle, cowering dejectedly.

"What's wrong, Bert?"

"I be a little scared, my lady." The boy was pale with anxiety.

"Everyone's nervous before a race. You'll get over it once it begins. Have you had anything to eat?"

"No, my lady. I wasn't hungry."

"Go buy yourself some tea and a bun. You'll feel better." She opened her reticule and gave him a coin. "Are your togs ready?"

"Yes, my lady. Me mum pressed them up nice last night. Here they be." He showed her the orange-and-white satin breeches and shirt neatly folded.

"Good, Bert. You're going to do just fine."

"Yes, my lady." He managed a faint smile.

"I'll be back to see you off."

"Thank you, my lady."

Whatever assurance Bert might have derived from Kate's

words was shattered by the sudden appearance of the Sovereign of his Realm. The boy dropped to his knees, quaking with fear.

"Come, lad, up with you. Your Fantastique is going to win, you know," said the Prince kindly, but the boy was near fainting and could not move.

The Prince, understanding, turned, and the whole company departed the stables. All except Donald, who had remained at the door when the party entered, and stayed there after they left. He called to Bert.

As the hour of the final race approached, Kate's nerves were at a pitch. She asked the Prince to excuse her that she might go back again to the stables. It had begun to rain, after holding off all day, and the wind had not diminished. She hurried along, holding up her skirts from the wet ground, her heart pounding with excitement. Fantastique, too, was excited, and Kate knew that he knew he was to race.

"You are going to win, amour!" she said, and he shook his long head as though to agree with her.

"Bert!" she called out, wondering what had happened to the boy. She was ready to speak encouraging words. Fantastique stamped his feet impatiently in the empty stall. She hurried down the aisle, and behind a partition found Bert stretched out flat on his back, fast asleep, breathing through his mouth. He had not dressed in his colours; the clothes lay beside him.

"Bert! Wake up! Get dressed! This is no time to be taking a nap. The race is about to begin."

The boy muttered in his sleep. From his open, sagging mouth came the odour of whiskey.

"Oh, no! It cannot be!" Kate shook the boy with all her strength. He flailed at her with his arms but soon lost his pugnaciousness and dropped back on the straw. With a grunt he turned on his side and curled up like a baby. As he turned over, a flask was revealed, a gentleman's flask made of silver, with a monogram she knew very well.

"Bert! Bert!" she shouted desperately, pommelling him with her fists.

Five o'clock.

Edward was at the start, wet with rain, directing the jockeys and horses to their places. The starting flag was in his hand. Where was Fantastique? he wondered. It was unlike Kate to allow him to be late.

Fantastique's place was second from the inner rail; the positions were chosen by lot. Kate hadn't cared where Fantastique was to ride because the colt didn't care; he rode well anywhere. It was Pasha, Wilfred's entry, who was next to the rail; he looked sturdy, set to go and come in first. Fourth from the rail was Trappist, Lord Easton's wild-eyed grey, rearing up. The pelting rain and wind annoyed him, and his jockey had all he could do to hold him in place. All the other entries were ready and were being held back by the jockeys, their bright satin habits turning deeper in colour from the downpour. Where was Fantastique?

All eyes were on Edward. The crowd, not a whit diminished by the elements, held its communal breath. In the royal box, the Prince Regent clutched his telescope. Edward wiped the rain from his lashes and, through the blur, saw Fantastique approaching, his jockey dressed in Kate's orange-and-white colours. Fantastique was deftly placed into position, and Edward raised the wet flag, hurled this way and that by the capricious winds. He looked once more to see that all was in order, and his eyes were drawn to something unusual: the grace of Fantastique's rider. He wiped his eyes again and perceived a delicate face beneath the peaked cap instead of Bert's blunt features. The flag was uncertain in his hand. After a few seconds of hesitation, Edward raised the flag firmly upright and then lowered it with decision. The horses were off.

Pasha shot out first, obediently responding to a whiplash, his muscular neck straining up and down with effort. From the grandstand, Wilfred Curtis let out a shout.

Trappist nervously pushed forward, breasting the wind, to become second.

Fantastique might have caught up, but Kate restrained him. "No, *cheri*, something isn't right."

What was troubling Kate was Trappist. His jockey was riding in the newly learned crouch position, knees up and head forward to increase speed. The boy had been unsure of himself at trial sessions, so that his horse had a tendency to sway from side to side, but Lord Easton had said that this aberration would be corrected with familiarity with the technique. Whether through lack of practice or because Trappist was skittish in the heavy winds and rain and muddy turf, no one afterward could say, but the boy and colt were moving uncertainly.

Third from the rail was Trafalgar, the admiral's entry, a favourite with no one but the admiral himself. With a spurt, he began to edge ahead of Fantastique. Kate shouted a warning, but jockey and horse kept going until they were on a par with Trappist. She could feel Fantastique's instinct to move faster. "No, amour, it isn't safe. Never mind, there will be other races, other times." She was speaking to herself as well as to the colt.

At the half, the accident occurred, and the crowd screamed as from one throat. Trafalgar had continued even with Trappist for several lengths, when Trappist swerved suddenly to the left, the legs of the colts met and entwined, and both horses crashed down into the mud, their riders holding on. Acting swiftly, Kate pulled Fantastique away from the wreckage and kept going.

"God, how horrible!" she gasped, appalled. "Oh, my God, Fantastique, it might have been you!"

By now Pasha was two lengths ahead, his firm hoofs industriously churning up mud, his jockey riding in the traditional posture. Kate crouched more tightly on to Fantastique's neck. "Shall we have a try?" she asked him.

Relieved now from restraint, Fantastique's answer was to let loose, his black tail straight out behind him. Witnesses said afterward that his hoofs seemed not to touch the dirty turf and did not even get splashing mud on them, but that was apocryphal.

As to the collision, both jockeys and Trafalgar had escaped serious injury, but Trappist was finished, a piece of leg bone protruding from the grey flesh like an ivory-handled knife. Edward handed Lord Easton a flintlock pistol. Easton studied his horse for a moment and then sadly gave him the coup de grace. "Greys are always unlucky!" was the folk opinion.

The crowd's attention was drawn to Fantastique, who had caught up with Pasha and surpassed him. Without a rival in sight, Fantastique ran on, rapturously, joy in every movement. As he passed the finish line, the crowd roared with excitement.

Kate slowed him down reluctantly. For a long moment she kept her arms clasped around him and did not move, her muddy face against his muddy neck.

The moment did not last. The reins were grasped, and she was lifted bodily from Fantastique. She tried to tear herself away and run, somewhere, anywhere, but there was no opportunity. She felt herself raised onto stalwart shoulders, and a large bouquet of spring flowers was thrust into her arms. She looked behind her and saw Fantastique decorated with a halter of flowers.

They were led to the grandstand, where the Prince was awaiting with his Silver Bell. He was puzzled that Fantastique's owner, young Lady Weyward, was not there to receive it; he had not seen her since she had left him to go to the stables. Servants were hurriedly dispatched to find her, and Edward let them go, uncertain himself as to what should be done. He stood next to the Prince, his eyes on Fantastique's muddied rider.

The crowd, boisterous with excitement, ended Edward's dilemma by taking matters into their own hands, literally. Kate was thrown up into the air and caught again. Her bouquet fell apart and flowers, as well as water, rained down.

"Hip, hip, hooray!" everyone shouted.

"Brave lad!" agreed their monarch.

Again Kate was thrown up in the air and caught. "Hip, hip, hooray!"

The third time the peaked cap flew off, and Kate's rebellious bright hair came tumbling down. "Hip, hip —"

With astonishment, she was caught and set on her feet. Everyone backed away.

The Prince stared in disbelief. "Is it—the Lady Katherine Weyward?"

There was a shocked silence for a few seconds, then voices began to murmur.

"Oh, no!"

"Oh, Kate!"

"Can it be?"

The crowd stayed away from her. Kate, her hair wild and blown by the wind, her face streaked with mud, stood in the rain alone before the grandstand, deserted.

Edward picked up the Silver Bell and handed it to the Prince. He knew that only the Prince Regent's approbation could save Kate's reputation this time.

"Will you award the trophy, sir?" he asked the amazed monarch.

The Prince pulled himself together. He had a sense of drama, and this scene appealed to him.

"Of course," he said. "Naturally." He descended into the rain and ceremoniously presented the Silver Bell to Kate.

"Not in a long time have I had such a pleasure!" the Prince said fervently, and he meant it. Kate accepted the Bell with tears coursing down her dirty face and curtsied deeply in her muddy orange-and-white outfit.

"Hooray!"

The crowd let out such a yell of released high spirits that it was heard for miles around Radburn Park. Some people said that the earth quaked, causing crockery to fall from shelves and horses to whinny. One housewife declared that her black cat turned white on the instant.

Certainly, many things were never the same again.

— 25 —

THE NEXT DAY was the first of May, the day Kate's legacy was to be bestowed, or not. It was also departure day for the many guests who had spent the week at the Radburn race meeting. All morning long, coaches rolled up to Coulder Hall for impromptu calls on Kate from visitors on their way home. Messengers arrived with letters from people Kate did not know, congratulating her on Fantastique's winning of the Silver Bell and on her own exploit in riding him. The Prince Regent himself sent her a note of regretful farewell, inviting her to call on him at the Brighton pavilion. By an oversight, he neglected to invite Donald.

The three solicitors, Pierce, Price, and Sharpe, remained in the background but were observed to be quite testy with one another. At one point, Sharpe leaned over from his eminence and dug his forefinger repeatedly into Price's shoulder to make a point. Obviously, they were of divided opinions. The meeting in the library to announce Kate's fate was postponed from ten o'clock until noon.

Lady Weyward's face was tight with restrained fury. "How could she have done it?" she muttered to Donald, scarcely moving her lips. Donald edged away. "On the last day, to jeopardise losing her fortune by playing the hoyden! After all we have done to help her!" Her frown intensified as she saw more wine being decanted for use in the drawing room. "More expense!" She turned to Donald in indignation, but he had disappeared.

The last of Kate's visitors were gone, and she took the Silver Bell down from the mantelpiece, where it had been proudly on display. "I hope that you were worth it," she said meditatively. The workmanship of the Bell was exquisite, but it was the meaning of the Bell that made her eyes shine. Reverently she replaced it on the mantel.

"Excuse me, my lady!" Nettie came hurriedly into the room brandishing a letter. "Another letter has come. This one from the mail coach. From Newmarket."

Kate smiled. "How could Papa have learned so soon?" She broke the seal and read, and the smile left her face. "It's from Mrs. Tattersall. My father is dead."

An oaken table had been set up in the library. With their backs to the empty shelves, the three solicitors sat in a row. On the other side of the table, of Uncle William's surviving family there were Lady Weyward, Donald, Lydia, and Adelaide. They were awaiting Kate. Mr. Pierce, who was to make the announcement, cleared his throat, as though testing to make sure that all was in working order.

A tall timepiece in a dark corner struck twelve solemn tones, and then its pendulum resumed its swinging for the post meridiem. Lady Weyward, noting that Mr. Price was staring at her, gave him a quick mechanical smile, more like a grimace. He did not respond. The pendulum continued its ticktock.

"Well," said Lady Weyward brightly, taking charge. "We'll have to send for her, won't we? Adelaide—"

The library door opened. Kate came in quickly and closed the door behind her. She was dressed in the shabby brown riding outfit she had worn that first day when she had arrived in the county; the battered tricorn was holding up her hair. Mr. Pierce raised his flexible eyebrows, Mr. Price remained passive, and Mr. Sharpe frowned.

"What is the meaning of this, my dear?" said Lady Weyward, sounding false, like an inexperienced actress.

"The meaning is," said Kate slowly, "that I am going

home, as I came, with nothing but Fantastique. Papa is dead."

"I am sorry to hear that."

"Accept my condolences."

"That is too bad."

"Oh, poor Cousin Kate!" said Adelaide, running to Kate and putting her arms about her. "I know how you feel."

Donald merely turned away.

"Well, these things happen, don't they?" said Lady Weyward. "What do you mean 'with nothing but Fantastique'?"

"It means that I am renouncing my inheritance." She turned to the three solicitors. "I am not even sure that you three gentlemen of the law, Mr. Pierce, Mr. Price, and Mr. Sharpe, appointed by my Uncle William, had decided that I was worthy and were ready to bestow it upon me. But that does not matter, for I do not want it now."

"If this is some kind of joke, it is not very funny" came from Lady Weyward.

"It is not a joke, and indeed it is not funny," said Kate. She turned again to the solicitors. "Under the terms of Uncle's will, I was to stay a year with Lady Weyward and prove myself a lady. I have tried to be a lady, according to her lights. To appear so, I have lied and I have deceived. And if you gentlemen were to award me the legacy on what you think you see me to be, you would be acting mistakenly through ignorance, and Uncle William's wishes would miscarry."

"She is mad!" exclaimed Lady Weyward. "Through grief, of course," she added, afraid to go too far.

"Give us an example of how you deceived us," said Mr. Pierce sternly, pulling his eyebrows into one straight line.

"It began the very first day. I arrived at Radburn Park dressed in these very clothes"—Kate motioned to her outfit—"and met the countess, who persuaded me that my clothes would not make a ladylike impression, although they are what I always wore for riding at Newmarket. She also thought it was not quite the thing for me to arrive on horseback, so we made up a lie about how I had arrived by the stage. She allowed me use of the wardrobe of the duchess of Conroyallan, who had discarded it when she left, and I have continued using it all year."

"I have worn many of those things, too," put in Adelaide. "If it was a fault, I am guilty, too."

"So that's where all that finery came from!" exclaimed Lydia. "I thought I had seen it before."

"What else have you done?" asked Mr. Price grimly. "How else did you deceive?"

"I kept Fantastique a secret. Lord Radburn permitted me to keep him at the Radburn stables. I would steal out before dawn in order to ride him, and, of course, I rode astride. But you know this; Donald revealed it to you—to everyone—at my coming-out ball."

"Of course he did!" said his mother.

"What else?" asked Mr. Sharpe impatiently.

"I became aware, whilst staying in Bath, that Lady Weyward had begun a campaign to smear my reputation. I assure you gentlemen that any evil gossip you may have heard from her lips, or relayed by ignorant parties, is utterly without basis."

"I never did such a thing!" protested Lady Weyward.

"You engaged in no —reckless behaviour with anyone?" Mr. Pierce eyed Kate closely.

"Never! Ever! Upon my soul!" Kate flushed in agitation.

"No one you became too fond of?"

"There is one man I learned to love this year, but in all innocence."

"You mean your husband?"

"Oh, no!" Kate looked shocked. "Oh no, no."

"Who is this man that you love?" asked Lydia.

"It doesn't matter. My love was unrequited. I married someone else, as you see."

"No, Kate, you are wrong!" blurted out Adelaide. "He *did* love you. Lionel told me. But we three were so much together, and somehow he got the idea that Lionel was courting you, many people did, whereas"—she blushed furiously—"it was really me that he was courting."

Kate stared at her, speechless.

"It's true, Kate. He would have proposed after Lionel and I announced our engagement, but by then you had married my brother."

"Who is this *he?*" demanded Lydia.

"Why, Edward, of course," said Adelaide, in wonder at her sister's obtuseness.

"I don't believe it!" Lydia cried.

"Lord Radburn!" said Mr. Sharpe. "So that was how things stood!"

"Let's see now," said Mr. Price, trying to piece things together. "Lord Radburn did not propose, so you turned around and married Sir Donald on the rebound."

"No, it was not like that at all," said Kate. Mr. Price looked at her doubtfully. "No, Mr. Price, all my deceptions are past. Why should I lie to you now that I have relinquished my fortune? What for? No, I married Donald to stop his and Lady Weyward's persecution. Donald tried to seduce me—if it hadn't been for Fantastique he might have succeeded. I was injured in the escape, which injury Donald made worse by handling me roughly at the ball. I believe he would have killed me rather than see me inherit."

"Do you believe her?" asked Lady Weyward with a cynical laugh.

"Go on, please," said Mr. Pierce, his heavy black brows knitted together.

"Once before, I had made up my mind to give up the whole thing, in Bath, when Lady Weyward was saying those dreadful things about me—and people were believing them—but then Papa's health took a turn for the worse, and it seemed desperately important to have money for expert medical care. You remember, I called on you in London to ask for an advance."

"Yes, yes, we could not help you. Go on!"

"I decided then to marry Donald. In that way, he and Lady Weyward would stop hindering me from receiving the inheritance—and possibly getting it for himself by having the will overturned—and start helping. It was the only thing I could think of to do."

"Let me get this straight," said Mr. Sharpe. "*You* proposed marriage to *him* and offered him part of the inheritance to do so."

"Half," said Kate.

"That is a lie!" shouted Donald. "I could have got the whole thing, if I had liked, by overturning the will!"

"That could perhaps have been, and might still be, possible, but it would be difficult" was Mr. Pierce's opinion. "If the legacy is to be refused to the first legatee, on the grounds of unworthiness, then there is the second to be taken up, Mr. William Weyward's business partner in the West Indies. If you were to challenge this, the case would no doubt wind up in Chancery, with no one receiving anything for a long, long time."

"Why *did* you marry her?" asked Mr. Sharpe.

"Because—I loved her!" he avowed.

Kate pulled out a paper from an inside pocket. "He married me for half of my expected fortune. I have it in writing."

She handed to Mr. Sharpe the document drawn up on her wedding day and witnessed by Nurse Amelia.

"You fool!" said Lady Weyward to her son.

Mr. Sharpe read it carefully. "You would be an asset to the legal profession," he said to Kate, handing the paper to Mr. Pierce, whose eyebrows did acrobatics.

"Then the marriage was never consummated?" asked Mr. Pierce.

"Never."

Mr. Pierce handed the document to Mr. Price.

"Disgusting!" was Mr. Price's verdict.

"Yes," said Kate, "I am. I used every means I could

command to achieve my inheritance. This was the foulest of all—to marry a man I detest because I thought he could help me, or at least not hinder me."

Everyone was silenced. Not even Lady Weyward protested. White marks had appeared on either side of her nostrils as she breathed heavily.

"You see clearly what I have become. A year ago I might have been worthy. I was a simple girl, brought up in the country away from Society, among horses. Although not polished in manners, at least I was honest and straightforward." She sighed. "I believe I prefer the company of horses."

"You are hereby formally renouncing your inheritance, then?" asked Mr. Price, in the tone of a man who wants to get matters straight.

"Yes," said Kate definitely. "I am not worthy under the terms of the will. I do not like what striving after the legacy has made me do. What might the money itself do? I do not need it now for Papa. It is too late—he is gone. I go now to Newmarket to bury him, and I shall stay there."

"But, dearest Kate, how will you live?" asked Adelaide, tears in her eyes.

"I shall do what I know how to do —train horses, like my father before me. Train jockeys. And perhaps teach ladies to ride astride—there seems to be an interest in it now. Good-bye, sweet Cousin Adelaide, I shall miss you very much. Farewell, all. Gentlemen."

From the threshold she added, "I was fond of Uncle William. I feel now I truly have his desires at heart."

She said good-bye to Nurse Amelia in the cavernous kitchen. The old lady wiped her eyes on her apron. "Now Guy Martin be gone afore me to the grave, but not by much. I fear I ain't going to see ye again, Miss Kate."

"Nonsense, Nanny. I'll be coming back to see both Miss Adelaide and you."

"Miss Adelaide will be getting married one of these days and moving on to the vicarage. And your old Nanny will be moving on, too, to the next world, one day soon. But there it is. Miss Meg left and I never seed her again no more, and now you be leaving. You ain't never coming back to Coulder Hall."

"Don't talk like that, Nanny. Of course we shall see each other again. Now dry those tears."

The old woman took a huge handkerchief out of a pocket and blew her nose.

"There be one thing I be asking ye to do before ye leave."

"Anything, Nanny."

"Make it up with Bert afore ye go. He be all cut up about what he did yesterday, crying and hiding his head."

"I promise I will, Nanny."

She kissed the old lady and left Coulder Hall.

As she approached the stables she saw Bert duck inside.

"Bert, saddle Fantastique, will you?" she called out. "Be sure the blanket is correctly placed under the saddle. We have a long journey, and I don't want him chafed."

She waited outside. Bert came out leading Fantastique, and his head was hanging.

"Come now, Bert, it's all right, it really is. No harm done, as it turned out. It was, after all, all for the best."

"Oh, my lady, I be so sorry. I didn't mean to do it. I ain't used to strong drink and on an empty stomach and all—I just passed out. It was because of Sir Donald, he sees me shaking and says I need bucking up and he hands me—"

"Don't tell me how it happened, I don't want to hear. It isn't necessary. I just want you to promise never to let it happen again."

"Never, my lady! I swear it! Ah, my lady, I feels so sick. My head feels like something is bursting in there."

"That's called a morning-after headache, Bert."

"I ain't never had a headache before, and I hopes I never gets it again."

"Bert, Fantastique and I are leaving now, for good. My dear papa died yesterday, and I am going to Newmarket to bury him. I plan to remain there."

"I heard about your father, my lady, and I be sorry, real sorry. You say you ain't coming back? Fantastique neither?" Bert looked shocked.

"No, Bert, most probably not."

The boy held on to the reins, looking stupefied, and then began to cry. "I'll never see Fantastique again!" he wailed. He put his arms around the horse's neck. "I'll never ride him again! I'll never race him again!"

"There, there, Bert. There will be other colts to ride and race."

"Not like Fantastique! There's none like him and never will be!" The boy put his head against Fantastique's rump and heaved with sobs, inconsolable.

"Bert, I have an idea. Would you like to come to Newmarket to work? I believe I could find something for you there. I *know* I could, for anyone with your way with horses."

Bert looked up through his tears. "Would I be in charge of Fantastique?"

"That could be arranged."

"You mean it, my lady? You truly mean it?"

"I truly mean it, Bert."

"Can I come with you now, my lady?" His round face shone with tears and gratitude.

"No, not now. You should consider the offer first, think it over, ask your mother and father, and if you still want to, then say good-bye to everyone and come. Say in a few weeks."

"If you say so, my lady, I'll wait. But I could protect you on your journey."

"Protect me? From what?"

The boy hesitated and looked down the road. "I just saddled Daisy for Sir Donald. Not five minutes past. He took the right-of-way south."

"He's going to a resort he fancies on the coast, no doubt."
"Yes, my lady."
"Good-bye, Bert. We'll see each other soon, then."
Kate turned Fantastique onto the road leading to the right-of-way. Bert watched after her and scratched his cowlick. The scratching made his head hurt, and he winced. He ran around the stables to the footpath.

Kate took the right-of-way through Radburn Park. By now the royal guest would have departed, and the countess and Edward would be alone at the Hall. But she could not face them now. She would write to the countess from Newmarket.

On either side the trees were impenetrable with their new pale green leaves. Among the branches unseen birds were calling and fussing. A hare darted across the road, and Fantastique threw back his head. Then the hare ran across their path again, as though he were drawing an invisible line beyond which they were not to pass.

Fantastique drew back. Kte patted his neck to calm him, thinking of that day (a year ago!) when Edward had stopped them just about here by shooting his rifle in the air. How she had upbraided him, and quite rightly, too. Fantastique and her father were all she had then, and now Fantastique was all. I must not cry, she said to herself, no self-pity.

"Come, love, we must be on our way to bury Papa." She urged him on.

Turning a bend, they came across a squirrel standing stiffly at attention in the middle of the road, her slanting Oriental eyes shiny with alarm. Through a mouth stretched wide, she let out a series of raucous calls, and her chest heaved. She did not run as the horse approached; it was Fantastique who pulled back.

"How odd," said Kate. "She's upset about something. Let's circle her carefully."

Ahead the right-of-way turned abruptly, and Kate

pulled on the left rein. Around the turn they faced a drawn and loaded pistol. Holding it nonchalantly was Donald, seated on Daisy. With a sense of foreboding, Kate pulled up.

"You didn't think you could get away so easily, did you?" he said, with an expression that was half-smile, half-snarl.

"Easily? You think it was easy?"

"Easy for you. You just wave away a fortune and ride away into the arms of the Prince Regent. I'm not blind, you know."

"I am on my way to Newmarket, not Brighton. I shall probably never see the Prince again. May I repeat, I renounced my legacy because I am not worthy of it."

"Fine sentiments. What about me? I was to have half."

"That can't be helped. And I don't much care. Let me go."

She lifted the reins, and Fantastique began to move.

"Stop!" He flourished the pistol threateningly, and Kate pulled the colt up.

"What good would it do to kill me now? I make no claim at all on Uncle's fortune. You are free to fight Uncle's partner over it."

"You imagine that I want to kill you! Oh, no, my dear wife, I am not going to kill you. I plan to hurt you worse than that. I am going to kill that damned horse."

"No, please, no, for the love of God!" begged Kate, looking with horror at the muzzle of the pistol, brought up to line with Fantastique's forehead. Above it, Donald's face was in a grimace, one eye closed to get an exact bead. Kate measured the path forward and back to see if she and Fantastique could make a bolt for it and realised that they did not have a chance.

Donald's forefinger closed on the trigger.

"No!" From out of the newly leaved foliage ran Bert; he gave a leap into the air and grabbed Donald's gun arm. The shot exploded, but was diverted from Fantastique. The shot hit Daisy, tearing off a piece of her ear. The old animal, wild with pain, reared up, her hoofs beating the air in a silent tattoo of agony. Donald, who had no grip on her, was thrown off, landing on the side of the right-of-way. Kate murmured a word of reassurance to Fantastique and jumped down. Donald was lying face down in the dirt.

"Donald?" When there was no reply or movement, she rolled him over. His mouth was open and his eyes glazed. With reluctant fingers, she unbuttoned his jacket and bent over to hear his heart. There was no beat.

In the branches overhead, the birds, who had flown away in the threatening noise and confusion, returned again when everything was still. As though from a place far away, Kate heard them chirp and renew their routine. Behind her Bert was holding the bleeding and trembling Daisy. She closed Donald's eyes.

"Be Sir Donald kilt, my lady?" Bert asked, awestruck.

"Sir Donald is dead."

"Be it my fault, my lady?"

"No, Bert, no, nor was it Daisy's, nor mine. It was Sir Donald's fault. In truth, he caused his own death."

"Yes, my lady."

"Bert, go back to Coulder Hall and get help. Take Daisy with you and tend to her ear. Don't let anyone hurt her. It wasn't her fault. I'll wait here and explain what happened. Hurry, Bert! I must be on my way to Newmarket."

Bert hesitated.

"Go! Tell them there has been an accident."

"Yes, my lady."

He led Daisy back along the road, his broad face solemn. Daisy kept shaking her head, as though to throw off the pain in her ear. Bert stroked her neck comfortingly as they walked.

Suddenly the boy let out a hoot. "Fancy being done in by sweet old Daisy!"

26

KATE UNLATCHED THE gate of the quiet cemetery at Newmarket, and it squeaked as she closed it behind her. In her hands was a bunch of red June roses, in startling contrast to her black dress. Overhead dark clouds were forming; she looked up at them and hurried to her father's grave. A cone-shaped tin vase inserted in the earth held yesterday's flowers. She pulled out the vase, discarded the wilted blooms, and filled the container with fresh water from the pump. Pushing the vase back into the earth, she knelt and arranged the deep-red roses tenderly. Grieving, she continued to kneel at the grave. If only Papa had outlived this year of trial, she thought mournfully.

Her worries had increased. With Bert's arrival came news of Donald's funeral, held the same day as her father's, and a vexing letter from the solicitors, who had been asked to remain at Coulder Hall to try to make sense out of Donald's snarled estate. His debts could be put off no longer, and his debts were now hers. She was requested to pay the solicitors a visit at their offices in London at her earliest convenience.

Messrs. Pierce, Price, and Sharpe put out the suggestion that she sell Coulder Hall, which now also was hers. But what of the occupants of the estate? Adelaide would marry soon and move on, but Lady Weyward and Lydia—what of them? They had some money of their own, but would it be enough to support them if their home was sold? Kate did not like the pair, but they were, after all, her kin. And the servants! Nurse Amelia, the faithful Nettie, Jack Hinds, and the others. And that whole tribe of children—what would become of them? Kate's hands clenched her black dress. She had indeed inherited a legacy, but it was a legacy of debts and responsibility.

The clouds overhead opened up and the rain pelted her, a hard spring torrent. The tin vase holding the roses overflowed, and the flowers, so carefully arranged, were forced out onto the earth. The petals became sodden and muddied.

She burst into tears as sudden and violent as the torrent. For days she had not allowed herself to cry, but now the pent-up tears were uncontrollable. She leaned over her father's grave and sobbed.

— 27 —

THE JOURNEY TO London was made in the coach of the countess. She had sent it to Newmarket especially to fetch Kate. The countess, rather than stay on alone at Radburn Park, had decided to follow Edward to London and open up her house there. She invited Kate to stay with her while Kate's legal difficulties were being settled. Unfortunately, wrote the countess, Edward would not be there, having gone with the Prince to Brighton. Where the charming Charlotte would be in residence with her father, thought Kate. But it did not matter. Nothing much did, anymore.

Her arrival at the countess's house in Portman Square was tumultuous. As the coach drew up, the front door was flung open, and Adelaide, dressed in mourning like herself but her childish face bright with happy expectation, ran down the steps; followed more decorously by a smiling Lionel; followed by a barking, frantic Frou-Frou, wearing a pink satin bow on her forehead; followed by energetic footmen, who opened the door, lowered the steps, and removed Kate's luggage from the overhead rack.

The countess, gowned in pink satin, rang for tea, and soon Kate was made to feel less forlorn in the company of warm friends.

"It's too bad of Donald to leave you in such straits," said the countess over her dish of China tea. "We all knew that he gambled but did not realise the extent of his reckless-ness. And now the piper must be paid. And by you, poor child. It isn't fair."

"What troubles me most about selling Coulder Hall is

letting the servants go. And Aunt Harriet and Cousin Lydia, too, will be out of a home."

"We plan to invite Mama and Lydia to stay at the Vicarage," said Adelaide. "It'll work out," she added doubtfully as Kate looked at her in dismay. "We'll find room."

"It is our duty," said Lionel firmly.

"As for the staff," said the countess, "I can find places for some of them in the country. Mrs. Wilcox will be happy to have some extra hands now that we have two houses open. Lady Curtis has promised to take the others. With her constantly increasing family, she truly needs them."

"And the stables?"

"Edward will buy the horses."

"Oh, countess, how you have relieved my mind. And Adelaide and Lionel, how very good you are. You could not be more so!" Kate's head fell back upon the high-backed chair in relief. "You have given me a measure of peace."

The countess observed her closely. "You look as though you need a good rest and some nourishment. It's been a trying time. I must say it was brave of you to give up your inheritance. More than brave—noble. But no more of that. You must start living again, and we want to help."

"Kate," said Adelaide, "we thought—Lionel and I thought—that since you and I are in mourning and cannot attend the theatre or balls, that we might see London, if you'd like to." Her face looked worried, so anxious was she to please.

"It's the best thing I can think of. Far better than going out socially. I really don't want to visit."

"Oh, Kate! London is wonderful. You'll love it! Lionel drove me around yesterday—such wonderful palaces and buildings and parks. There is a park named after the Prince Regent—Regent's Park, it's called, and it's beautiful. And there are libraries and exhibitions and, oh, all kinds of things we can do."

"It does sound wonderful, but first I must make arrangements to see Messrs. Pierce, Price, and Sharpe, and get this unpleasant business under way."

"Let it go for a few days, my dear," said the countess, "and get a good rest first. Solicitors have this curious habit of expecting you to do everything immediately, while they take infinite time to do anything at all. Take your leisure, just as they do. It will all come out in the end."

"You are all so very kind," murmured Kate, feeling warm and protected and a little sleepy.

Mrs. Wilcox placed the breakfast tray on the table next to Kate and raised the shade. "Lovely day, my lady!"

Kate blinked at thc light and wondered for a few seconds where she was.

"Excuse me, my lady, for waking you. But Miss Adelaide said to tell you that the exhibition opens at ten o'clock, and as it is so very popular, it's better to be early than not."

Through the open door waddled Frou-Frou, her nails sounding like an industrious woodpecker against the bare floor. Without ceremony she leapt on the bed and attempted to wash Kate's face with a pink tongue. Fortunately she was distracted by the homely smell of the breakfast tray and put two fat legs up on the table, the better to sniff it.

"I am to be spoiled like Frou-Frou, Mrs. Wilcox, I can see that. Shall I grow fat like her, too?"

"You could stand some more weight, my lady, if I may say so." Mrs. Wilcox lifted the silver cover from a large plate to reveal a generous piece of steak, chicken livers, sausage, eggs, and fried tomatoes. Frou-Frou became so excited that the covers fell from the bed, and the hangings too were in danger. Mrs. Wilcox removed Frou-Frou bodily to the countess's room, where an equally rich meal awaited her.

The days in London were full. Each day Adelaide read through the papers for notices of exhibitions and pored over a map of London, drawing up an itinerary for them to follow. At teatime they described to the countess all that they had seen and done. In the evenings they read aloud or sang, with Adelaide at the harpsichord. Kate was kept so busy that her sorrow gradually eased, and she had nearly forgotten the reason for her coming to London.

The day of reckoning came when on her breakfast tray she found a letter marked "Urgent." Messrs. Pierce, Price, and Sharpe wrote that it was necessaray that she call on them that morning.

Kate sighed as she donned the black dress and fastened the tiny buttons on the bodice and wrists. The day had come, and she must do what had to be done. She placed the heavy black veil over her bonnet.

"Would you like us to accompany you?" asked Adelaide sympathetically.

"No, dear Adelaide. I don't imagine there will be much to do except sign some documents. They will see to the rest."

The countess insisted on lending Kate her coach, and as Kate rode through London to the rooms of the solicitors, she was surprised at how familiar those streets had become. London seemed like home to her. But where is home now, she asked herself. Newmarket, without Papa? Coulder Hall, soon to be up for sale? No, that never was.

Mr. Price, his face as bland as ever, greeted her and ushered her into a wide inner office where three desks were arranged before a window made of rectangular panes. Kate was deposited in a chair facing the window; the solicitors were three silhouettes seated before her, as though regarding her in judgement. She lifted her veil, and her eyes squinted against the glare.

"Lady Weyward," began Mr. Pierce, "we want you to know that we sympathise with your recent losses." His moveable eyebrows were for once level.

"You understand that it was the loss of my father that most affected me."

"Of course," said Mr. Sharpe, distinguished from the others in that his silhouette was taller and narrower. "Your union with Sir Donald was a *mariage de convenance.*"

"Less than that, if anything could be less. I married him solely to ensure his cooperation in gaining my inheritance.

It was obvious that he and Lady Weyward had been trying to prevent this from happening, for their own ends."

"Lady Weyward," said Mr. Price, "may we ask you a few questions concerning the Weywards. I assure you that they are pertinent to your financial problem."

"Very well. I see no reason why not."

"We would like to have your opinion of Harriet, Lady Weyward. We ask that you be candid."

"I am afraid I cannot say anything very good about her—because of my experience, you see," said Kate hesitantly. "Why not be candid, indeed? I find my aunt—small. More than small, malicious."

"Expound on that, if you please."

"She is a selfish woman, mean spirited and cruel."

"Cruel? In what way?" put in Mr. Pierce.

"In her treatment of Adelaide Weyward. Adelaide was a favourite with Sir Joseph, Aunt Harriet's husband. After his death she was left a virtual prisoner in the nursery, without kindness or education. Naturally she became underdeveloped and—odd. They were about to abandon her to an institution when I came to Coulder Hall."

"And you laboured to save her from this fate?"

"It was no labour! I enjoyed every moment of it. Adelaide needed encouragement, was thirsty for knowledge far beyond what I could supply. I enlisted the aid of the vicar, with the results you have seen. She is now far beyond me, her intellectual curiosity and capacity far surpasses mine. Even the greatly endowed vicar must work hard to keep up."

"Yes," said Mr. Pierce meditatively. "She is a fine young lady."

"May I ask, gentlemen, what these questions have to do with the sale of Coulder Hall? Surely my opinions of the dwellers there cannot change the fact that it must go?"

"Would you be patient with us for a little, Lady Weyward, and answer just a few more questions? I assure you, they are important."

Kate sighed. "Go on, then."

"You will answer honestly?"

"I would answer in no other way, I assure you. My days of dissembling are past."

"Ah, yes, I see. Harriet, the Lady Weyward—would you consider her a lady in the commonly accepted meaning of the term?"

"If the commonly accepted meaning is that of a veneer that covers up anything disagreeable, yes."

"A hypocrite?"

"Yes."

"Not a genuine lady?"

"Never!"

Mr. Price looked at Mr. Pierce who looked at Mr. Sharpe. "Are we finally decided, gentlemen?" asked Mr. Pierce.

"Just one moment," said Mr. Price, who had joined his fingers together at the tips and was making a whistling noise through them. "Who is your idea of a lady, then?"

Kate answered promptly. "The countess of Radburn."

"Why?"

Kate considered. "She is kind, honest, and moral."

"Those are the characteristics of a lady, then?"

Kate smiled wanly. "The necessary requirements."

"You are staying with the countess here in London, are you not?"

"She has kindly asked me to visit until my legal affairs are taken care of."

"Her sons are there, too?" asked Mr. Sharpe.

"Only the vicar. Lord Radburn is with the Prince Regent at Brighton." For the first time Kate lowered her lids against the strong light.

"The Prince Regent returned from Brighton some days ago," said Mr. Sharpe.

Kate looked up, startled. "Oh—then I do not know where Lord Radburn is."

"Perhaps he is staying at his club," suggested Mr. Price.

Kate sighed. "Yes, no doubt."

"Then there is nothing between you and Lord Radburn?" asked Mr. Sharpe. "No—understanding?"

"Not at all. I believe that Lord Radburn will ask for the hand of the Princess Charlotte."

"The Princess Charlotte! How can that be? Have you not heard the rumours from the Court?" Mr. Pierce's eyebrows shot up nearly to his hairline.

"Rumours? I hear no gossip at all. I am in mourning and do not circulate in Society."

"It is more than gossip—it is history. The young Princess is enamoured of Prince Leopold of Saxe-Coburg, and an announcement from Carlton House is expected momentarily."

Kate caught her breath. "I did not know."

"This is beside the point, Mr. Sharpe," said Mr. Price severely. "Let us conclude this business. I am sure Mr. Coulder would not countenance any more delay. Your uncle's will is unusual, Lady Weyward."

"Of that I am well aware."

"It is even stranger than you think. Let me read a part of it." Mr. Price turned sideways to get the light. "Let's see now, 'I, William Coulder, of the West Indies, being of sound mind,' et cetera, et cetera, 'do bequeath my entire estate to my niece, Katherine Martin, of Newmarket, daughter of my sister Margaret,' et cetera, et cetera. Here is the important section, '. . . on the condition that she remain a year under the direct supervision of my sister-in-law, Harriet Coulder, Lady Weyward of Coulder Hall, and if at the end of that time, said niece remains direct, honest, charitable, and courageous, in the true sense a lady, after a long period of association with that dissembling, ruthless, ambitious woman. . . .' "

Mr. Price turned around.

Kate stared from one to another and shook her head in disbelief.

Mr. Pierce explained. "Your uncle came back to England

a few years ago and paid a visit to Coulder Hall. He was appalled at what he saw, especially of Lady Weyward, whom he had once considered marrying himself—at one time she had been quite beautiful, I believe. He found her ugly, the result of her mean thinking and low actions. The whole atmosphere of Coulder Hall was changed—it had become disagreeable and hypocritical. His brother by then was a miserable shell of a man whose only pleasure in life was his youngest child Adelaide, who was indeed his only child, as he had come to know. Lady Weyward had made the two other children, offspring of a certain draper's assistant in Lewes, into replicas of herself, selfishly empty."

"Good God!"

"Your Uncle William then visited his sister Margaret, your mother, at Newmarket, who although in straitened circumstances, maintained a happy, pleasant, encouraging atmosphere in her home. He was particularly taken by you, his niece, but wondered what you would be like if transplanted to Coulder Hall under the particularly evil influence of Lady Weyward. The test was this—could you maintain your own identity despite her malevolent direction and the promise of great gain by being just like her. If at the end of the year you were unscathed, then indeed you would be worthy of his fortune."

"You mean to say that by deliberately marrying Donald and doing all that I could deceptively to gain the legacy, I was only ensuring my losing it."

"That's about it."

Kate began to laugh. "Oh, that is just, it is just!" She laughed until the tears came, and took out a black-edged handkerchief from her cuff to wipe them away.

The three solicitors did not laugh.

"But then you refused the legacy," said Mr. Price.

"And made that remarkable confession," Mr. Pierce reminded her.

"And denounced Lady Weyward," added Mr. Sharpe.

"So I did."

"So don't you see?" asked Mr. Price. "At the end you were worthy of the inheritance, after all."

"But I renounced it only because Papa had died. If he had lived—I would not have renounced it."

"We have taken that into consideration, and we understand. And more important, we believe our client would have understood."

Kate gazed from one to the other of the solicitors, unbelieving. "Are you gentlemen trying to tell me that I have come into Uncle William's inheritance?"

All three nodded affirmatively.

"Yes," said Mr. Price, not a man to waste words.

"Exactly so," said Mr. Pierce.

"Congratulations, Lady Weyward," said Mr. Sharpe.

Kate looked uncomprehending. "Then I don't have to sell Coulder Hall?"

"Not if you don't wish to, Lady Weyward. Your husband's debts are great and will certainly have to be paid, but your liquid assets can easily take care of them. No need to sell anything."

"And Aunt Harriet and Lydia can remain there and not move to the Vicarage?"

"I am sure they will be happy to accept your generosity."

"And I don't have to disperse the servants?"

"*Believe* me, Lady Weyward, with your wealth you will not. But these items are all negative things. You should start thinking of what you *can* do."

"All I ever wanted to do was to get medical care for Papa. Now it is too late for that."

"That is all past now, Lady Weyward," said Mr. Pierce guiltily.

"Look to the future," said Mr. Price cheerfully. "It could not be brighter."

"You might think of a second, happier marriage," said Mr. Sharpe. "After a suitable period of mourning, of course."

"Never!" said Kate, jumping to her feet. She felt angry

and, needing fresh air, went around the desk to the huge window and opened it herself. She breathed deeply. When she turned around to the solicitors, she was in shadow and they in the glare.

Mr. Price's expression remained bland.

Mr. Pierce's eyebrows contracted over his eyes.

Mr. Sharpe looked sad.

— 28 —

"You still won't tell me what we are going to see?" Kate smiled.

She and the betrothed couple were riding along behind Lionel's greys. Turning away from the busy streets, they entered Hyde Park.

"It wouldn't be a surprise anymore if we told you what it was," said Adelaide.

"It can't be an exhibition, or a gallery, or a palace, or a new bookshop. We've left them all behind us."

"No, none of those. I'll tell you that much."

"What can it be then?" Kate, perplexed, looked around at green lawns and greener trees. "I know! It's a beautiful view!"

"You might say that," said Adelaide cautiously.

"You're getting warm," said Lionel.

On they drove for yet another half-mile, Kate consumed by curiosity. "If we keep going, the day will be gone and we'll be late for tea!"

"Days are getting longer," said Lionel. "The light will last for quite a while. Don't worry about tea."

In a shallow valley Lionel slowed the greys. On one side was a stretch of grass and on the other a copse of oaks.

"Come, ladies," said Lionel, helping them down. "This way, please." He led them into the trees and seemed to be looking for something on the ground, his eyeglasses glinting this way and that.

"There they are!" said the sharp-eyed Adelaide, pointing. Kate lifted her veil and peered. Before them was a field of violets, their colour exquisite against shiny green leaves.

"How lovely!" exclaimed Kate. "So utterly beautiful!" She sank to her knees to breathe in their perfume. "Thank you for this surprise, you dear, dear couple."

Bending over the flowers, Kate did not notice when Adelaide and Lionel tiptoed away. With her lungs full of delicate fragrance, she turned to one side and saw a pair of shiny brown boots on the ground next to her. Her glance travelled up the lean figure and rested on the questioning black eyes of Edward. Instinctively, as though for self-protection, she pulled at her veil, letting it fall over her face.

"Kate," he said, taking her hands and drawing her up to her feet. "Don't you think we have had veils between us for long enough? Unnecessary walls caused by misunderstanding? Let me lift them, once and for all."

Gently he raised the heavy veil that hid her features and draped it back tenderly over the bonnet. "We must always be honest with each other, always be sure that the other knows the truth." He ran his finger down the flushed cheek. "I love you, Kate."

"I love you, Edward."

His thin lips stretched into a smile. "Is that the truth?"

"It's the truth. Oh, it is as much truth as there is!"

— 29 —

THE COUNTESS BREATHED a sigh of content. Back again at Radburn Hall, which she loved above all of her homes, she could relax and savour her happinesses.

First, the marriages of Edward and Kate, and Lionel and Adelaide, a double wedding, with the bishop of London officiating, to take place just as soon as the mourning period for Guy Martin was over. And for Donald, of course.

No, the countess corrected herself, I must put the security and happiness of England first. Wellington had defeated Napoleon at Waterloo! Everyone's immense relief at the news had been followed by celebrations in London such as she had never witnessed before. Days and nights of exuberance: church bells pealing, singing in the streets, parties and balls, and fireworks making the night sky brilliant with light and colour. Napoleon had been like one of these displays, lighting up the sky for a while, she thought, then fizzling out. He had been banished to still another island, called St. Helena, far away. Edward had assured her that the Dreadful Man was now tired and ill, and that there was no chance of his rising up again. England was safe.

The Countess scooped up Frou-Frou in her arms and left the morning room for the double-storied Great Hall. She looked about her, trying to see it through Kate's eyes, and wondered what changes would be made. They would be good changes, she knew, for Kate had the taste and intelligence—and the wealth now—to do everything right, to the

Hall, the stables, the Park. The countess would be leaving Radburn Park in good hands.

Edward loved Kate so, she thought with affection. He had a habit of holding on to her as though he might lose her again.

"Let's go out into the garden, Frou-Frou." The countess returned to the morning room and, by way of the long glass door, entered into glorious spring sunshine.

"You are getting too heavy for me to carry. I spoil you." She placed Frou-Frou on the path with a little grunt. The dog sneezed at the fresh outside aromas. "Perhaps soon I'll have grandchildren to carry and fuss over."

But Frou-Frou didn't care. She was fascinated by two butterflies somersaulting in the air, and she tried very hard to jump up and down, as though joining them.

If you have enjoyed this book and would like to receive details of other Walker Regency romances, please write to:

Regency Editor
Walker and Company
720 Fifth Avenue
New York, N.Y., 10019